THE URBANA FREE LIBRARY

P9-CBR-052

The Urbana Free Library

DISCARDED BY THE
URBANA FREE LIBRARY

To renew: call 217-367-4057
or go to *urbanafreelibrary.org*
and select "My Account"

CAJUN WALTZ

ALSO BY ROBERT H. PATTON

FICTION

Up, Down & Sideways

Life Between Wars

NONFICTION

*Hell Before Breakfast: America's First
War Correspondents*

*Patriot Pirates: The Privateer War for
Freedom & Fortune in the American Revolution*

The Pattons: A Personal History of an American Family

CAJUN WALTZ

ROBERT H. PATTON

THOMAS DUNNE BOOKS

St. Martin's Press ⋙ New York

THOMAS DUNNE BOOKS.
An imprint of St. Martin's Press.

CAJUN WALTZ. Copyright © 2016 by Robert H. Patton. All rights reserved. Printed in the
United States of America. For information, address St. Martin's Press, 175 Fifth Avenue,
New York, N.Y. 10010.

www.thomasdunnebooks.com
www.stmartins.com

The Library of Congress Cataloging-in-Publication Data is available upon request.

ISBN 978-1-250-08899-4 (hardcover)
ISBN 978-1-250-08900-7 (e-book)

Our books may be purchased in bulk for promotional, educational, or business use.
Please contact your local bookseller or the Macmillan Corporate and Premium Sales
Department at 1-800-221-7945, extension 5442, or by e-mail at MacmillanSpecial
Markets@macmillan.com.

First Edition: June 2016

10 9 8 7 6 5 4 3 2 1

For Vicki, of course

and for the memory of Tudor Leland—"Cap"

Baby you're too cute to do anything wrong.

—*"Allons à Lafayette"* by Joseph Falcon
Columbia Records, 1928

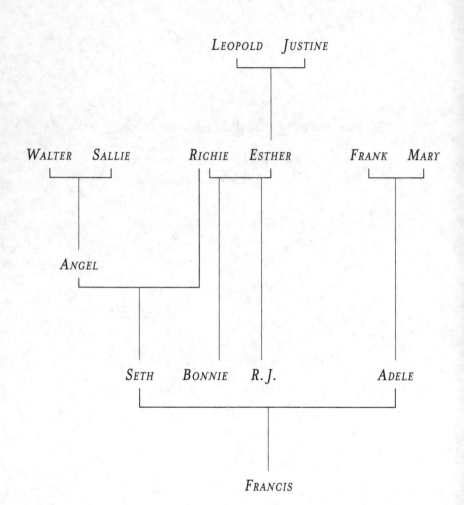

CAJUN WALTZ

Richie, Esther, Angel

Imagine the odds against a traveling musician from East Texas and the spinster daughter of an elderly French widower meeting across a store counter in Lake Charles, Louisiana, in 1928 and each thinking that here might be someone for me. But it happened.

Neither was much to look at. Richie Bainard's face was often in shadow under his wide-brim Stetson, and he carried himself with the twitchy presumption of an undersized bird at a feeder. Esther Block was blond as a Bavarian milkmaid and easily sixty pounds overweight, though her forebears were Jewish peddlers from Alsace-Lorraine with a long history of going hungry.

Being thirty-six and unmarried was fine by her but for her father's sighs whenever young couples browsed for cradles and nursing bottles at Block's Dry Goods on Ryan Street. In the years since Esther's mother died his desire for a grandchild had become a grumpy lament. Things took a pitiful turn when after a recent doctor's appointment he'd declared that his tacky heart was frail as paper and how sad it was that he wouldn't live to see his daughter become a wife and mother. Now whenever lone male customers came into the store, Esther found herself sizing them up like a judge at the Brahma bull competition in the Lake Charles country fair. The abstraction that filled her face at those moments was the first thing Richie saw after adjusting his squint from the bright morning outside. He tipped his hat blearily. "Ma'am."

"Miss," she corrected.

Richie had been fairly sober after last night's show. The damage came afterward at a house party whose tribal crush of dancing and moonshine ran past four A.M. He hadn't slept, the notion of this morning's errand nagging him as he'd scrunched on the seat of his Model T runabout. Finally he'd said screw it and driven around till he found a colored fry shop to kill time over coffee and waffles in wait for the shops to open. "Heard me a squeeze box first time last night," he said. "Was thinkin' I gotta get one."

"An accordion," Esther said.

"Place down the way said you had 'em."

"We do. A couple." There was a stack of straw boaters for sale on a table in the center aisle. An open umbrella hung upside-down from a crossbeam above it, neckties and kerchiefs draped over the ribs like harem veils. Esther possessed no eye for prettiness and had conceived the display for its efficient hawking of mixed accessories. Her father said it made his shop look like a Bourbon Street speakeasy, though positive receipts had calmed his complaints.

"Thing played louder'n a brass band," Richie said. "A hunnert frogs couldn't squash it."

"A hundred bullfrogs?"

"Frenchies."

"Ah," she said. "You mean Acadians."

"Bull's-eye. Barnful o' Cajuns . . ." She glanced sideways as he spoke. A white-haired gentleman in a banker's suit sat on a rocker in the back corner. The chair's motion had slowed. ". . . dancin' like goddamn monkeys till the sun come up."

The old man snorted. "Acadian no French! We are French."

Richie looked over. "They talked it plenty last night. Talked and sung both."

"*C'est patois. Illettré.*"

"Be nice, Papa." With age, Esther's father increasingly fell back into his childhood tongue, aggravating and worrying her in equal amounts. "They work hard, same as us."

The old man swatted the air. He was right about Cajuns insofar as their roots lay less in France than in French-speaking Canada, from where the British had expelled them as seditious vagrants in 1755. The reputation endured—how they kept to themselves, talked their muddy dialect, caroused like gypsies, and persisted in living like bucolic refugees rather than normal Americans.

Richie leaned over the counter toward Esther. "He okay?"

"Oh, he's just getting on." Her dress collar was unbuttoned. A swell of flesh, possibly more fat than bosom, drew his eye down. He wondered if it was hard carrying that weight around. And he wondered how soft she must feel against you.

Leopold Block pulled himself out of his rocking chair. He was stooped but imperious in his charcoal suit, as if he wore this casket attire specifically as a dare to the reaper. He'd left Alsace-Lorraine as a boy after the province was ceded as war booty to the hated Prussians in 1871. New Orleans was a haven for French émigrés. There he'd got his start in retail and belatedly into marriage and fatherhood. But the city's rude vitality intimidated him, and he'd moved with his wife and daughter to Lake Charles on the benignly featureless coastal plain of southwest Louisiana. A rural backwater by New Orleans standards, Lake Charles was home to a small Jewish community that had worshiped at a Masonic lodge till Leopold and some fellow businessmen built Temple Israel near the middle of town. The structure's bell tower was felled by a hurricane in 1918. Subsequent years saw its congregation likewise cut down, members leaving or marrying outside the faith. The synagogue lacked a full-time rabbi now and offered only a puny remnant of Jewish sons to court his aging daughter. Leopold had abandoned his religious hopes and was ready to receive any man short of a criminal as a potential son-in-law. He said to Richie, "You purchase accordion."

"Thinkin' maybe. Course I don't know how to play it." Richie turned to Esther. "Can't hardly play guitar neither, but don't tell my band." He knew three chords total, and usually got so caught up in his vocals that he stuck with just one, damping the strings with his fingers and scratching along in rhythm.

"I'm not much for music," she said.

Two women entered the store. Leopold went to intercept them.

"Name's Richie Bainard."

"Esther Block."

He spun a finger around the room.

"Yup. Block's is me," she said.

"And Papa sweeps the floors?"

"He's the owner. Obviously."

"Be yours in time, though."

The tease went too far. "You want an accordion, we got 'em for sale. You wanna talk like a jackass, move along."

Richie took the jab in stride. He wasn't sure why she intrigued him; he never looked twice at the large girls in the bordellos. But no question this Esther had grabbed his attention. He was tired of hustling town to town with the Texas Ramblers, a cowboy trio of two guitars and a fiddle whose thirty-dollar bookings were getting fewer and farther between. Early success had bought him the Ford, but dry spells of late made the motorcar his home and bed, no money to spare for a room. He was open to alternatives.

Richie was twenty-eight. His father, a Houston oil speculator with grand ambitions based on blind luck, had bet all he had on a mineral lease near the Spindletop gusher in Beaumont. When the money ran out at a thousand feet down, he'd cleared his debts by selling to the fledgling Texas Fuel Company and persuaded his son to enlist with him to go fight the Germans in 1918. They went overseas as a couple of doughboys whose family patriotism was praised in the Beaumont *Enterprise* the day they shipped out. Only the son came back. Richie disembarked in Port Arthur under a serrated skyline of oil containers emblazoned with TEXACO in big block letters, his father's old well now one of the company's top producers. His next several years as an oil rigger deepened his sense that great fortunes had come out of his hide.

Prohibition enforcement, never rigorous, ran thin as near

beer south of the Bible Belt and was all but a joke by the time you reached the Gulf. Noisy nights in the saloon gave rise to someone's observation that Richie could carry a tune. Two local players asked him to form a string band with them. They worked the East Texas boomtowns before venturing into Louisiana, where people went for music like nobody's business. Now more acts were crowding the circuit along with any number of pickup groups of family and friends. The Ramblers increasingly had to set aside their instruments for stints canning shrimp on the coast or working the sulfur mines along the state line. His bandmates talked about quitting the road and taking oil jobs back home. It was hard to disagree.

Leopold returned, leaving the ladies at the cookware table. He slapped his hands together. "Now we get accordion."

"See it first. Buy it maybe."

"Have special for you, make right here in Lake Charles."

"No," Esther said. "Show him the Hohner."

Leopold frowned. "Is German. Very bad."

"Papa! *C'est faux.*"

With a petulant grunt Leopold fetched the Hohner accordion from a shelf and placed it on the counter. It was the size of a carpenter's toolbox. When he undid the straps that clamped shut the bellows it sprung open lazily, white and black keys on one side, multiple rows of pewter buttons on the other. "Lot bigger'n what I seen last night," Richie said.

"Acadian ones are smaller and noisier," Esther explained.

"That's what I'm lookin' for. Cajun style. Had the crowd goin'."

"We can order you a Monarch. It's the brand they like."

"From Germany," her father scowled. "Junk."

"Gettin' the idea you don't like Germans," Richie said to him. "I done my part, if it makes you feel better."

"In war?"

"Was a while ago."

"Not for him," Esther said.

"You kill Boche?" Leopold pressed.

"I did try."

Leopold returned the Hohner to its shelf. He pushed aside some boxes till he found what he was looking for. It seemed a child's toy, less than half the size of the Hohner, its cardboard bellows covered with burgundy cloth and boxed with varnished red pine, a row of brass-plated buttons on each side. "No German," he said. "America."

Richie asked Esther, "Why'nt you show me this first?"

"The Hohner costs twenty dollars, the Monarch sixteen, and we guarantee them both. This one's made local from scrap parts."

"How much?"

"Twelve dollars."

"Ten," Leopold said. "My cost."

"You mean it?"

"He does not," Esther said. "It's twelve dollars."

"Ten," Leopold insisted. "And tonight you dine at my house. We will discuss the dead Boche."

"Papa," Esther warned. *"Ne soyez pas sournois."*

His voice turned impish. *"Je meurs, me rappelle?"*

"You'll live forever."

"Il est beau."

"Papa!"

The ladies from cookware approached, one brandishing a

cast-iron skillet. Leopold said to Richie, "Come tonight. My daughter is superior cook."

Richie removed his hat, placed it over his stomach, and cocked his head toward Esther's pie face. "Bull's-eye."

MORE THAN A quarter million French soldiers and civilians died as a result of Prussia's invasion of France in 1870. The carnage accounted for Leopold's vengeful joy in Richie's tales of fighting Germans on the western front in World War I. After Esther's meal of *andouille* sausage with peas and brown rice, the three of them passed the evening on the porch of the Blocks' dollhouse Victorian on the east bank of Lake Charles. Father and daughter listened as Richie deployed every tavern trick of witty narration he knew to describe a wartime experience that in reality had been six months of tedium and one morning of fright until shrapnel in his leg put him in a hospital where he convalesced through Armistice six weeks later.

Esther had changed to a sleeveless dress in the summer humidity. Her bare arms drew Richie's gaze like a magnet. She was no beauty, but her slender wrists and ankles refined the heft spilling over her chair into something classically ripe.

"Boche," her father mumbled sleepily. "*Sauvage.*"

"Got him a one-track mind, huh?"

"Not always," she said. "There's the store. There's me."

Richie lucked into a perfect response. "Fathers fret for their daughters."

"You know from experience?"

"Not a bit. But what I seen, men want sons. Me, I want a lil girl. Way they love their daddies."

Leopold drowsed in his chair. Cicadas creaked in the trees at the edge of the property. A ruffle of moonlight glittered on the lake beyond. "I imagine that could be so," Esther said.

Leopold's breathing deepened. Richie perked his ear. "You hear that?" He went to the porch railing.

"There's your accordion."

The sound of the instrument floated bare on the breeze— someone playing in solitude before an open window in one of the cottages nearer the lake. It was reedy and alternately faint and full, like a city siren heard from a distance. Its underlying drone mingled with high notes in a melody more drifty than tuneful. "Remind me of France," Richie said. In Westlake on the far shore of Lake Charles, fires flickered atop the exhaust stacks of the town's chemical factory. "We heard it at night on the German side."

"Probably Hohner," she said. "Like the one today."

Her practicality popped his reverie. The accordion sound faded.

Esther's face had lifted to his with the same dull and willful combination he'd observed in the store that morning. *I'm not much for music,* she'd said. Factual, capable, steady—just what he needed in many ways. But looking down at her, he knew he'd end up mistreating her for being too boring, too nice, too fat. "Ramblers playin' Pinefield tomorrow," he said. That part was true. The band was opening for a local act at the Pinefield City Auditorium. "We get done, I'd like to call on you again." That part wasn't true.

"I'll be at Block's, same as ever."

"Maybe I'll know some songs on my new accordion."

"Either way, we don't take returns."

Her brisk tone almost turned him around. It was like a challenge, daring him to try and get her mind off commerce and onto unfurling her sweeter self. He shook off the notion. "Tell your daddy thanks from me."

Esther's expression didn't show her disappointment at Richie's noble exit. She would have liked him to make a pass, if only just to see, for her own curiosity, how she would have reacted.

A MONTH EARLIER, a publicity photo of the Texas Ramblers had come into the hands of the promoter putting on the Pinefield show. They were posed beside Richie's motorcar, the band's name chalked on the spare tire along with the exchange number of the fiddler's mother. Worried that a strictly Cajun bill might not fill the place, the promoter had booked the Ramblers based on the cowboy getups they wore in the photo, big hats and chaps and tasseled vests borrowed from a high school theater's costume trunk.

Pinefield was far from the Ramblers' usual turf. The drive east from Lake Charles took half a day, the three men crammed in the Ford with guitars on their laps and duffels strapped to the running board. Their mood wasn't helped by the promoter complaining, when they got to the auditorium, that he'd expected them to perform in the Tom Mix outfits they'd worn in the publicity shot. Surveying their matching white shirts and white trousers, a spiffy look Richie had pressured the group to adopt to widen its appeal, he growled that tonight's crowd was expecting the *Texas* Ramblers so they'd best put some cowboy into their act. "We playin' more hillbilly now," Richie explained.

"Hillbilly? Y'all look like a damn glee club."

The other band members glowered at Richie. They'd hated the change of style. Right now he pretty much hated them.

The promoter lit a cigarette and exhaled with purpose. A sheriff's deputy stood at his shoulder. The young man's name was Hollis Jenks. He was muscular-stout with buzzed hair and a forehead broad as a tractor cowl. The florid bulbs of his nose and scalp suggested things cooking inside him. "Let's see how the show goes," the promoter said.

It turned out that most of the patrons had no interest in the opening act, preferring to picnic on the grassy lot behind the building until the headliner came on. Knowing they'd be facing an empty house freed Richie's mates to go hard on their pharmacy liquor backstage. Richie pushed through "John Henry" and "Wreck of the Old '97," but sloppy play behind him and no pretty girls in front made it hard to give a damn. When "Red River Valley" came around on the set list, he sang the chorus lyric, "and the *cowboy* who loved you so true," with a wink at the promoter watching in the wings, who understandably took it as snotty.

Applause came in pockets from folks who'd wandered in to find seats for the main performance. Richie knew he was done with the Ramblers before the clapping stopped. He slung his guitar over his shoulder and edged toward a side door on the calculation that letting his bandmates split tonight's meager take was a fair swap for leaving them flat. A rush of incomers swept him back—families with grandparents and little kids, teenagers in packs, couples out on the town and done up for Saturday night in clean shirts and stubby neckties, the gals in patterned frocks and shiny shoes, most of them chattering in the same French drawl he'd heard at the house party in Lake Charles. He retreated down the aisle to slip out the rear of the building, feeling now totally foolish in his soda shop whites. But curious about the cause of the fuss, he paused backstage to get a glimpse of the headliner.

The promoter should have known that Joe Falcon could sell out any venue in south Louisiana without help from of an out-of-state string band. Joe and his fiancée Cleoma Breaux, him on accordion and her on guitar, had recorded two sides for Columbia Records in a hotel suite in New Orleans last spring. Now every area jukebox featured the thirty-five-cent 78 of *"Allons à Lafayette"* and "The Waltz That Carried Me to My Grave," as did all the tumbledown households that had found dollars to buy a hand-cranked Victrola from the Montgomery Ward catalog or a Silvertone Super Deluxe from Sears Roebuck so they could hear Joe and Cleoma's Cajun crooning whenever they wanted.

Smoking cigarettes and sharing discreet sips from a flask, the couple looked like Jazz Age swells from New York or Chicago rather than the sharecropper and housemaid they'd been before social sing-alongs brought them together and led Cleoma to leave her husband and hit the road with Joe last year. He was Richie's age; his tailored suit and rimless glasses made him seem older. And Cleoma was nothing but cute with her red lipstick, black curls spilling out from under a slanted hat, and tiny feet in audacious heels that pushed her height to barely five feet, putting her eyes level with Richie's slack mouth as he stared at the couple.

"Mes compliments."

It took him a moment to realize she was talking to him.

She continued in English, "You sung real good, we like so much."

Joe nodded beside her. "*Mon amour* was dancin', she was." Their accents were burred and smoky—Cajun accents, which next to Richie's Texas twang was like weathered driftwood compared to Formica.

"Nice o' you to say, pros like yourself."

"We play," Joe said. "It pay some, we happy."

Joe removed his jacket in preparation to go on, smoothed down his shirtsleeves and straightened his tie. Resembling a stockbroker holding a toy, he fitted his right thumb through a leather loop on one side of his black-lacquered Monarch and his left hand under a strap on the other side. It was as precise and comfortable as a ballplayer donning his glove, Joe's pull on the bellows while playing a reflex riff equivalent to a last smack of the pocket before taking the field. Cleoma was equally dapper in unpinning her hat and passing her guitar strap over her head without mussing her hair. The guitar, a National steel resonator, looked big as a cotton bale in her arms. She strummed a chord and tuned the strings to Joe's accordion notes.

A dispute broke out at the back of the room. Richie's bandmates were bitching to the promoter about tonight's fee. The man scornfully pulled bills from his clip. Richie saw his mates take the money and scoot out the far door, dumping him before he could dump them. The promoter pocketed his clip. Seeing Richie watching him, he gave a snide wink to match Richie's earlier—paid in full, it said. Richie wasn't upset and in fact felt bleakly affirmed, like a priest watching sinners behave as expected.

Joe and Cleoma had observed the exchange. "Not right," she said.

Richie shrugged. It was time to get a real job. "He hated me from the start."

"Us same," Joe said.

"Come on. You sold out the joint."

"'Cept he say Walter can't play with us. We ain' go for that."

"Don't know no Walter."

"Be me." A young man dressed in a suit and white shirt had come up behind them. "I'm the Neg in the show." It was an amiable term in Cajun circles. "Walter Dopsie." He carried a scuffed cardboard suitcase in one hand and in the other a flour sack holding—you could tell by the mismatched shapes inside—a violin, bow, and corrugated washboard. He set the bags down and reached out.

They shook hands. Richie liked black women but preferred the men at a distance—though this Walter was black only if you looked for it. His hair was brushed in slick waves against his temple and his color was like the fingerboard on Richie's guitar, originally dyed dark to mimic the ebony of pricier instruments but which heavy use had worn back to maple. A girl slouched beside him in a pleated white dress and brown Oxfords. Europe infused her features—green eyes, honey skin, raven hair in loose ringlets so shiny they seemed oiled. Twelve or thirteen, she was stunning by any measure. "My daughter," Walter said, watching Richie. "Angela. Go by Angel mos' time."

"Pretty."

"Talk about. Need me a shotgun soon."

Richie, unable quite to pull his eyes off her, directed the

only words he could think of to a vague spot above her head. "You love your daddy?"

"Nope. Wanna go back Shreveport."

Her father laughed. "Shreveport? You a Creole girl. B'long in a field, or a pogie plant makin' that fish meal all day long."

Her mouth formed a tough pout. "Not gonna."

"Oh no?" Walter tried to look mad but couldn't sustain it. He said to the others, "Twenty dollar a month cuttin' 'cane, packin' fish? She hate that shit much as me."

Hollis Jenks, the young deputy sheriff, was scanning the house from behind the curtain. He barked over his shoulder, "Cut that talk, boy." His glance hung a second too long on Angel, Richie thought.

"Yes, sir," Walter said. "My 'pologies."

The promoter announced it was showtime. When Joe and Cleoma didn't respond, he got the hint, licked his thumb, and pulled bills from his clip, leaving each one wet with saliva. "How I be sure you gimme the full hour?"

"They our people," Joe said. "We go all night for them."

Cleoma slid her guitar to one side to give Walter a parting embrace. "Come see us in Eunice. We make a new song for the radio."

"I needa do a little earnin' first."

"I know, an' we so sorry for this."

"Boss make the rules."

An idea came to Cleoma. She whispered in Joe's ear.

He nodded. *"Après 'Lafayette.' "*

She turned back to Walter. *"La seconde,"* she promised. *"Pour vous."*

———

THE CROWD CLAPPED politely when the two musicians took the stage. The cheering swelled when they commenced *"Allons à Lafayette,"* the popular side they'd cut in New Orleans. Without spotlight or amplification they held every eye and filled the hall with sound. Joe's accordion, its effortless volume, dominated, the flight of his fingers contrasting with his torso's imperceptible flex as he worked the bellows in and out. Cleoma was barely more animated as she strummed, the sway of her body visible to the first few rows at most. Yet the tune bounded along in cheerful two-four time that soon jammed the aisles with hand-holding Cajuns twirling in a snug little mob. Joe and Cleoma seemed not to notice. They gazed out from the stage with blank intensity, like blind people hearing their names called across a room.

Joe sang in a clipped, almost conversational tenor whose plaintive cast would have made even good-time lyrics sound bleak. Cleoma came in on the chorus with a whiny warble that shimmered at the high end. They looked spellbound and slightly embarrassed by the dynamic effect of their sound. Richie had no idea what the French lyrics were saying. Walter sighed beside him. "Sad, sad."

"The song? Coulda fooled me."

"Tha's Cajun. Broken hearts, bound for the graveyard, still they gonna dance."

"What's it about?"

"Man wanna marry his girl even he know she trouble."

"You know French?"

"I *am* French. Much as them."

"*Lafayette*" ended and the applause was loud. "Boy!" It was Deputy Jenks. He'd been jiggling to the music and now in the lull reverted to previous fixations. "No nigras allowed back here."

"Okay we listen one more?" Walter asked.

Jenks sighted over his pointer finger. "One and git."

"Yes, sir. Thank you, sir."

Onstage, Joe and Cleoma conferred before starting the next number. She gave Walter a warm glance over her shoulder. From the song's first notes it was clear the crowd wasn't sure how to take it. Cleoma played a progression of minor and seventh chords, and her vocals, in French, were mournfully strained. Joe added bits here and there, accordion fills behind the melody that echoed her ragged wail. The song's volume was low. People leaned toward the stage, trying first to determine what the music was and second to decide if they liked it.

Certainly Hollis Jenks didn't like it. At the sound of Walter singing along behind him, he dealt him a nasty glare. " '*Blues Negres*,' " Walter said, answering the question before it was asked. He put an arm around his daughter. " 'Nigger Blues.' "

Jenks pointed to the exit door.

Walter took up his suitcase and flour sack. "Blues ain't nothin' but a good man beat down," he said to Angel. "Them's the words Miss Cleoma singin'. My words." And to Jenks: "My song."

He put his shoulder to the steel exit door. He was on the scrawny side, and Richie reached across to help push it open. Then Richie followed Walter and his daughter outside, somehow sure he'd regret it if he didn't.

WALTER DOPSIE HAD first met Joe Falcon and Cleoma Breaux at the Columbia sessions in New Orleans last April. Occasionally crossing paths since then, they'd done a broadcast together at Shreveport's KWKH two days ago. Walter got fifteen dollars for backing them on fiddle while they did *"Lafayette"* for the radio audience, a nice payday he'd blown on a room at the colored hotel and a thrift-shop dress for his daughter. Shreveport was Paris as far as Angel knew; she'd never been out of Hancock Bayou down on the Gulf where she lived with her mother. Now it was time to get her home—Walter liked liquor and women and she wasn't an asset in those pursuits. When Richie mentioned he had a vehicle after they left the Pinefield Auditorium, Walter calculated that free transportation and access to any *fais do-dos* on the way were good reasons to befriend him.

"*Fais do-do.*" Richie had heard the term before. "Be a dance hall, right?"

"Dance *party*," Walter said. "One settin' up on the highway I seen comin' in." He unlatched Richie's trunk to put his suitcase inside. Angel climbed onto the leather seat from the passenger's side. "Pay good, too."

The notion that these two expected to ride with him settled on Richie agreeably. On the brink of quitting music, he found Walter's zeal for it encouraging. Too, there was something about Angel that made him reluctant to look at her but also reluctant to give up the chance, as if maybe proximity would build up his immunity to whatever hazard she posed.

"What you got here?" Walter lifted Richie's new accordion out of the trunk. "Hooboy, we make some money now."

"Ain't learned it yet."

"Leave that to me."

"Thought you was a fiddle player."

"I play it all, boy."

"No colored call me boy, we straight on that?"

Walter doffed his jacket and laid it atop his suitcase in Richie's trunk. He slipped his hands into the straps of the accordion and peeled off a giddy melody as he walked around to the front of the vehicle.

Richie was too bewildered to be angry. Apparently they were a duo now, heading off to play some damn barn dance. "Least tell me you got dough for the pump," he said, but again received no reply.

Walter and Angel had caught a ride here from Shreveport earlier today in Joe Falcon's touring car. On the road into Pinefield, Walter had noticed a tin-roofed meeting hall with hurricane shutters hinged over its windows. Men were hoisting the shutters and hooking them open. That was the signal, plain as neon, that a *fais do-do* was on tap tonight. Two bits a head, children in free, homebrew for sale by the dipperful, music by whichever act, out of the several that invariably showed up at these things, best filled the dance floor and drew the biggest cheers.

"They pass the hat, do they?" Richie asked as he climbed in and punched the starter. Angel was squeezed between him and her father. Richie's guitar in its case lay across their knees. She folded her arms on top and rested her head. Her dark hair fanned across her face and touched Richie's wrist as he shifted gears on the steering column.

Walter noodled on the accordion as he directed Richie down

the road. Twilight washed the trees and buildings gray in the Model T's headlamps. "Best band take the pot," he said.

"Don't tell me us. With no kinda practice."

"You be white. I do the rest." At Richie's look, Walter explained, "Got to be. No Neg gettin' in 'cept a white man vouch for him. But ain't nobody play Cajun like me."

"Even Cajuns," Angel said drowsily.

Richie looked down. Her face on her arms was turned his way, the curve of her mouth reflecting passing lights from outside. She easily, her father too if he worked at it, could have passed for white. Richie wished they'd give it a try, drop the "Neg" and the "Nigger Blues" at least while traveling with him. When Angel moved in her sleep, her hair tickled his forearm. He slid his hand up the steering wheel to make it stop.

There were more wagons and horse buggies than motorcars outside the meeting hall. Folks milling about in the dusk had a spectral glow from the yellow-lit windows and the flare of cigarette lighters. Ladies collected admission at a front table. Walter told Richie it was early yet, the music wouldn't start till nine or ten, after the heat of the day subsided. Richie parked beside a shallow flood gully, grabbed his guitar and got out. Walter removed his fiddle and bow from the flour sack and put Richie's accordion inside to go along with the washboard. He slung the sack over his shoulder like a hobo. Angel fished six thimbles from the suitcase and gave them to her father to keep in his pocket. "Who play the washboard?" Richie asked.

"Rubboard, we call it," Walter said. "She feel it more'n she play it."

"It's easy," Angel said.

"Easy 'cause you good at it."

"Tellin' me she on with us?" Richie said.

"Girl lay a spell," Walter said. "You'll see."

Walter found the *fais do-do*'s organizers, introduced Richie and himself, and asked where they could store their instruments till the show started; where, too, they might get a sip of something beforehand. The head man's face and forearms were leathery from outdoor work. "I seen you in Ville Platte one time," he said. "Played good."

Walter scanned around. "Crowd pretty thin."

"Joe Falcon in town. He done, all them folks be here."

"What you think, then?"

"Fill the place, we get you twelve, fifteen."

"Throw in some hooch?"

The man put it straight. "Neg need his own cup."

Walter made his way to a parked flatbed where booze was being dispensed from jugs off the back. Men standing around it took slugs from shared containers. Before they could react to Walter's intrusion, he removed a tin cup from his sack and held it out. They flicked their eyes twice from his face to the cup before obliging him with a pour. He raised his hand in a genial toast before taking a good long drink.

Richie and the *fais do-do* organizer watched the exchange. "You an' him partners long?"

"Not long," Richie said.

The man's voice turned stern. "Keep him sober."

UNTIL JOE AND Cleoma's performance ended in Pinefield and their fans began showing up to continue the party at the *fais do-do*, the crowd inside the meeting hall remained sparse. Walter opted to let a local combo go on first—mom and dad on guitar, daughter on fiddle, son on accordion. Watching through a side door as they twanged away, Richie appreciated Walter's strategy, for the dance floor was mostly kids horsing around and oldsters getting in a few steps before heading home to bed.

Kerosene lamps slung from nails in the wood framing threw greasy light this way and that. Birds nested in the rafters. Smelling of sawdust and creosote, the hall was built on blocks off the ground. There was no raised performance stage. The band stood level with the dancers just a few feet away from them, as if playing in somebody's parlor. "Get any fuller," Richie said over the clattering floorboards, "how people gonna hear us?"

Walter pointed to some large wood crates by the wall behind the band. "Git up on 'em, shout it over they heads."

"Stand on them things an' play?"

"Feel like you flyin'."

Walter took a swallow of moonshine. He passed the cup to Richie, who, in trying to avoid touching his lips to the rim, poured more into his mouth than he'd meant to. Shuddering with the 140-proof burn, he handed the cup to Angel.

She took a sip, clamping her eyes till the fire subsided. Her forehead was damp with perspiration and strands of hair stuck to her skin. Richie reached over unthinking and brushed them aside. Her glance caught his before he looked away. In the corner of his eye he saw her smile, which annoyed him because she was mixed race for one thing and a mere child worse than that. When she handed back the cup he accepted it brusquely to remind her of her place.

The next hours passed in a blur. People came from the

Falcon show and filled the hall. Late as it was, mothers with infants and children repaired to a side chamber that had chairs to sit on to nurse the babies and cots for sleepy kids; the mothers spelled each other babysitting in order to take turns with their men on the dance floor. Benches lined the sides of the hall. Older women, the widows and matriarchs, sat chaperone as teenagers touched hands and whatever more they could manage in the dim-lit whirl, the twining of arms, the soft collision of hips and torsos. Spouses kissed on the dips, the music breezing overhead like fresh air after rain. Young men and women, nervous hawks and willing prey, surveyed the scene from opposite corners.

Richie observed it all from his perch on a produce crate between Walter and Angel, his center position dictated by Walter so no one would doubt that a white man headed the band. Richie's balance was wobbly at first—from the moonshine and also the strangeness of the scene. He was strumming tunes he didn't know, chasing the lead of Walter's accordion and Angel's rubboard rhythm. He looked at her often. Her silver board hung from a cord around her neck, clasped to her front like makeshift armor. Her eyes were shut as she played and her body moved in waves. She wore a thimble on each thumb, pointer, and middle finger. Her hands flew across the board's rippled surface, giving smacks on the downbeat and a syncopation of zips and runs that made the music jump. Glancing down, he saw that sweat at the small of her back was making her dress cling in the cleft.

They made a peculiar sight—a white man dressed like a soda jerk playing alongside a Creole dandy and a Spanish-looking girl with the allure of French Quarter jailbait. People refused with hoots and hollers to let them yield to another group. The sea of celebrants thickened and the action grew frenetic. Richie had only to fumble along while Walter did the work of singing and playing. He was free to enjoy the booze in his blood, the music fueling his uplift rather than weighting it with any need to be coherent. Only when Angel looked over in amusement did Richie realize he was grinning.

He didn't know the song titles or the words. They were Cajun, with traditional lyrics that no doubt changed every time Walter sang them. But Walter's vocals, like something cried from a scaffold, gave Richie all he needed to know about *"Mon Coeur T'Appelle," "La Valse Criminelle,"* and *"L'Amour Indifferent."* At the end of each number, Walter would immediately start the next. The accordion was tuned in C, a fortunate thing since the key incorporated the only chords Richie knew: C, F, and G. So off they'd go, Walter setting the pace, Angel hopping aboard, Richie hanging back till he got the chord sequence and joined in.

At some point he became aware of the Pinefield deputy sheriff watching from the side of the dance floor. Hollis Jenks had heard about the *fais do-do* after the Falcon show and come by with some pals, swapping his khaki uniform for dungarees and madras short sleeves. They stood in a huddle whose dour contrast to the prevailing mood few but Richie noticed. For Jenks and his friends, seeing Walter excite the room killed any fun they might have found here. Walter's skin shone darker in the lamplight. He sweated like a field hand through his suit and his greased hair had loosened into wiry coils. Cajuns showered him with cheers that seemed to give the deputy personal offense. Richie played on, trying not to let foreboding dampen his good time.

A young woman brought them alcohol between songs. Walter yipped, "Oh darlin'!" each time she appeared, no one caring anymore whose lips touched the communal cup. The moments seemed a ripple in the room's noisy wash until Richie noticed Jenks watching with stony reproach. He hoped that Walter would smarten up and let the woman be. She didn't make it easy, lingering in front of him with her eyes cast dreamily upward. Richie glanced again at Jenks. The deputy's attention had switched to Angel, where it remained as if hypnotized.

People waited for Walter to start the next tune. He called out to the room, "Y'all gonna let a Neg take a leak?" Laughter erupted. Walter hopped off the crate and darted through the side door to relieve himself outside. Tonight's celebration was nothing if not a call of nature.

Angel took the moment to lift the rubboard from around her neck. It got warm under that sheet of metal. Perspiration had turned her dress wet and sheer across small pointed breasts naked beneath the material. She seemed unaware of the nubile vision she made. Holding the rubboard in one hand, she raked the fingers of her other hand through her hair to cool the back of her neck. Richie turned away in embarrassment. His eyes fell on Jenks, who was still staring at Angel. The deputy looked lost in wonder till he realized Richie was watching him. His reaction might have been milder if he'd only been leering. But getting caught in a state of rapture over a nigger's daughter was something else again.

Walter bounded back inside like a vaudevillian taking an encore. The room's energy had cooled. Families and couples made to leave, thanking him as they headed out. The moonshine woman went up to him. She withdrew a handkerchief from under her bodice and dabbed his brow. There was cause for surprise in this—white woman, black man. But the real rarity came when she refolded the hankie and returned it inside her dress, his sweat against her skin. Few saw the exchange; she rejoined her kin leaving the hall and disappeared into the night. But Deputy Jenks took note.

He and his friends waited till the wagons and motorcars thinned out around the hall. It was after midnight. Walter and Richie had collected their pay and were loading up the Ford. Angel had climbed in and was already half asleep with her head on her arms. The plan was to stop at an all-night diner and then continue southwest toward her home on the Gulf, resting at roadside and hopefully hitting another *fais do-do* somewhere on the way tomorrow. Richie and Walter stood by the trunk of the motorcar, counting out the money. "Turn you Cajun yet," Walter laughed.

"Or colored," Richie said, taking his half.

Footsteps hissed in the long grass behind them. Richie and Walter were turning to the sound when blows came down with thuds and cracks, hardwood hitting muscle and bone. Driven to the ground, Walter received extra pounding while Richie sprawled facedown beside him with his brain ringing and someone's boot on his neck. Men stood over them in the dark, panting and grunting as if breaking rocks. Walter curled up to shield himself but his forearm was snapped by one swing of an ax handle and the side of his head was next.

It was too dark to see much blood. The men threw Walter limp into the gully. They got behind the Ford and with a rowdy heave pushed that in, too, Angel still inside; Richie later wondered if he'd heard her scream or was it in his head? Walking away, one of the attackers gave Richie a last kick that caught him square in the throat. Meanwhile Walter was drowning in six inches of swamp water at the bottom of the gully, though he never knew it.

Richie woke to a woman's voice somewhere in the air above him. "You in Lake Charles Hospital. Been here three days." It hurt to open his eyes, the lids leaky and crusty both.

He couldn't form words. She bent over him and he smelled the bleach in her uniform. He tried moving his tongue. He pushed air through his lips. "Lake Charles?" came out in a whisper.

"Lake Charles, yes. You got people here? Must be worried sick."

Lake Charles. The words took meaning slowly. A name came to mind. "Esther Block," he murmured before falling back into sleep.

They were married four months later at Lake Charles City Hall. It seemed a natural next step after he convalesced at Esther and her father's house and began helping at their store as his health returned. Before long they were as good as husband and wife but for the paperwork and wedding night. Leopold witnessed, paid for the license and dinner for three at the Majestic Hotel. Esther went straight to her room after they got home. Leopold poured cognacs for him and his son-in-law until enough time had passed to assume she'd got herself ready. His goodnight wink about killed Richie with embarrassment.

Though it was her first time compared to maybe a dozen for him, all with professionals in their establishments or in his motorcar, he was the nervous one. He'd rarely done it without protection. The feel of Esther's fingers slotting him in place and the yielding clasp when he pushed inside brought him to a fast finish. Propped on his elbows in the dark above her, his mouth fell open and some saliva dropped onto her cheek. She teased him about it afterward, saying she took it as a compliment that he'd lost himself that way. Humiliated, he curled to the wall. She lay on her back with her knees up as instructed in her pregnancy pamphlet.

Being Esther's husband turned out okay. Thanks to the store, there was ample food and money around, and scented powder she ordered from New York always aroused him when he undid her nightgown at night. Damage to his throat had left Richie's voice a sandpaper rasp good for telling funny stories but unable to sing a note. His memory of performing with Walter Dopsie at the *fais do-do* was like an itch at the end of a severed limb, not terribly hard to put out of mind once he accepted that it always would be there. *Feel like you flyin'*, Walter had said before they'd climbed on those crates to play. True at the time, but never again.

The sheriff's inquiry into Walter's death had come to a finding of drunken mishap. The details of the attack were lost to Richie. He had a dim recollection of one face at the scene, swollen and shiny with a nervous mean look that makes for the worst kind of bully, but it was no more substantial than a ghost glimpsed in a window. Pinefield teenagers had hauled his vehicle out of the gully and picked it clean of its tires, upholstery, and engine; it was a rusting skeleton by the time Richie got back there weeks afterward. And his concern for Walter's daughter was too awkward to bring up. Someone said she'd been returned to her mother down on the coast. Her face he pictured clearly.

THE TWINS WERE born the next summer. Justine first, followed moments later by Richard Junior. Richie was absent due to unloading deliveries at Block's, he said, though being unmissed at the occasion by his wife and father-in-law made their doubt a non-issue. Esther's pregnancy had been her and Leopold's show from the start. Richie had assumed he was forever golden in their eyes for having rescued Esther from spinsterhood; their acceptance of his drinking and carousing throughout her pregnancy seemed almost amiable. But coming home to find his wife in bed with an infant at each breast and her father and the midwife looking on with pride, he realized he was extraneous here. He turned on a heel and went back to the bar.

He and Leopold worked at the store while Esther stayed home with the children. Leopold kept him at laborer status, barely letting him talk to customers much less man the register or deposit the day's cash at the bank. Richie reminded himself that marriage and fatherhood were a game he was running— no money problems ever again, freedom when he wanted it, and a wife who let him have relations with her if he bathed and shaved and treated her nice that day. Condescension from some old Jew was nothing he couldn't handle.

Those relations predated Esther's pregnancy. Hands off during it he'd understood; the continued halt in the weeks and now months afterward was vexing. She'd become gigantic carrying the twins and had stayed that way since, but her size in daylight gave way to splendor at night when the press of her knee or backside under the covers posed a cushiony promise. He'd wait for a hint confirming that it wasn't by accident. Sometimes he thought Esther too was waiting, lying there with breath held just like him. Then sleep would take over and the moment would pass unregretted.

Lately she'd become careless of the sour milk smell that attached to her after nursing. Richie in turn didn't bother to rinse the bourbon from his mouth or pass a washcloth under his arms before bed. She would jolt awake when the babies cried in their nursery at night. He'd hear the floorboards groan under her weight and think malicious thoughts. Leopold would appear in the hallway in his robe and slippers, holding the latest electric lantern he'd purchased from some supplier or other. Their silent collusion as they went to tend the children irritated Richie more than if he'd heard them whispering about his faults. He accepted that they thought he was useless. He disliked that they preferred it that way.

His chance to assert himself came when his father-in-law brought up religion one day at the store. "Jewish from the mother," Leopold said. "Her children."

"*Our* children," Richie said.

"You not religious, what I can see."

"Your daughter neither."

"We are a people. *Hébreu*. Justine and Richard, same."

Richie shook his head. "I gave in on her name, that's it."

"Justine?"

"Wanted Bonnie, you know that."

"Justine is beautiful."

"Ain't American. They're Bainards. American. And the boy," Richie said, "want him called R.J., not Richard."

"I no like."

"R. J. Bainard is a rich man's name."

"You not rich. I not rich."

"Look around, Mr. Block. You made a nice business. I can take it big."

Richie, who'd only been trying to get under Leopold's skin, was surprised when the old man seized his arm. "You will do? For the children?"

"Just said, didn't I?"

"I have worried on this."

Richie tried to keep up. "Talkin' about your store, right?"

"Maybe your store."

Leopold's meaning sunk in. "Bull's-eye," Richie said.

Expanding Block's had been Esther's idea originally. She didn't care which faith if any her children adopted and seemed not to care much about them except as a point of duty. She couldn't wait to get back to the business. She wanted to improve the space and open locations in other towns, make Block's the popular stop for household goods and also farm tools, feed, and fertilizer. Hearing her excited plans when they came home after work was the one time each day that Richie and Leopold laid off bickering to share agreement in dismissing her.

She began interviewing prospective help, ladies endorsed as righteous and non-thieving by their pastors or previous employers. It was inconceivable to Leopold that she might so abandon her children—his grandchildren, raised by a stranger! Richie dreaded the idea of Esther bossing him around at work.

He was relieved that Leopold was of the same mind to keep her home. That he might put Richie in charge, make him *the owner,* was an unexpected bonus.

A small law office had recently opened a few doors down from Block's. Leopold had gathered from its fancy sign that it was a firm of two attorneys, Abelard & Percy. He'd seized on the idea that the former was of French and possibly Jewish descent. But when he asked inside for "Monsieur Abelard," the lone gentleman there rose from his desk chair and said with drama, "While I'm honored to be on a first-name basis with you, sir, I confess that Messrs. Abelard and Percy are but one humble soul." He gestured toward his front window and the shingle displayed outside. "My middle initial was rendered a virtual Chinese ampersand by the so-called calligrapher and as a consequence I've endured no end of confusion about my business, my name, and my very identity."

None of this got through to Leopold. "You make will?"

Abelard "Abe" Percy—in his forties, portly, with a red pocket square peeking out from his threadbare suit—gave a bow. "But of course." Seemingly full of display, the gesture in truth was grateful. This was Abe's first client since setting up shop in Lake Charles after being expelled from his position as a state attorney in New Orleans. By his own admission in retrospect, he'd become overkeen in giving shelter and comfort to street waifs thrown to charity while their parents did time in jail. Shelter and comfort he considered it still, but people had whispered revolting things. Out here in the sticks, he hoped to leave all that behind.

———

LEOPOLD, WHEN CUSTOMERS entered the store, had developed a tendency to rock aggressively in his chair in order to propel himself to his feet. Richie got a kick out of seeing him, at the ring of the front bell, gather momentum with his face turning red and his white hair flying. One day the old man launched and kept going, hurtling forward like a toppled tree and smacking the floor face-first. The comedy of the pratfall preceded its seriousness by several seconds. Richie was still laughing when the realization dawned that his father-in-law was badly hurt. It was markdown day at the store. The crowd of shoppers recoiled in horror from Leopold's lifeless body and Richie's pealing laughter.

Block's Dry Goods was a Lake Charles fixture and Leopold an eminent figure. Dozens of mourners came to Orange Grove Cemetery to pay respects. Richie felt them eyeing him at graveside as the lout who'd found this funny. The feeling got worse during the reading of the Kaddish prayer of mourning. The strangeness of the Hebrew spoken by Leopold's temple colleagues brought home to Richie how bizarre it was that he should have wound up connected to this old dead foreigner.

He studied Leopold's uncovered granite casement. It was built half out of the ground on account of the region's high water table, the varnished casket inside looking like a long shiny shoe in a shoebox. He wondered what he was doing here, how in hell he'd fathered two children with a woman he barely knew, and did he really see himself running a department store for the rest of his life? The questions posed their own answer. He would escape first chance he got.

The Kaddish was gibberish to him, what he imagined Apaches or Zulus talked like around their heathen fires. The

lingual murk set his thoughts adrift. He heard a woman's murmur inside the Kaddish's monotone. He turned to the sound
with hazy joy that some angel had come to save him. It was
only Esther whispering, "I don't get a word of it." He blinked at
her as if unsure who she was.

"Amen," several men said abruptly. Richie thought the Kaddish was over and chimed in, "Amen." But the responses were
part of the ritual, standard avowals of something, and the
prayer resumed with no end in sight.

"Lord," Esther said under her breath. "Could it be any drea-
rier?"

"That kinda day," Richie said.

"Was Papa's time. Gotta accept it."

Her composure spooked him. "Your time now," slipped out
accidentally.

She put her hand inside his. "Thanks for saying that, Richie."
She rarely addressed him by name; it seemed a warning of sorts.
"But really it's *our* time." She brought his hand to her lips and
kissed his fingers one by one.

Two hours later they were having intercourse in their bedroom at home with clothes thrown around and Esther heedless
of the bedsprings groaning or the nanny she'd hired being
just down the hall with the kids. Richie was torn between self-
consciousness over their racket and fright at his wife's weird
passion on this fraught afternoon. She clamped him so hard
into her breasts that he had trouble getting air. Things were
slippery down there as never before. Her cries in his ear became continuous. He looked over his shoulder to make sure
the door was shut. He caught a glimpse of her bare legs, thick,
pale, bent at the knees, jutting upward around his hips in the

afternoon light. The sight astonished him, her open thighs flexing each time he pushed into her. He heard his own cries mingle with hers.

They retreated to separate sides of the bed. At length he asked, "Gonna tell me why?"

"A wife needs a reason?"

"A daughter kinda do, day like today."

"Not one no more. Could be that's why."

Dusk in the window signaled the end of a long day. Richie pictured the fresh-laid slab on Leopold's tomb going dark on this first night of many. A baby's yelp in the nursery startled him. Esther began to get up before falling back on the pillow. "Help's here now, I forgot."

"Who she again?"

"Sallie Hooker. Told you ten times."

"Surprised you went with a colored."

"She's half only. Bayou gal. Up from trouble, lookin' for better."

"You know some man got to do with it."

"Long as she's straight now."

"Ain't like we need her," Richie said.

"I'm back the store tomorrow."

"Your father did not want that."

"He's got no say anymore, God rest him."

"I don't want it neither."

Esther tucked against him. "Don't start, Richie. Not after such sweetness." One breast lay huge across his chest. Moments ago he'd been trying to inhale it into his mouth. Now it made him feel queasy.

"You know he seen a lawyer." Esther rose on one elbow as

Richie spoke. Her blond hair framed her face and he appreciated how flawless her complexion was up close. This accounted
for his hesitation, as of a gently applied knife, when he added,
"'Bout me takin' over the business."

After a pause she said, "Please tell me that's a lie."

LEOPOLD'S WILL STIPULATED that Block's proceed under Richie's
control with Esther as a limited partner. When the children
turned twenty-five, they would share in the operating profits
or the net proceeds should the business be sold. Abe Percy,
wearing his usual linen suit with a pastel shirt and matching
pocket square, explained the terms to Richie and Esther in his
office.

Richie had expected to inherit the store outright. In his
mind he'd already sold it and banked the money after leaving,
as he saw it, a fair fraction to his wife and kids; now he'd have
to stick around to gather his cut piecemeal. Esther saw betrayal
where her father had seen tradition. "I don't understand how
he can reach out the grave and make me do what he wants
even then."

"You could file an objection with the court," Abe said.

"Kinda shit is that?" Richie said. "You wrote the will, now
you wanna tear it up?"

"I say it *because* I wrote it and *because* it's a fact. I warned
Mr. Block that churches and government can mandate perpet-
ual property rights, but not always individuals."

Esther clasped Richie's hand. "Then we'll fight it."

Richie pulled free. "Your father had a right—"

"Block's is *my* right!"

Richie turned to Abe, a fellow man in the room, like-minded and sensible. The lawyer acknowledged, "Be hard for her to prevail without your consent."

The subsequent silence said everything. Richie talked anyway. "I run it. Kids get it. Wife stays home." He turned to her with the calm of a man holding aces. "Like Papa wanted."

"Let me just work the store like I always done." Tears came. "You need me there, you'll see."

It occurred to him she was talking sense. "Long as I'm boss." Her sniffling quieted.

"Make suggestions, okay. No opinions."

She nodded.

"Because I *will* be the goddamn boss."

"Whatever you want."

"Whatever I want." Richie pointed at Abe. "You heard it."

"I did." Overweight himself, Abe had sympathy for Esther on many levels, marriage to this grabby hayseed heading the list.

"Little test," Richie said. "We been callin' her Justine, don't ask me why."

"Her? You mean your daughter."

"Well, that's just it. I wanted Bonnie, but I got overruled at the time."

"Because you were out drinking," Esther said.

"I'm talkin' to the lawyer here."

She lowered her eyes. Abe hurt at the sight of it.

Richie went on, "And I cannot get right with Justine. Bonnie's my girl. Miss Bonnie Bainard from Lake Charles, USA."

"You're saying you want the name changed," Abe said.

"In the paperwork, yes I do. Make it official here on out."

Abe looked to Esther. Her face was splotchy from crying earlier, as if slapped by a clumsy master. "Justine was my mother's name," she said.

"Then surely out of respect—" Abe began.

"No," she cut in. "Bonnie's fine." Abe saw that she had little choice but to feed her husband this concession, but that she felt obliged to sweeten it with "In fact I like it better" made his heart sink.

"See," Richie grinned. "I was right all along."

Abe leaned back in his chair. When Richie took Esther's hand in a possessive grip, Abe's gaze was there to meet hers as she mutely begged him to pity her plight. Recognition lit their faces too tenderly for Richie to notice. You could say Abe and Esther found each other at that moment, as friends rather than lovers—but either way, for life.

WITHIN A YEAR of taking over Block's, Richie opened stores in Shreveport and Baton Rouge, closing the latter after a few months but opening three more around the state in 1937 and 1938, when the worst of the Depression seemed past. Tailoring their wares to the needs of each locale, he otherwise patterned the establishments after the original. The sign and outside façade were indistinguishable among them. Even their staffs were alike. Richie hired female managers, an idea he got from watching his wife run the main store while he concentrated on the big picture. He judged candidates on the basis of his image of Esther. Salesmen needed charm and brass. Managers had to be diligent, organized, and invisible. Like her.

He let underlings do the daily retail slog while he hobnobbed with bankers and local bigwigs, a crowd he was pleased to discover enjoyed a drink and a laugh same as him. Esther planted herself at the Lake Charles store, squeezed into her father's old rocking chair with a ledger in her lap, monitoring accounts from throughout the Block's chain. Richie did the hands-on management, driving store to store in a canary Packard, striding in slick as a Federal agent and peppering staff with questions supplied by his wife. His black workers out back in the storage yards enjoyed his banter and the dollar bills he put in their hands. Whites in the front showroom remained gratifyingly cowed. His wife urged him to fire weak performers, but at worst he only cut their wages. Letting them keep their jobs allowed him to think well of himself and less of Esther, the heartless sow.

Neither had any touch for parenting. Richie's affection for his daughter began with her name, "Bonnie Bainard" meeting his ideal of the saucy all-American gal that any daughter of his surely must be. Esther's sense that the girl was a sourpuss was closer to the truth. The genetic misfire that caused Bonnie to shoot up in height to where she stood a head taller than the tallest boys in her class didn't help. Being neither cute nor popular despite belonging to one of Lake Charles's most successful families was bound to promote a glum attitude.

Her brother R.J. was more personable but rare to show it, a genuine loner but for interaction with the nanny, Sallie Hooker, who stayed on as the Bainards' live-in help as the children grew. Sallie, out of fondness, mistook R.J.'s quiet for introspection and his time spent with her in the kitchen and laundry as showing sensible regard for her hard-won country wisdom, rather than what it was, a way to hide out from his family. R.J.'s one certifiable virtue concerned the money she mailed each month to her home in Hancock Bayou down on the coast, the purpose of which, she let slip one afternoon, was to help her daughter being raised there by Sallie's mother. It didn't occur to R.J. to ask about the girl's father, but Sallie told him anyway. "He gone. Dead in a ditch."

"Fell?"

"Or got push. The drink done it either way, you can bet."

R.J. was too young to give this fact its full due. But keeping secrets was natural for him, and, compelled by Sallie's grave expression, easy in this case.

RICHIE WASN'T ONE to mark turning points or reflect on the past. His memories of the war in 1918 meant no more to him than the steak he had last night or the whiskey he shortly would quaff. A whore, afterward, was the same as his hand, and the esteem of his family was less a factor in maintaining his mood than having a nice automobile to drive and at least twenty bucks in his pocket at all times. But in the summer of 1938 he received two jolts that put him in mind of regrets and desires not even a new car could assuage. It felt like the hand of fate in action, spurring him to better his life while giving pardon in advance for any outside hurt it caused. Like a dog that somehow learns to read, Richie underwent a miracle. A simple man became less so.

It was a Wednesday in August when Joe Falcon entered the Lake Charles Block's with a guitar in one hand, a suitcase in the other, and a length of rope looped around one wrist. Richie, who rarely came to the store and was only there to get some petty cash out of the register, recognized him at once despite the musician's thinning hair and ratty suit. Joe's singing partner Cleoma Breaux walked a few steps behind him. Richie wouldn't have recognized her if they hadn't been together. Her hair was a tangled bird's nest and she wore an ill-fitting dress and dirty tennis shoes. She carried a baby of maybe six months in the crook of one arm, carried it with unnerving vigilance, like a girl so afraid of dropping her doll that she almost breaks it from squeezing. Cleoma's free hand gripped the rope tied around her waist, by which Joe led her as if on a leash.

Richie stood behind the store's front counter. Joe dropped his end of the rope to the floor and stepped on it while he opened the guitar case. Cleoma continued past him with a rapt expression until the rope tightened and tugged her back like a balloon on a string. Richie wondered what had happened to the lively girl with the knowing smile he'd met ten years ago. Her gaze drifted to his. *"Mes compliments,"* she said before looking off elsewhere. He felt sick to see such strangeness.

"My wife tell that to everyone," Joe said. "She mean only kindness by it."

"You got married," Richie said.

"We acquainted?"

"I seen you two play. After *'Lafayette'* come out."

"Them days done." Was this a reference to Cleoma? Richie regarded her worriedly, taking in once more the vacant gaze and rope around her waist. "Hard times," Joe said, reading his thoughts. "Same as everywhere."

"True that." Richie's suggestion of shared struggle rang false even as he spoke it. The Depression hadn't touched him. His life had never been easier. "New baby?" he asked to fill the space.

"Lil girl, yes sir. Lulu. Near lost 'em both right after she born. Wife snagged up her shawl in a Greyhound door. Drug her a quarter mile, her holdin' the child whole time."

"You pullin' my leg now."

"God's truth. Lulu, not a scratch. Cleoma took the hurt."

Richie looked at her again. "Seem okay now." He looked harder. Brain damage, plain as day. Retarded. He'd met her only once in his life, still it horrified him to see what bad luck had dealt her. "Damn."

The rope around her waist was the obvious next question. "She wander some," Joe explained. "Forget what she about. Not on Lulu. With Lulu she sharp."

Richie shook his head in utter sorrow. "You got a heavy load."

"Oh no, we fine. Grateful every day." Behind his glasses Joe's eyes told another story. He set the guitar on the countertop. Richie recognized Cleoma's National resonator, fingerboard ebony with pearl inlays, its metal body polished, cut with a pair of tapered f-holes, and etched with magnolia blossoms. Joe, watching Richie's admiring eyes, ran his hand along the neck. "She make a pretty noise, I guarantee."

Joe's drawl returned Richie to that evening backstage at the Pinefield Auditorium when he and Walter Dopsie had watched Joe and Cleoma perform *"Allons à Lafayette."* Walter had translated: *Man wanna marry his girl even he know she trouble.* A love song that Richie, it occurred to him now, could never sing on account of his voice and whatever else about him was broken. "Still got your accordion?" he asked.

"Still got me, better to say. But the National no need, so here go."

"Not interested." Esther had lumbered up from the rear of the store. It was the exact wrong person for Richie to see. He hated her right then. It had nothing to do with her size. He'd reveled enough in her lushness to know it could work him up every bit as much as the skinny girls he paid for in East Lake Charles, though they were available whereas Esther, by mutual indifference, no longer was. "Block's don't take consignments," she told Joe.

"Prefer a straight sell anyhow."

"We're not a pawnshop here."

"Forty'll get it. Worth double at least."

"It's not about the money, sir."

It was the "sir" that set Richie off, so upright and professional. Plus he'd had a couple drinks, it being past noon. He banged open the register, removed two twenties, and thrust them at Joe.

Esther whirled on him. "Dammit, Richie!"

He slapped her hard with his open palm. A first for him, it felt and sounded perfect. She buckled but didn't go down. Her eyes filled from the sting and her cheek burned red around the redder shape of his hand. Store patrons gaped in shock. Down the passway to the storeroom Richie saw his nine-year-old son and daughter watching with frozen faces, Bonnie taller, her head a brunette bulb on a stalk, R.J. wiry like his father but on the way to being handsomer thanks to his mother's blue-blue eyes. Richie marveled at the coincidence of the family all present to see this. It confirmed that a crossroads was at hand.

Esther's friend, the lawyer Abe Percy, pushed through the Block's front door carrying a stewpot wrapped in a towel. The pot held whatever kitchen concoction the two were sharing today. Both liked to cook. Lunching together on obscure recipes was one of their pleasures, others being coffee and pastry each morning and tea and more pastry each afternoon. Abe froze midstep as he took in the scene.

"Mes compliments," Cleoma chirped to him, the greeting now as spooky to Richie as a talking skull. Her baby started to fuss and she jiggled it. Something unseen beckoned her and she ambled after it down one aisle until the rope gently called her back.

Abe rushed to Esther, setting the pot on the counter and putting his arm around her. "Essie! What'd he do to you?" Only now did she begin to cry.

Richie's first thought was that the food smelled good, some kind of pepper stew. His next thought was a notion ludicrous but usefully rude: *"Essie?* Whatsat, lil pillow talk 'tween you two?" He felt the eyes of his children shift between himself and their sobbing mother.

Abe glared at him. "I told her it was only a matter of time."

Joe laid the two twenties on the countertop and started to put away his guitar. "Keep the money," Richie snapped. "And the National."

"Ain't lookin' for charity." Joe pocketed the bills, left the guitar, picked up his suitcase and led his wife and baby out the front door. Cleoma waved airy good-byes to all. Through the store window, people inside saw her husband kneel on the sidewalk to untie her. Their business at Block's concluded, he took her hand and led her down Ryan Street to catch a bus going wherever, forty dollars to the better in the quest to rebuild their lives.

Esther stopped crying. A shopper picked up an item in a show of considering to buy it. Richie lifted the National's strap over his head. Though he hadn't played in a decade, the G chord came instantly to his left hand; it sounded awful when he strummed. R.J. sidled over to see the guitar up close. On impulse he silenced its tuneless clang by grabbing the neck in a wraparound grip. His thumb clamped the strings to the fingerboard. When Richie strummed again, the sound was beautiful.

The boy let go and his father plucked a perfect G chord with open strings. "I'll be damned. Open tuning. That's a colored thing." For a moment Richie lost himself in playing, sliding his left hand in a flat bar up and down the neck, sometimes dragging a finger to turn a major chord into a sixth or seventh, fluid touches he'd never tried in his days with the Ramblers. His rhythm took a shuffle pattern as a melody returned faintly to mind. R.J. had never seen his dad with a guitar, had no idea he played. Richie's dreamy expression made the boy not nervous to be with him.

Richie paused and looked around sheepishly. " 'Nigger Blues,' give or take. Walter be proud." That no one knew what he was talking about sharpened the revelation that struck him: his present life stunk and change was required.

He handed the guitar to R.J. "Pawn it or play it. Yours either way." He beckoned Bonnie, who froze when he reached to embrace her but relaxed when it proved benign. Richie opened the register and gave her two twenties. "R.J. get the guitar, you get the cash. Been thinkin' you got a head for business." He'd thought no such thing but wanted to make the gifts even. "Turn it double, I bet."

"Bribing their loyalty," Abe said. "How touching."

"Best you not address me or my kids," Richie said to him. "The wife you can talk till you're sick of it."

Esther's face had begun to bruise. Richie caressed her shoulder. "I am sorry. I'll try never to do that again." He clapped his hands to conclude the matter and she flinched as if from a gunshot. Only Abe, his arm still around her, realized Esther was trembling.

All this was preamble to the second jolt that hit Richie that summer, the first half of a one-two punch that softened him up to the idea that coincidence doesn't happen by chance. Seeing Joe and Cleoma brought low by misfortune seemed a sign meant directly for him, a warning to get out and get satisfied while he still could. He wouldn't hesitate when the chance came.

HANCOCK BAYOU IS on the Gulf beach highway on the western end of Cameron Parish, fifty miles south of Lake Charles. It's the kind of place called nowhere by people who would never go there by choice—seashell roads, scrub-covered flood plains, few trees or structures predating the leveling crush of water and wind that had been the 1918 hurricane. Hundreds of thousands of wetland acres lie north of the town, laced with wooded cheniers and dark twisty channels spilling into the Gulf of Mexico on one side of the highway and wide, brackish bays on the other.

Hancock Bayou owed its existence to a commercial marina and adjacent pogie plant that rendered the inedible baitfish down to oil, fishmeal, and fertilizer, fouling the air if the breeze blew wrong though disagreeably only to visitors, who didn't appreciate the jobs and wages it signified. The town had a filling station, a movie house, two cement churches—Baptist and Catholic—and a combination druggist and general store where Richie agreed to drop Sallie Hooker when he drove her home a week after the scene at Block's with the Falcons.

Usually Sallie took a bus there on her breaks, but Richie had business in Cameron Parish. Last year the government had claimed vast tracts of Louisiana wetlands as protected habitats for fish, wildlife, and waterfowl. Richie and his cronies were furious at the Federal grab. They didn't golf or travel or do anything leisurely beyond private vice or public churchgoing except to hunt and fish. Hunting's high holiday was duck season from November to January. You could pay rice farmers for access to their ponds and paddies, but lately out-of-towners had started buying property and building private lodges. Most were tin-roofed bunkhouses with chicken-wire kennels for the barking retrievers; the hunting was spectacular but the accommodations strictly Jim Beam in a jelly jar and steel cots from army surplus. Richie's group of business partners planned something finer, with veteran guides and gourmet food along the lines of Scottish estates that offered shooting in the royal style to Hollywood stars and Texas oilmen. They'd bought ten thousand acres of marsh near the Sabine National Wildlife Refuge— like owning a bar next door to a brewery, Richie said—in order to construct a plush refuge of their own to be called the Section Eight Gun Club.

Richie had come to Hancock Bayou with one of his Section Eight partners, a Lake Charles builder named Burt Meers, to begin laying out the project. The men rode up front in Richie's

Packard. Sallie sat quiet as a mouse in back with a travel case
on the seat beside her and her hair pinned up under a Sunday
hat. A larger bag was in the trunk. She'd tried to smile when
Richie teased her about how much stuff she'd packed for a
week. The Bainards had treated her decently, after all, and she'd
raised the twins from infancy. It'd be a lie to say she wouldn't
miss them.

The years of having Sallie living under his roof had taught
Richie that ignoring servants on a personal level was how they
seemed to prefer it. When Burt Meers started quizzing Sallie
over the noise of the motor about whether Lake Charles blacks
needed a public school or couldn't they just get their learning at
home, her unease at being brought into the conversation made
Richie cut in sympathetically, "Got no kids, what she gonna
know?"

"They talk. In the hair shop, church."

"You just lookin' to get the project."

"Build a nigger school? Pay me, I'll build 'em a damn palace."

Richie drummed up a laugh but couldn't help glancing at
Sallie in the backseat. The splash of sunlight through the car
window turned her complexion almost creamy. With mild surprise he was reminded that she was part white. Mixed blood
was common in these parts, and in any event his indifference
to matters outside himself freed him of social prejudice. He
turned frontward and drove on.

"I got a child." Sallie's declaration was nervous and quick.
"Growed now."

Richie looked back around. "And you ain't never said a
word?"

"Girl too much for me. My mama raise her."

"My wife know?"

"No, sir."

"Smart."

"Oughtn't keep secrets from the lady of the house," Meers said.

Richie asked him, "Would you'a hired her to raise your kids with a child no daddy back home?"

"She didn't say no daddy."

"She ain't got to."

"Then be a couple reasons I don't hire her. Good Christian number one."

Sallie turned her face to the window as they discussed her. The last stretch of road into Hancock Bayou wound through a patchwork of rice and sugarcane fields mostly worked by tenant families like the Hookers. She'd left almost a decade ago on the excuse that her prospects were better in Lake Charles to earn wages to support the daughter she'd had with a no-account tomcat who'd drunk himself to death upstate. In truth she'd left her in her mother's care after painful reminders of the man started showing up in their child, teenaged by that time, in the form of allure combined with uncaring. The girl was selfish and blithe yet people adored her, a mystery that made sense once you took her looks into account. "Beauty" didn't capture it. "Knockout" was more the effect.

Sallie said nothing to Richie about quitting the Bainards when she exited his car at the general store. A letter could say it later, silence just as well. He retrieved her bag from the trunk. She lied that she would return by bus to Lake Charles next week, and took a seat on a sidewalk bench awaiting her kin to come fetch her.

Richie was about to back his car into the street when a Chevy flatbed rumbled up on his left. An old lady drove, gray hair, nut-colored skin, her head barely higher than the steering wheel. The passenger on Richie's side was a young woman with dark ropy tresses that flew like a pennant over her bare elbow jutting out the truck window. Pulling alongside, she surveyed Richie's Packard as if sure it was stolen. Her expression turned sly when she met him eye to eye, the message being that no way did he rate such a classy ride but to his credit had swung the trick. Meanwhile his expression showed near religious amazement.

He recognized Walter Dopsie's daughter at once, though her eyes were hooded and her hair had taken copper glints that spoke of southern sun and not the smoky music hall in which she'd first impressed him. Ten years had puffed and rounded her features—she was in her early twenties now—but oh, it was her. "Angel," popped from his mouth like a gulp.

She cocked her head. "You."

His joy at being remembered didn't even embarrass him. Surely it proved that his feelings were pure, his miracle girl now probably some sharecropper's wife and still he'd surrender his soul to win her. "Just down for a visit," he said. The explanation rang absurd in his ears.

"Didn't imagine you here permanent."

His thoughts hit a wall. Acknowledgment was called for. "Was a bad night we had. At the end."

"I don't think about it."

"I guess me neither."

She was silent. Evidently it was his job to do the talking.

"So it's your mama been workin' for me all these years?"

"News to me."

He nodded, stymied again. It annoyed him to have to make small talk when fate clearly had big things in store for them.

Angel Hooker (her parents hadn't married) peered down at the Packard as though at a lifeboat she might deign to let save her. Her softening expression suggested she was starting to sense how much her life might change in the next moments. She wasn't a wife, let alone one tied to a sharecropper. But she was, like Richie, in the market for rescue.

Her mother had risen from the bench and was watching from nearby. Sallie hesitated to approach, her daughter's long intimidation of her now reinforced by Angel's strange bond with Mr. Bainard. Her own mother stood beside her, hand resting on Sallie's arm for support and in unspoken gratitude that her daughter had finally come home for good. Old Mrs. Hooker was full of the cancer but still the family's proud matriarch, driving a truck, scolding the men, farming rice for landowners she'd never met. Her one failure, she would have said, was in not getting her granddaughter to value herself above whatever slick piece of traveling trash came through town. But then Sallie too had been a handful in her day, getting pregnant by that charmer Walter Dopsie, who was as wrong for faithful fatherhood as he was for tilling dirt in Hancock Bayou all his life.

Richie shut off his motor and climbed out of the Packard. The move was unwelcome to Meers, who wanted the hell out of there, but also to Sallie and her mother, whom Richie approached with an earnest stride. They recoiled warily. He belonged here no more than did his big fancy car all covered in dust in front of a ramshackle storefront. But the car spoke money, he had plenty, the Hookers much less. It gave him the courage to be direct. "Ma'am. Sallie. I knew Angel's daddy. I knew Angel some, and I hope to reacquaint if she'll have it."

The Hooker ladies were speechless.

"And if she's married," he said, "well, no secret—so am I."

There was silence till Angel broke it. "Shouldn't you be talkin' to me?"

Richie turned and put his hand on his heart. "Afraid what you might say."

"How about take me to Shreveport?"

The questioned staggered him thrillingly, like being hit with a handful of rose petals. "Wherever you say, pretty girl."

Angel's smile, cute as it was, held a sliver of letdown, his ardor too predictable, too easy, another man with a teenage brain. She rested her chin on her arm but kept her eyes on him. They were a paler green than what he recalled, like a new seedling before it buds with flowers or prickers. "Now remind me your name again," she said.

HE INSTALLED HER in a suite at the Youree Hotel in Shreveport and spent so much time there the staff took to calling them Mr. and Mrs. When she gave birth to his son fourteen months later, he got her a cottage with a trellis and carport not far from the Block's on Texas Street. She was electric in his arms from their first time together, giggly and coarse and just a natural to do things to. She gave weepy cries during lovemaking that hardened him whenever he replayed them in his head. She liked to drink and even when she was pregnant would dance naked for him to the wireless. She laughed at jokes that made him blush and dared him, though he refused in appalled disbelief, to let her give him an orgasm with her hand while they waited for her doctor to arrive in a taxicab to deliver the baby. Afterward, Richie wanted to name the boy Walter, but Angel insisted on Seth.

"Seth? Where you get that?"

"It come to me."

"Now goddamn, Angel, if it some ol' boyfriend—"

"Stop. I like the name."

"I'd kill the guy, you know that."

"Big talk."

He smiled, mostly. "Thought you'd want him called for your daddy."

"I hardly knew the man. Took me travelin' a couple times when my mama tired o' fightin' me."

Propped on feather pillows in bed, she shifted the baby to her other breast. Richie glanced down warily but found it not so bad. "Lookit that sonofabitch work! And still you want every time I see him I got to wonder who he named for?"

"If you so worried, don't see him."

"You know I will, whatever he called."

"In the Bible, Richie! Seth is Adam and Eve's number three child. Sent by the Lord after Cain killed Abel."

"Well, if it out the Bible, okay."

"Little gift from me to you. No matter what else. 'Cause you been good to me and I love you."

In that moment Richie loved her back a hundredfold. He beheld the vision of her and their child with cosmic wonder that men like him often aren't built to acknowledge. But he knew it the instant he felt it, and he knew that it was rare and he would never let it go. In the shaded glow of her bedside lamp

Angel's caramel shoulders and the slope of her breasts were something out of a classic painting he'd never seen. His baby's pink head made him want to cry for its preciousness. In fact he did cry a little, Angel too, and when he bent low to give her a kiss their lips made a beautiful fit.

THE COMPANY'S GROWTH slowed only a little during the war years, with Block's stores opening in Houston and Jackson. Esther, from her father's rocking chair relocated to a headquarters office near the Lake Charles city hall, oversaw the selection of sites and distribution centers and the standardization of products and services throughout the chain. Richie was her eyes and ears, making the rounds from place to place in a performance mixing the strut of a corporate boss with the skitter of a traveling salesman. It was an efficient partnership in which they spent little time together, and it came to an end just after New Year's in 1946, when Esther choked on a mouthful of crawfish pie and died at age fifty-four.

Abe Percy had prepared the dish as a pick-me-up for his friend, who was nursing a cold at home. He was sitting beside her while she ate in bed when something caught in her throat and caused a spasm that took her life right there in a blue-faced thrashing silence. He would never get over it. He would never forgive himself. Richie made a special trip to his office a week after the funeral to let Abe know that he wouldn't forgive him either. "I loved the woman," Richie said. "Now you gone and orphaned her children."

"They're not orphans. They have their father."

"Listen to you, talkin' legal at such a time."

Abe clasped his hands in front of his face to keep them from shaking. "What do you want from me? I can't feel worse than I already do."

Richie had specific wants in mind. Sympathy intruded. "Hell, everyone knows it was an accident. Show me a crawfish pie ain't got a shell in it. Woman ate like a damn horse."

Abe's hands tightened.

"I'll be straight," Richie went on. "I didn't love Esther that much. Not like I love my gal in Shreveport and it's a magical thing, lemme tell you."

"Come again?"

"Gonna marry her. Our boy, gonna be his daddy official."

"You have a son with another woman?"

"Almost seven now. Seth. Smart as a whip."

"Poor Esther."

"She not part o' this."

"Clearly."

"Don't be smart or we done here."

"Done for what, Richie?"

"The store. The paperwork. Who know that shit more?" Abe had drafted most every legal contract for the Block's chain since Leopold's death. Cutting loose such a client would mean starting over in his profession, a humiliation at middle age after he'd been sacked from the state attorney's office almost twenty years ago, a death sentence if it happened again. "I need you to school Bonnie on the business," Richie said. "The whole shootin' match."

A fantasy teased Abe's mind of continuing to work for Block's in order, like a secret saboteur, to hurt Richie someday for his mistreatment of Esther. But he knew he'd lose fire once the money kept coming. "She's in high school," he protested halfheartedly.

"No more. Asked her to quit, she jumped on it. Hates that goddamn place. Girl likes makin' money."

"You don't?"

"I like havin' it."

"And your son? Esther's son."

"He out the toy army come spring." The term was Richie's take on Esther's insistence that R.J. enter the East Texas Military Academy as an eighth grader in 1942. Wartime conscription had been revving up and she'd wanted to shield him from the draft on an education deferral. A *military* education, so nobody could call him a shirker—first at high school and then, she'd hoped, in the Corps of Cadets at Texas A&M, giving him eight years out of harm's way should the fighting drag on in Europe and the Pacific. The precaution had proved unnecessary once the war ended last summer. "I reckon it's college next," Richie said. "Stay drunk at the fraternity on my dime."

"You can afford it."

"Yeah? That your money gone for piss at that prep school?"

"It'll be his money eventually." The lawyer smiled, knowing it would annoy. "Leopold's will, remember? The grandchildren become owners at age twenty-five."

"Why I got to get on it, make my plans." Richie leaned forward. "For Angel and my lil boy."

"Her name is Angel?"

"It fit, trust me."

"You're serious about this."

"Best you be, too."

"May I ask, have you told Bonnie and R.J.?"

Richie nodded, though it didn't mean yes. "That's got to come, I know."

HE PREPARED FOR introducing his elder children to Angel and Seth by buying a residence big enough for them all. He called it Georgia Hill after being informed it was of Georgian revival design and thinking it needed a plantation name. Located outside town not far from the lakefront, the place rather strained for glamor, its whitewashed pillars and portico overmatching the brick façade like too much icing on a cake. But it appealed to Richie for its view—the view of *it,* from the road. The main house sat among several outbuildings on a rise overlooking lawns and established plantings. Two southern live oaks guarded each side of the driveway entrance, trunks gray and hefty as an elephant's hindquarters. Entering between them in a long-hooded limousine and seeing the Georgia Hill grounds unfurl before you was to understand that nothing beats money sometimes. It was a lesson that his daughter Bonnie, the older twin by minutes and by temperament, instinctively endorsed. Not so her brother. The difference went far to explain why they'd never got along.

Rather than warm to the child most like them—one prudent, one feckless—their parents had each favored their opposite. There'd been something poignant about this in Esther's case. Her feelings for her son held a bit of whatever once had been positive in her marriage to Richie. She'd wanted mainly to give Leopold a grandchild, but Richie had attracted her with his energy and chatter. He was even romantic when he made the effort. Their early times together, he would slide down her big body and lay his head between her legs, her pubic hair a tickly pillow under his cheek, and declare, "I could die here with a smile." She would pull him on top to stop him from talking. Embarrassment felt like love in those moments.

Where R.J. disappointed was in traits he shared with his father—his evasiveness, his third-rate friends. But Esther tapped the same indulgence toward him that she'd shown Richie in the beginning. It wasn't easy; she was happiest when working in solitude at matters of business. Nor was it easy to ship him off to boarding school at age thirteen. Eluding the draft had been only one reason. Esther had begun contemplating removing R.J. from his father's influence the second Richie had hit her that first time in Block's. Subsequent incidents—slaps on her cheek or backside much harder than playful, maybe a grip on her arm tight enough to remind her that he could draw blood if he wanted—had made fierce her desire to give R.J. a life beyond Richie. She'd done it in small ways already, letting the boy dabble at playing guitar and slipping him catalogs to purchase the race records he liked listening to, frivolous wastes of time in her view but worth allowing if it made him think of his mother as not some all-business robot. She did hope military school would sharpen him up some. More than that, she wanted it to happen away from her husband.

Esther didn't miss R.J. in his absence; nor did he miss her. But when each on occasion thought of the other, it was with generosity enough to suppose that mother and son might have become close in the future. R.J.'s were the only moist eyes at Esther's funeral other than Abe Percy's. Richie had arranged the event to be held at the Baptist church; accommodating his wife's Jewish heritage was too much trouble given her non-practice and the continuing dreary news out of Europe about death camp survivors and hollow-eyed peasants that no one knew what to do with. Richie was well known in Lake Charles, but few of the funeral attendees had any sense of Esther beyond her being plainspoken and obese. R.J., on bereavement leave from the military academy, was praised by his father's friends for showing maturity in the face of what everyone agreed was his mother's pathetic death by gluttony. He knew their praise was based mostly on his cadet uniform, its crisp formality an improvement on his hometown reputation as a rich man's shiftless son. The contempt this aroused in him tempered his sorrow and enabled him to keep tears at a minimum.

At just under six feet, R.J. was taller than his father. He had his grandfather Leopold's high forehead and long nose that gave an intellectual effect not borne out in the classroom. The look was enhanced by his cigarette habit, the hang on the lip, the curling blue cloud, the clack of his Ronson lighter contributing to the impression that he was a young man of world-weary mind. He'd been aware from childhood that his family was well fixed. He knew that in time he could claim his share of Block's. It didn't matter if he deserved it or not.

His father had bought Georgia Hill after R.J. returned to the academy following Esther's funeral. R.J.'s first visit there was on his midwinter break. Bonnie, employed full time at Block's now, met him at the Lake Charles bus depot in an MG convertible that Richie had recently bought her. She was striking rather than pretty, with an angular jaw and thick hair that fought the aluminum curlers she applied grudgingly at night. Teenage vogues of pleated skirts and square-shouldered blouses gave her the appearance, because of her height, of a librarian who might also coach basketball. She was taller than her brother and much taller than any girl she knew, an unwelcome distinction that made leaving high school a relief and gave sweet satisfaction to zipping around town in a ragtop roadster and pointedly not waving to former schoolmates standing like fools at the bus stop.

Bonnie loved working at Block's. Her father had assured her that she would run the operation eventually, a pledge he'd reiterated to allay her concern, earlier that afternoon, on meeting the "houseguests" he'd invited down from Shreveport. In her car at the depot waiting for R.J., she recalled today's introduction with a smile, sort of, as she pictured R.J.'s shocked face a few minutes from now, when he too would meet his new mom and little brother.

"What's funny?" He climbed into the MG beside his sister, his rucksack on his lap. "That you got a car and I don't."

"Just all the changes."

"Like the house?"

"Well, it's big. We've got staff now." She pulled onto the road. "We come from a rich family, R.J. More than I knew."

"You're the expert."

"Getting there. I met bankers, suppliers, store managers, and I've been sitting with the lawyer to learn the particulars."

"Suppose I want some of that?" He didn't, but was curious what she'd say.

"To work in retail? I thought college for you. Go be the smart one."

"Let you be the boss."

"I do the work, you get the money. Not so bad."

He bent to light a cigarette. "Could be I'll just stay home, play guitar on the porch. Maybe summon the staff now and then."

"We don't have a porch, R.J. We have a terrace." Bonnie wheeled into the driveway, the live oaks like dark sentinels at each side. "Georgia Hill," she said, her expression losing its humor. "Home."

RICHIE HAD ARRANGED Angel and Seth on a sofa in the front parlor awaiting R.J.'s arrival with Bonnie. There was an endearing quality to his agitation that was lost on Angel. She didn't like seeing Richie fret over something in which he held the power. A month from thirty (he was forty-six), she wondered why he couldn't just command his older children to love their new family. She wanted nothing from them that wasn't in her possession already. She was Mrs. Richie Bainard, married in the Shreveport courthouse with little Seth passing the wedding ring after his daddy gave him the high sign. Issues of inheritance and hierarchy that had leaped to Bonnie's mind when they'd met today didn't trouble Angel at all. She expected her husband to take care of her and their child in proper fashion whether the others liked it or not. Ultimately she was sure they *would* like it. She'd never met anyone she couldn't charm.

And really, things went pretty well that night. Bonnie had absorbed the news already, and shocks in general tended to register with R.J. as interesting breaks from boredom. Their father made introductions even before R.J. laid down his bag. Angel hopped off the sofa and approached so fast that R.J. had time to discern only a beaming face of almond complexion and jade-colored eyes. She threw her arms around him in her habitual way of pushing good things to the limit. He was almost seventeen and alert to her curvy shape and the scent of her hair as he awkwardly returned her embrace. Fearing to look past her lest he have to acknowledge the kid sitting in the chair, he let his gaze drop over her shoulder. She arched slightly and lifted one foot off the carpet. The small of her back tightened under R.J.'s hands. Her upraised calf flexed in its stocking and her bottom did the same in its tight skirt. He looked up dizzily and found himself gazing at a neatly dressed boy sitting erect and dutiful on the sofa behind her. They stared at each other for maybe two seconds. R.J., at a loss for what to do, winked. Seth winked back.

The two of them—half brothers, odd as that sounded—had another exchange at the end of the evening. It turned out their rooms, new to each of them at Georgia Hill, were on opposite sides of the third-floor landing. Angel went to say bedtime prayers with Seth. R.J. waited till she returned downstairs to say goodnight to his father, sister, and Angel; he kept the last standoffish in case she made a move to hug him again. He grabbed two bottles of Jax and an opener from the kitchen. He opened his bedroom window and put the beers on the sill alongside a lighter, ashtray, and cigarettes. The movers had brought his guitar and Philco from the old house. A gift from his mother last Christmas, the Philco doubled as a radio and record player. His 78s were in a box on the floor and he took one out and inserted it in the front slot. Big Joe Williams's "Crawling King Snake" came out grainy and raw, a lone guitar and an evil voice.

I'm a crawlin' king snake, woman, gonna drag all 'round your
door,
You had the nerve to tell me, baby, you don't want me 'round no
more . . .

R.J. picked up his guitar, Cleoma Breaux's old National steel, and began noodling to the music. It was his first time playing in months. He was more than pretty good, and in any case the guitar's open tuning complemented Williams's Delta style. It could make mistakes sound like slick improvisations, make an off note sound soulful instead of bad—and R.J. only played for himself anyway, a few beers in the better.

Seth appeared in the doorway wearing red pajamas with feet. R.J. lowered the volume. "Didn't mean to wake you."

"Not asleep." The boy had a compact, earnest face that resembled their father's more than did R.J.'s. "I didn't know what it was," he said, glancing at the record player.

"Blues music. Negro blues."

This made no impression.

"Easy to play. Hard to play good." R.J. swigged his beer self-consciously. "You should go back to bed. I'll stop."

Seth fiddled with the door latch.

"How about this house, huh?" R.J. ventured. "Big as two houses."

"Will you live here?"

"I'll be away mostly. You'll have the run of the place." R.J. had no idea how to talk to children, so went with something that mattered: "You like your daddy, Seth?"

The boy nodded.

"Why?"

"He's nice to my mother."

"Good reason."

"Your mother's dead." It wasn't a question.

"She is," R.J. said. "He wasn't too nice to her." He saw this troubled the boy and added quickly, "It's different now. He's gonna be fine with you."

Seth dropped cross-legged to the floor, eyes upraised.

"Guess we ain't sleepy." R.J. lit a cigarette, flipped the platter to the B-side and reinserted it in the player. "Meet Me Around the Corner" had a country bounce with lyrics murky and ribald. R.J., amused by Seth's vexed expression, explained over the music, "Guy likes a chubby woman, you get that? More she wobbles, more he wants her." He blew smoke out his window. "No one we know, of course."

The song ended. R.J. took some 78s from the box and shuffled through them on his lap. He opened the other beer. They listened to Leadbelly, Robert Johnson, and Reverend Gary Davis. R.J. invited his brother to slide the empty beer bottle along the strings of the National, creating a fluid beebuzzy hum that wove easily through the blues chords. He resumed playing himself only after Seth fell asleep and he'd carried him to bed. He didn't want the kid telling his father, *their* father, about R.J. enjoying such foolishness as playing along to a record. Not because Richie would mock it; on the contrary, he would declare with smug vindication that R.J.'s mother would *not* have approved. What's more, Bonnie would agree with him, making R.J. further resent them for what they'd never known.

———

OF EVERYONE IN the snapshot taken in front of the Houston
Municipal Airport in June 1952, R.J. showed the least change in
appearance from the night the family had first gathered at
Georgia Hill six years earlier. This may seem odd since he was
still in uniform and looking thin after seven months on the line
in Korea. But consider the others. Richie was a full-blown alco-
holic now, though late hours, rich food, and frequent expedi-
tions of hunting and fishing were as much to blame as bourbon
for his rheumy eyes and ruddy complexion. Bonnie's rising authority in the Block's store chain had awakened a cool regality
almost avant-garde in style. She'd discarded the makeup and
pleated skirts in favor of silk blouses, cuffed slacks, and jew-
eled barrettes the size of a jackknife to hold back her side-
parted hair, everything serving to dramatize her height, long
legs, and masculine features. Then there was Angel. Her hair
was flipped at the shoulder and dyed silver-blond. In a further
nod to Marilyn, the few pounds she'd put on had gone to good
places; if her earlier allure, dusky and wild, was diminished by
this conventional sexiness, there weren't many men making
that argument in 1952. As for twelve-year-old Seth, he was perfectly average, perfectly nice, yet shone like a movie star in his
parents' eyes, a distortion that applied to their sense of his over-
all brilliance and which, to his credit, he realized was much
inflated. He was smarter than they were. It led him to doubt
their praise and drew him to people he deemed better than he,
more talented, more magnetic, more heroic. His brother topped
this list. R.J.'s absence away at college and at war had burnished
the boy's spotty impression of him, turning obscurity into legend
and mere survival into storybook gallantry. In the photo taken
at the Houston airport, Seth isn't smiling. He's staring across

at R.J. with wonder, still not believing that his idol is home at last.

How he'd wound up leading a rifle platoon in the Korean War was a story R.J. later was able to make amusing because he'd survived and because memories of fallen marines and of enemy he killed, two in the latter case, by a single short burst of a BAR midway through his deployment, recurred to him only rarely; he was a solitary person but not a brooder, one of those who can truly think about nothing while pondering the night sky. During his college sophomore summer in 1947, it had been announced that the draft, suspended since the end of World War II, would be reinstated. Richie imagined nothing better than for his elder son to serve in the enlisted ranks, but Angel, eager to be helpful, had noted R.J.'s alarm and proposed a clever alternative. A marine program called the Platoon Leaders Class invited college boys to spend summers training at Quantico, Virginia, in order to become second lieutenants in the Marine Corps Reserve. A few years of monthly meetings and field exercises would exempt them from conscription into active duty in the peacetime service. Bonnie had pegged the plan as too good to be true, but there was no way her brother could resist Angel's giddy encouragement. So the PLC it was.

He graduated in May 1950 and was duly commissioned in the reserves. The North Koreans invaded south across the 38th Parallel a month later. Angel was more upset than R.J. about his subsequent mobilization; he took it as fair comeuppance whereas she saw it as a fateful trick hatched to make her look unfit as a loving stepmother. "Come back to me safe," she'd told him in tears, arms tight around him, when he'd left to join his unit. That "to me" was confusing, a private clue of remorse or endearment, and lingered in his mind more than it should have.

He'd unpacked his rucksack and seabag in a fortified bunker on the reverse slope of a snowy Korean ridgeline in November 1951. The ground leveled at the floor of the valley before ascending to mountains on the far side. The mountains held dug-in Chinese and North Koreans who through the winter of 1951–52 faced off against forward elements of the First Marine Division. Each side eyed the other while diplomats worked out international peace terms. Heavy combat was over. The previous year's huge swings of momentum, of attack and retreat up and down the Korean peninsula at the cost of thousands of casualties, had slowed to a stalemate of fitful barrages and small unit probes. For R.J.'s platoon, the mission to keep the resistance line static until the final boundaries were demarcated meant night watch, sentinel duty, and staying alert while mostly staying in trenches within the wire perimeter.

He led roughly one recon patrol per week across no-man's-land during his seven-month stint. They would move out at sunset and return at dawn. On his first one, he stepped on a mine under deep snow, was thrown ten feet with a concussion but nothing broken or bleeding. The legs of the marine behind him were shredded. R.J.'s consciousness returned with the image of his men's faces lifting from their stricken comrade to the rookie lieutenant who'd fucked him up. It was a bad start to R.J.'s tour that might have been worse had not his platoon sergeant blamed himself for not noticing that the men had bunched too close as they'd walked. The sergeant's name was Alvin Dupree. He'd fought in the Pacific in the last war and was from New Orleans. You couldn't call him and R.J. close; officers and noncoms don't do that. But Alvin came to respect the lieutenant's diligent command. And he appreciated that R.J. liked Negro blues, which Alvin played on harmonica, played well, with the tender restraint of someone trying not to cry, though the sergeant would never have made the claim himself.

Sergeant Dupree took the photo of the Bainard family that day at the Houston airport. He and R.J. had flown from San Diego where they'd disembarked from the troopship *General M. C. Meigs*, which soon would return to Korea with the next replacement draft. R.J. had already been processed back to reserve status. Alvin was to finish out behind a desk at a Marine Corps recruiting office in New Orleans before being discharged next year. They addressed each other as in the field, "Sergeant" for Alvin and "Mister Bainard" for R.J. This confused Richie when he heard it. "Ain't it *Lieutenant* Bainard?" he asked Alvin after they'd shaken hands.

"We use 'mister' sometime," Alvin explained. "Marines do."

"Army here. World War One. Rough stuff."

"Sergeant Dupree was in the Pacific in 1945," R.J. said to his father over Angel's shoulder. She'd rushed to embrace him and it took time to peel her off.

"'Forty-five? So you missed Iwo Jima an' all that."

"I did," Alvin said. "Okinawa was all I seen."

"Can we least get a picture?" Angel said. "These boys won't never look finer. I'll mail it," she told Alvin. "Give it to your girl, she'll thank you good."

"Not necessary, ma'am." He offered to photograph them.

Angel gave him the camera and lined everyone up. Alvin looked down in puzzlement. "*Dog*," he muttered.

Bonnie came over. "It's a Rolleiflex. The top pops open."

She showed him. "They're complicated. I doubt my stepmother can work it either."

"Brownie's more my speed."

"That's why they're popular."

They stood close. Bonnie liked not having to look down at him. She was over six feet but he was much taller, a huge fellow with a sleepy face and shoulders like sandbags stuffed inside his olive tunic. His dark hair was so thick it was opaque where it was buzzed at the temples. She returned to the family group. In the resulting photo her eyes aren't on the camera or on anyone in particular. They're adrift, skittish of where to land.

The sergeant would take a bus to New Orleans from here. He gave R.J. a sharp salute. Seth watched in pride, glad to see his brother's stature affirmed.

The Greyhound idled nearby. The two marines walked over together. "You ever need a job, Alvin," R.J. said, "my dad could help."

The sergeant ignored the switch to first names. "Most kind, Mr. Bainard."

He slid his seabag into the luggage compartment and stepped aboard the bus. Cigarette smoke clouded the air. Almost all the seats were taken, none available on the side facing the airport. Alvin made his way up the aisle, head bowed below the nicotine-stained ceiling. There was chagrin on his face until he came to a young Asian couple. "Speak English?"

"Of course," the man said, though it seemed from his wife's silence that perhaps she didn't.

"Gonna need you to move from there."

"There are single seats left."

"All yours."

"We're together," the man said. "You must see that."

"I see two gooks and a U.S. marine. Two live gooks, not even burned to death."

The couple moved. Alvin helped the wife stow her bags in the overhead rack. He eased into the seats they'd vacated and draped one leg over the armrest, reclining against the window. He cocked his head for a view outside. The Bainards were walking toward the parking lot. Alvin tracked them through a squint; tracked Bonnie, that is, as she strode apart from the others. *"Dog."* His sigh fogged the glass.

As the bus lurched ahead he took his mouth harp from his breast pocket and blew something soft and aimless. The Asian woman, in her seat a couple rows back, heard the music and liked it, not knowing what sort of man was playing.

To CALL ANGEL Bainard flighty would be unfair. Her whims resisted alternate fancies until they were accomplished. Nor was she a tease; what she promised, she gave. Her life was a series of passion projects achieved through deliberate steps often as unwise as they were brave. Becoming Richie's mistress, for example, had all but guaranteed that she would bear his child. Becoming his wife after Esther died had likewise assured that she would be Mrs. Bainard to the hilt—mom to the children, smoking hot on his arm, bitchy or nice to his friends and underlings as the mood, her mood, dictated. By 1953, she'd done all those things. It was time for something new.

The first project that seized her was to revamp the Kilties, Lake Charles High School's all-girl marching drum corps. Founded on the eve of World War II to promote school spirit and female fellowship, the outfit performed at parades and football halftimes. Angel wasn't a sports fan and only attended the game because Richie was being honored for funding school repairs from a lightning fire the previous year. Led by three blond "colonels" flashing silver batons, the Kilties high-stepped onto the field to a patter of drumbeats. They wore Scottish kilts, white trim, and red plumes in their hair, and pranced around in choreographed columns that formed eagles and stars and other national symbols to the crowd's enthusiastic applause. Angel watched with dismay. They looked pathetic. She was the person to help them.

Something raw in her blood reacted against the Kilties' dewy propriety. Emboldened by her looks and her husband's prominence, she blew into the office of the school's athletic director with a load of suggestions, none of which could have passed school codes or the sensibilities of the Kiltie parents. She wanted the girls to add horns and cymbals for pizzazz and wanted the hem of the skirts raised to the knee with six inches of fringe below. "That way, when they march they look proper and when they kick they look sexy."

The AD's name was Frank Billodeau. The varsity basketball coach in addition to this job, he had a reputation and also a look of rectitude, like Lincoln before the beard. "Not sure sexy's what they're after," he said from behind his desk.

"I'll pay for the changes. Or make my husband. He's Richie Bainard."

"My wife works at his store. On Ryan Street."

"I'll put in a good word for her."

"Mary can take of herself."

Angel smiled. "Sounds like a sweetheart." She'd heard her

husband complaining that the original Lake Charles Block's had become a poor performer. Area commerce was shifting away from lumber and agriculture. Chemical production was flat, and expanded refineries for the Humble and Union oil companies remained in the talking stage. Bonnie, Richie's co-boss these days, urged closing the store and opening new ones in Alabama's peanut belt and the poultry cradle of central Arkansas. Angel said to Frank, "Your wife comes to trouble, keep me in mind."

"I'll do that, ma'am."

"Now here's my other idea," she went on, returning to topic. "W. O. Boston? They got marchin' girls, too?" She was referring to the Negro high school that had opened two years ago in East Lake Charles.

"Probably just a band, be my guess."

"So put 'em together. Their band, your girls."

Frank gave a laugh. "Maybe my daughter'd join up in that case."

"Too boring now, right? Like little soldiers. What the hell is a Kiltie anyway?"

"From the skirts."

"You get my drift." She placed her hands on his desk and bent toward him, hair down, a button undone, provocative but in no way pretend.

"I do. But you realize that can't happen—black boys and white girls."

"Be a better show."

"I'd pay to see it."

Angel straightened. "You're a nice man," she said.

He crossed his arms as if to protect himself. "Not always," he said kind of sadly.

Persuaded that her plan to jazz up the Kilties couldn't fly, Angel moved on to another project. Next time she heard her husband and Bonnie discuss closing down the Ryan Street Block's, she suggested they refurbish the store and use the occasion to rechristen the entire chain Block's *Home* Supply. "No more o' this farm baloney. Your biggest sucker is a young family man with a crappy-built house in a hardware store on a Saturday. That's whose coin you're after." Rebranding was only part of her new idea, but Richie liked the bit she told him—postwar growth across the South would bring many such men to many such houses. He approved the plan over a raised glass at Georgia Hill. Bonnie gave her approval as well, though no one exactly had asked it.

ON THE NIGHT that Richie made the decision to transform the Block's business, his older son was meeting Alvin Dupree in New Orleans, where R.J. often visited for what he couldn't get in Lake Charles. Alvin had contacted him after his marine discharge, and R.J. proposed they meet at an upscale parlor house on Conti Street. The venue illustrates R.J.'s social clumsiness, for Emily Post surely advises that one shouldn't visit a brothel with a colleague one doesn't know well. Alvin was from the city's Ninth Ward, reared by the state after his mother died. He was quite aware of such establishments but had never been a customer. It turned out that R.J.'s choice of a congenial spot made the sergeant intensely uncomfortable, putting a crimp in their reunion.

Alvin didn't drink. He sat stiff as a vestryman in the chintz-papered lounge, sipping seltzer and listening to the Victrola. It rankled other gentleman-visitors suspicious of virtuous company. A street cop came in to collect the monthly Police Board donation. He asked R.J. if his friend worked for the district attorney. Thinking it a joke rather than a comment on his starched demeanor, Alvin attempted a clever reply: "Sure, and you're busted." It brought no laugh. Blows ensued, furniture was broken, and the policeman wound up apologizing with Alvin's hands on his throat. The madam roundly cussed R.J. for bringing such a thug to her place. She declared them banished, adding in a gratuitous jab that R.J. would never see "Miss Katie" again.

Miss Katie was a prostitute. Alvin caught a glimpse of her when she came downstairs with the other girls to see what was the ruckus. She was buxom, had platinum hair, and was painted with makeup and powder to lighten her mocha skin. Seeing the lieutenant's distress when told he'd been cut off filled Alvin with remorse for not getting into the swing of things earlier.

His chances of finding work with the Bainards seemed shot. They walked down the street toward what Alvin figured would be good-bye. R.J. surprised him by offering to arrange a job interview with his father. "He'll like you. He prefers people around him with clean habits. It lets him be the show."

Alvin gushed thanks and apology until R.J. waved him off. "I'm just sorry 'bout your girl," Alvin insisted.

"Who?"

"That Katie girl there. Pretty lil thing."

"Are you blind? She's forty if she's a day."

"*Dog!* I'm thinkin' she eighteen, nineteen."

"In 1935 maybe." R.J. was embarrassed. "She reminds me of someone, is all. Guess I'm back to the genuine article now."

"Give you trouble, that one?"

"Other way round, I'm afraid."

"That I cannot believe, Mr. Bainard. Fine gentleman like you."

"I just took you to a whorehouse, Sergeant."

"An' I made a mess of a nice evening."

It touched R.J. to see the superbly sharp noncom he'd depended on in Korea so flummoxed in a civilian setting, a natural-born warrior now awkwardly costumed in a cheap suit and steel-toed shoes. "The only mess here is me," he assured the sergeant, "as you oughta know better than anyone."

They walked east toward Bourbon Street. It was well into night, but passersby, even those walking eyes-down as if fearing to be identified, moved with the quickness of a day just beginning. Scarves and veils, grandiose cloaks and eccentric jewelry gave an air of mannered disguise that was R.J.'s favorite thing about the Quarter, a constant passing parade performed under balconies arrayed like theater boxes on the upper floors of stucco row houses. Alvin, with no mystery about him, seemed out of place despite being a city native. It made R.J. uncomfortable, like the host of a party whose honored guest refuses to mingle. "Got something in mind you'd care to do?" he asked.

Alvin considered. "Still like them nigger blues, Mr. Bainard?"

"I do."

Alvin turned down a dark alley. "I know some places," he said.

———

BLOCK'S HOME SUPPLY in Lake Charles held its grand reopening in February 1953. Richie blocked off the street and made it a party, with punch and hard cider, hush puppies and horseradish, shrimp creole, red beans and rice; and for dessert, hot candied yams with cinnamon glaze and praline ice cream, all served free to any who cared to partake. The weather had warmed enough for men to shed their jackets and ladies to slide up their sweater sleeves, pale arms entwining and separating like pulled taffy as the band out front of the store played banjo bluegrass and accordion waltzes. Kids stayed home from school to attend. A magician did card tricks and took burning balls of cotton into his mouth. A troupe of foreign gymnasts tumbled on a horsehair mat while their women hawked shawls and potholders to people looking on. The black folks in attendance kept apart in cautious deference. They carried tin plates to the food tables in lulls between waves of whites, as if worried a bill might yet be presented them.

Richie presided over the festivities with Angel on his arm. Strolling about with his necktie loosened and his houndstooth fedora tipped back, he resembled a politician working a county fair—though that's a poor description given whose eyes we're looking through here. Seth Bainard, like most fourteen-year-olds, had no notion of politics beyond the popularity feuds of high school. He likened his father to a football coach or, what he was, a small-town bigwig with a gravel laugh and a trailing scent of cigars and whiskey; his mother to a butterfly, flimsy and buoyant on breezes of breathless impulse. Seth was fond of his parents. But lately he'd got the sense that loving one more required loving the other less. He detected no rift between them, no side to take in a domestic dispute. His allegiance felt tested nevertheless. He spent more and more time on his own as a result.

He trailed them as they toured the store's widened aisles and new ladies' section, the latter featuring kitchenware and housecleaning items as well as a selection of "hits for hubby" such as fishing gear and auto parts. Richie had confided to Seth that he had zero expectation of the store's success and likely would end up closing it—it was a playtoy for Angel, who'd overseen the renovation as a diversion to keep her busy. Seth resented being drawn into dismissing his mother's pride in the project. Bonnie was worse. She openly ridiculed Angel on the presumption that all agreed she was a silly goose. His resentment intensified whenever that presumption was borne out by his mother's behavior. Like now.

Angel's arm not linked with her husband's encircled the waist of a prim-looking lady anyone could have told was her opposite. The lady's name was Mary Billodeau, and Seth observed from her body language, her torso tilted away as from a wall of wet paint, that she disliked being clutched so familiarly. He sympathized. His mother had drunk quantities of "special punch" in the rear of the store, fueling her usual emotiveness to operatic heights. Mary Billodeau by contrast was on duty today. She was the store's new manager. Richie usually reserved such positions for women unmarried and severe. Mrs. Billodeau failed on the first count, but Angel, for reasons unclear, had lobbied her husband on Mary's behalf and now was pleased to tell everyone that Mary owed her job to her.

Mary's husband didn't mingle. Frank Billodeau, "Coach" to everyone in town, huddled with some earnest old-timers to discuss an upcoming basketball game between Lake Charles High and a reform school team from Baton Rouge. Basketball surpassed even football as a life-or-death matter around here; the men worried those prison boys might be ringers or possibly black. Frank had a chiseled, hawkish look at odds with his mild voice. "We play any squad what shakes our hand and honors the Stars 'n' Stripes," he said to the men pestering him.

The comment brought an eye roll from Adele Billodeau, Frank's daughter, watching nearby. From the moment Seth first spotted her today he'd tried not to stare lest she catch him. Sixteen and looking powerfully slutty in a party dress and jean jacket, Adele wore her hair in a pixie cut as if to keep it unmussed on a motorcycle. She was a Lake Charles junior even the lords of the locker room circled cautiously. Seth, a year behind her, was one of the school's invisible nobodies. He was fascinated by her and needed only to be in her vicinity to feel the pull of her presence, like an unseen moon that draws all tides toward it.

Concluding their inspection of the store, his mother seemed to have toned down her patronization of Mary Billodeau, who strode beside Richie pointing out this or that display in a rapture of incontestable competence. Seth saw Angel slip away to the back where the booze was. He followed, determined to be the grown-up to her perennial child. Outside the storeroom he heard a sigh and saw shadows against the wall. He inched closer. His mother was embracing Frank Billodeau, their open mouths together, her hand gripping his crotch in a rhythmic squeeze. Like a movie played backward he lurched in reverse to the front of the store. He had no idea how to handle what he'd just seen, only knew it was bad and that it made his heart crack in his chest. He crashed into Bonnie by the entrance.

"Another drunk," she said. He used the idea—swaying, summoning a burp—to repel her in the other direction.

Not yet twenty-five, Bonnie seemed almost middle-aged to Seth. The arrival of R.J. and Alvin Dupree at the Block's event introduced another opinion. It was shortly after their big night in New Orleans, and it was the second time Alvin saw R.J.'s sister. The impact amplified his first impression, for qualities about Bonnie that gave some men the willies answered Alvin's every dream. He stared at her like a dog tracking pork ribs from platter to plate. When R.J. went to find his father, Alvin summoned every bit as much nerve as he'd shown in combat and asked if she was in the hardware biz or just here for the grub. She recognized him at once from Houston last year. "Do I know you?"

"Sergeant Dupree. From Korea."

"Alvin."

Big smile. "Miss Bonnie. The boss's daughter."

"I prefer to think of him as the boss's father."

"Maybe I talk to you instead."

"About what?"

"A job, ma'am. Your brother's tryin' to work it."

She didn't like being leapfrogged in the hierarchy. "What are your skills?"

"Can fix a motor and clean a carbine, but none like you mean."

"How do you know what I mean?"

"Sayin' you need a fella can fix a motor and clean a carbine?"

"I'm saying don't count on my brother. The guy needs a job himself."

"Count on you then?"

"Unless you have obligations elsewhere."

"I need work, ma'am. Only obligation's myself and my future employer. *Dog!* Whassat ol' whore doin' here?"

"I beg your pardon?"

He pointed. "Miss Katie from the bordello!"

Angel was approaching with Richie. With flaxen hair and figure like an hourglass seen in a funhouse mirror, she was the spitting image of R.J.'s Conti Street favorite. Bonnie smiled. "That would be my stepmother."

"*Dog,* but it's a likeness."

"I'm sure she'll be thrilled to hear it."

R.J. walked next to his father on the opposite side from Angel. Seth shuffled behind them, his thoughts lost in wondering which was worse, his love life or that of his parents. The group was nearly in earshot of Bonnie and Alvin when Bonnie told the sergeant one more thing:

"By the way . . ."

"Ma'am?"

"You're hired."

HE BECAME THE Bainards' general assistant, living in the carriage house at Georgia Hill, on call to the family twenty-four hours a day. In time his duties came to include assignments for Block's. He was management's designated deliverer of bad news to sub-par employees in stores across four states. His large physical size helped in the role, as did his being of exceedingly deliberate mind. It lent him a calm, implacable poise that discouraged excuses or protest.

Another of his tasks was to drive Seth to and from school

each day. They grew familiar as a result. Conversations in a Cadillac with the stolid ex-marine were the closest thing Seth had to a social life. Many times when they were alone together he almost blurted the secret of seeing his mother in Frank Billodeau's arms. The urge hit hardest when watching her behave in ways that screamed of her infidelity now that he knew to notice the clues, the casual excuses and credible reasons for her lateness, flushed cheeks, or buoyant mood that no one but Seth understood were bald lies.

That December, his parents were to spend a weekend at Richie's hunting lodge, the Section Eight Gun Club. Completed down in Cameron Parish several years earlier, it was a swanky setup, its members local high-achievers fond of spending self-made money. Angel backed out at the last minute. She urged Richie to go alone. It was that insistence more than her change of plan that upset him; he couldn't fathom wanting to do anything or be anywhere without her. Their subsequent argument shook the house. Though ignorant of her full betrayal, Richie's resentment of her inattentiveness to him had been simmering for some time, needing only the prospect of a few days apart to trigger its eruption.

He complained, she called him an ass, and he took a roundhouse swing at her that missed only because of the bourbon. Alvin restrained him as Seth whisked his mother away. Within an hour the lovebirds were smiling and smooching as they apologized for their ugly display. They'd decided to stay home together, and wanted Seth and Alvin to take their place on the trip.

Seth's knowledge of his mother's affair with Frank Billodeau made a farce of her perky façade, how she clung to Richie's arm and wiped lipstick from his cheek. Picturing her hand on

Frank's dick, Frank's knees buckling under her touch, Seth wanted to be rid of the sight of her, to flush her from heart and mind. The Section Eight marsh, where he'd often hunted with his father and R.J., was a good place to do that. But it also invited some careless unburdening as he scrunched next to Alvin in a frozen duck blind that weekend. "You like my sister," he began.

"Respect more the word," Alvin said.

"I can tell. Way you watch her."

There was an old guide in the blind with them, his torn canvas jacket spilling insulation from the elbows, a duck call hanging from his lips like a stogie. He scanned the horizon in gruff irritation at his chattering clients. Their three shotguns aimed skyward as if awaiting enemy bombers. At length Alvin said, "She outta my class, Miss Bonnie."

"That don't stop people, what I've seen."

"You fifteen. You seen nothin'."

"Yeah?" From there it was automatic for Seth to say what he'd seen, if only to hold up his end of a dialog about what's bad about love. It was also automatic that Alvin, out of loyalty dating back to Korea, would tell R.J. first chance he got.

Tipped off by Angel's resemblance to Miss Katie of Conti Street, Alvin had detected in countless hangdog stares that R.J. was spellbound by his young stepmother, feelings lustful at minimum yet possibly stupid with real affection. He took care to be sensitive in reporting Angel's affair, maintaining a respectful veneer of obliviousness to his lieutenant's secret stake in the matter. "I figured you the one to handle this," he said, "bein' your daddy's namesake an' all."

R.J.'s face had gone to stone. "My father'd kill for love of that woman."

"You'll talk to her?"

"Talk to someone."

"Don't wanna see nobody hurt."

"Better close your eyes," R.J. said.

Next stop was the library at Georgia Hill, a masculine, wood-paneled sanctuary housing, if not many books, a firearms cabinet full of shotguns, rifles, and pistols. Opening the cabinet's glass doors, R.J. inhaled the tangy scent of solvent and gun oil and was seized by the poetry of using one of his father's weapons on the man cuckolding Richie and, in his mind anyway, cuckolding R.J. as well. He selected a lady-size snubnose .22, stuck it in his belt under his shirt, and went off to visit Frank Billodeau in his athletic office at Lake Charles High School.

He never drew the gun. Frank stared him down, shamed him with righteous indignation, an impressive maneuver considering Frank was a two-timing skunk who hated himself every day. "You're drunk," he said after R.J. accused him of seducing Angel. "Go home."

R.J. indeed had stopped off at a bar. He felt embarrassed to have needed the boost, though it was probably to his credit that he couldn't take up a pistol and run around making death threats cold sober.

"Angel told me you watch her," Frank said. "Stare at her like a damn pervert. Your daddy's wife! Now git the hell outta here 'fore I call Richie myself."

"Stay away from her or I'll kill you." The words sounded idiotic to R.J. the instant he spoke them.

Frank stood up at his desk as if to make a better target of his heart. "Go on now. Get some coffee. Be all over come mornin'."

R.J. left, driven back inside his doubts like a bear into its cave. Frank sat down and put his hands to his temples as if to crush his skull. He picked up the telephone and dialed Angel at home, an act that in its directness doesn't fit a man looking to continue an illicit affair. But the question of whether he intended to end things with Angel can't be resolved because Alvin, vigilant in his household duties, answered the phone at first ring. Recognizing the voice of the husband of Mary Billodeau, manager of the Lake Charles Block's, he informed Frank that Mrs. Bainard wasn't at home. It would prove a consequential lie.

THERE WAS A basketball game at the high school that night. R.J. sat in the bleachers behind the Wildcats' bench with the .22 jammed in his pants. The raucous gym was a conducive environment for a troubled man to sit and stew. Picture him studying the back of Coach Billodeau's head while caressing the pistol under his shirt and you get the gist of his state of mind.

The game proceeded in a fog. R.J. stared at Frank as if at the sun until red spots appeared and replicated. The crowd noise yielded to a clocklike tapping of his upper and lower teeth. He didn't want to shoot anyone. It was about confronting a cliff he must jump off or not. Mooning over his stepmother had to stop. Lying around Georgia Hill drinking beer and playing music had to stop. The Korean War was over, his reserve commitments concluded. Next year he would inherit a major interest in a million-dollar enterprise. He ought to accept his good fortune and go be content for a while.

His attention fell on Adele Billodeau, Frank's high school daughter, sitting by herself nearby. She wore blue jeans tighter than the fashion and cuffed at the ankles above a new pair of Keds. She had a slight double chin and dimples across the pale tops of her knuckles, suggestions of succulence she highlighted with a jazzy hairdo and clothes she spilled out of by choice. She leaned on her elbows and studied the game until she turned to the guy watching her. "What?"

"Your ma runs Block's."

"So."

"Must have a lot of gumption."

Adele gave no reply.

"You got good genes, is my point."

She glanced down uncertainly. "They're Lees."

R.J. smiled. "And Daddy's the coach."

"Hope he loses, too."

"What'd he do?"

"Not him. My boyfriend. The center."

R.J. surveyed the court. "Big fella."

"It ain't everything."

They gazed forward for a bit. R.J. slid down the bench next to her.

She asked him, "How do you know me?"

"Your parents, not you. Yet." It doesn't get much plainer than that. Unless next you ask, "How old are you?"

"How old are *you*?"

"Twenty-four. I feel older."

"How come?"

"Sitting here alone on a Friday night watching a high school basketball game? I'd say it's about over for me."

"I seen you before."

"I'm Richie Bainard's son."

"Then my mom—"

"Works for my father. Poor woman."

These asides were too slippery for her. Part of their meaning seemed a fair warning to run. "I'm Adele."

"Nice." They shook hands. "Nice," he said again.

"Gonna tell me your name?"

"I'm Lieutenant Bainard."

"An army man."

"Marines."

"Ooh. Scary."

"Korea kinda was."

"You're braggin' now."

He laughed. "You're pretty fast."

"My boyfriend's mom says that." She scowled. "Bitch."

"Wanna go?"

Adele looked at him.

"Said you don't care about your daddy's team."

"I care. He's the best man in the world. It's my boyfriend I wanna kill."

"Come on with me anyhow."

"Where?"

"Does it matter? You know I'm respectable. I'm R. J. Bainard." He raised his hands and turned the palms upward to show they were clean. "Could be your chaperone."

"I seen a few of them was worse'n their sons." If further deliberation occurred to her, it didn't show on her face. Adele stood and strode down the bleachers and out of the gym in a manner almost royal. He waited before following on the assumption that she wanted him to—to wait and to follow, that is.

He was driving one of his father's Cadillacs; it felt like a carriage to her when he opened the door to invite her inside. He took her dancing and drinking. Secure that she was running the show, Adele expected him to make a move before the night was over. Her wariness when he parked on a side street was that of an athlete confronting a challenge. She knew her way around the back end of a date. She knew how to say yes and no, how to deploy her body to amaze and intimidate. In a clinch with a boy she held all the cards, nervous but never afraid.

Except R.J. wasn't a boy. He knew he didn't have to take no for an answer. He reached over and grasped her wrist. Gentle at first, but still odd—that he took her wrist not her hand; bones, not soft flesh, in his grip. "Okay," he said. "We're gonna do it now."

He drove her home afterward. At curbside he tried to kiss her goodnight. Her snarling rebuff warned him that she might do something reckless. "Call you tomorrow?" His breezy tone was a reflex toward charm under pressure. She bit back defeated tears, got out of the car, and climbed her front steps like any teenager home too late.

ADELE NEVER WOULD have told anyone if she'd had time to collect herself. She tried to lift the latch quietly, to cross the floor with a weightless tread as if literally lightened by what she'd lost tonight. But ambushed by her mother's angry relief to have her home safe, she lost the will to lie.

Under the bright hallway bulb her red eyes and beginning bruises on her upper arms couldn't be explained away. The truth blew out like a drowning man's last air. "He raped me, Mommy. I'm sorry." Mary Billodeau's expression curdled, for her daughter was now a certified tramp. The next question came from Adele's father, who'd fallen asleep in his chair while compiling stats from tonight's basketball game. To hear "R. J. Bainard" in answer was as stunning to Frank as the violence his daughter had suffered. He took her in his arms. His gaze over her heaving shoulders was directed far away. "Jesus Christ, forgive me."

Before going to wash off R.J.'s filth, the girl and her mother exchanged looks so probing the moment would stay with Adele all her life. The understanding was that they would never speak "rape" again. It would only hurt Adele's future in this town and in this house—hurt, too, it didn't need to be said, Mary's management position at Block's Home Supply. Adele got beat up by a boy—that was the story. It happened more than people admitted, and Mary trusted that in the eyes of God a woman is ennobled for enduring it.

Frank helped his daughter undress for a bath under a quilt he draped around her. Seeing the abrasions on her skin brought a wave of fury. He yanked her from the edge of the steaming tub and threw her clothes at her. "We're going to the doctor and we're going to the police. They gonna see you like he left you."

"No one'll believe it," Mary said.

"Look at her!"

He dragged Adele out the front door. "You're hurting me," she said.

His face looked distorted in the light from the kitchen window. "You swear it happened like you said?"

"Daddy, it did."

He shook her by the shoulders, her head snapping back and forth. "You swear it was R. J. Bainard?"

"Why's it matter him?"

"It matters!"

She tried to embrace her father for both their sakes but he wanted an oath from her, something solid he could defend and lean on, like a wall to a wounded soldier. "It was him, Daddy. I wouldn't lie." He lifted her into the cab of his truck and closed the door with grim resolve more frightening than if he'd slammed it.

On the drive to the doctor's house, Adele's head lolled with the road's rhythm. She hurt between her legs, inside her jeans. She studied herself sluggishly. How had R.J. removed her jeans? They fit so tight, she'd had to lie flat on her bed to zip them before going out. Uncertainty seized her. The liquor that had clouded her night threw confusing clues. A teenage dossier of feels and fingerfucks made shame the surest thing.

The doctor, a white-haired gentleman whose office was decorated with Norman Rockwell prints that he could have modeled for, examined Adele through her clothes. Nothing broke or bleeding, go home and rest with a wet cloth over the eyes. Outside in the waiting room he told her father, "You wanna claim her boyfriend thumped her, I'd say you got a case."

Frank remembered his argument with R.J. earlier that day and accepted that his only honorable course was to kill him; the thought was exhausting, like last chores to do before bed. First there was more to ask about his daughter's condition, if he could get the words out. He couldn't.

"He raped me," Adele whispered in the next room.

The doctor's wife, who attended all her husband's examinations of women, was folding towels by the sink. "Dear?"

"R. J. Bainard raped me. In his car."

"Do you know what you're sayin'?"

Adele's eyes tilted upward to keep tears from spilling. "I know what's rape."

The woman handed her a robe from a hook on the door. "Bottoms off. Put this on." She summoned her husband. "Girl says there's something more."

He examined her closely this time. Wincing as he straightened his back, he closed her robe and asked without looking at her, "Were you a virgin before tonight?"

Her mouth crumpled. "I've had . . . I've let them . . ."

The doctor's wife cut in. "Have you gone the limit, dear? He needs to know."

There was a split-second interval, as between the plunger and the dynamite, before Adele answered, "Never."

Frank was brought in to hear it from his daughter's mouth. He asked to use the phone to dial the chief of police at home. It was late. The Chief was a recent appointment by the Lake Charles City Council, brought in after a long stint with the sheriff's office in Pinefield. There he'd gained a reputation as a lawman who'd bend the rules for those that deserved it and never for those who didn't, exactly the discretion the elite of Lake Charles preferred in their public officials.

Hollis Jenks, yawning and scratching his hairless head, listened to Frank without urgency until he heard R. J. Bainard named as the perpetrator. Though new in his position at the department, Chief Jenks was aware that the Bainards were big in Lake Charles and that sex accusations against an heir to the Block's retail chain would reverberate statewide. He told Frank to stay put until he and his deputy arrived to question his daughter. Showing keen understanding of how things worked around here, the Chief then called Richie Bainard, whom he knew by reputation if not yet personally, to tell him what had happened and that his son better get his story together. It was a short conversation on account of Richie smashing his handset through the telephone dial.

Richie had composed himself by the time he addressed reporters outside the Block's headquarters after Adele's story came out. He was lavish in praising Mary Billodeau, assuring that he bore no ill will toward the woman on account of her crazy daughter. Bonnie stepped forward to add that if Mary wished to stay on as manager of the Lake Charles Block's, the company would welcome it. Abelard Percy, the family lawyer, formally denied all charges against R. J. Bainard. The accused, out on bail, stayed home.

ABE PERCY LOST sleep and gained weight as he became ever more nervous that this case would crown his career. He wasn't a trial lawyer. State law permitted him to conduct the defense if his client so desired. Richie, who was paying the bills, did; R.J. didn't care. Abe took it on out of loyalty to R.J.'s late mother, whose death he blamed himself for.

He deposed Adele Billodeau gently, presenting his questions like a benevolent uncle seeking to clear up a misunderstanding. He knew he'd have to attack her in court. She must admit to drinking that night, to having welcomed the prospect of backseat foolery with a handsome older man and semi–war hero. Her thighs and pubic area had been bruised; her jeans and underwear, stained from when she'd put them back on after intercourse, were otherwise clean and not torn. A minor point alongside other evidence, Abe planned to highlight it on grounds of common sense. You don't remove pants that tight without a struggle or help from the girl. She should have thrashed like a deer in a trap. She should have seized the moment of his trying to get her pants off to break free and save herself, had she wanted to. Her reputation suggested she hadn't.

Adele began to doubt her own memory. From a distance she saw R.J. on a street corner one afternoon. In bed that night she remembered how, before he turned scary, he'd kissed her neck, his hand warmer than the skin of her breasts as he'd caressed them under her blouse. She might have let him go further had he kept that tender tack. She squirmed under the covers almost feeling his embrace, almost tasting his tongue. R. J. Bainard on a winter night in her seventeenth year—why not? She'd pleased enough boys other ways, it seemed silly to withhold, not least to satisfy her own curiosity, the prize contained inside her.

And she felt sorry for him. Dropping offhand clues of melancholy and solitude, he'd behaved nicely through much of that evening. Her deepest dread was that she may have invited the assault, tempted him somehow. Had she ruined his life even more than he'd ruined hers? She went to her father with her fears. Frank shook his head fiercely. "Bastard raped you. Never doubt it."

"It's just sometimes I wonder if boys think with me it's okay."

"I told you he done it. Now drop it."

"He's not the first to try."

"Goddamn you, girl!" Frank raised his fist before burying it in shame behind his back. He leaned into his daughter, pressing roughly against her to force from inside his chest the secret he didn't want to reveal. "R.J. done it in revenge against me." His voice was spooky at her ear. "I am so sorry for that."

He'd told no one about his affair with R.J.'s stepmother. Nor had he followed through on his impulse to kill R.J. out of fatherly duty. He'd rationalized his lapses in honorable terms. Adele had suffered for his misdeeds, but Mary, his wife, was unscathed. Richie had retained her as store manager—finding out about Frank and Angel's affair would surely change that. Wouldn't it be better if Richie and Mary never learned of their spouses' betrayal, if the whole lousy business faded away quietly and R.J. was convicted on evidence already at hand? Frank thought it a fair hope until his daughter's self-blame broke his heart and forced him to come forward. He sat down with state prosecutors and explained that R.J. had somehow discovered his and Angel's affair and threatened to take revenge. He gave the same statement to Defense Attorney Percy. He resigned as Wildcat coach and after a difficult dialog with his wife, packed a bag for a room in town.

Abe telephoned Richie with these revelations, prompting a savage reaction that gratified Abe with its vision of the Bainard world collapsing. Richie's vow to Abe that he would see Frank Billodeau dead was a forgivable reflex. It turned out that Frank was exactly that by dawn the next day. From the sprawl of his body beside his truck outside town, investigators judged that he'd been leaning against the radiator when he put the pistol to his head. He left no suicide note, though the care he took to spare his family from finding his body suggests contrition for disappointing them so.

It shattered Adele. She couldn't face a trial supported only by a mother she distrusted and lawyers she didn't know; she decided to drop the rape charge against R.J. It never happened officially, however. He jumped bail before she notified the court of her change of mind. Informed about it afterward, she was so offended by his gutless flight that she decided to let the charge stand and make him run like a dog for the rest of his life.

Frank's testimony would have sealed the verdict—that was R.J.'s thinking when he bolted. The decision proved over-hasty, since Frank's suicide and Adele's second thoughts came less than twenty-four hours later. It also proved tragic following another call from Abe on that same confused day, this time to tell Richie that in light of the new evidence the prosecution, citing a motive, would base its case on R.J.'s hatred of Adele Billodeau's father.

"No crime in that," Richie growled.

Abe, in his Ryan Street office with the phone sweaty at his ear, savored the moment joylessly. "R.J.'s *jealous* hatred, I should say."

Richie had taken the call in the library. Seth was home and heard cursing, steps bounding upstairs, and his mother's shrieks in the master bedroom. He rushed in and was shocked by the scarlet smears across the wallpaper. His mother's face was al-ready pulp. His father's continued blows threw vivid spatters such as Seth had never seen. He pulled Richie off her and pinned him to the floor. Angel crawled like a drunk toward the door.

Seth screamed for her to get the car while in his ear his father howled about knowing she was Frank Billodeau's whore, *but now with my own fucking son!* Misunderstanding obviously figured here. That's why it might have helped if R.J. had been available to clarify things. He wasn't. He was bombing out of Lake Charles in his sister's car with some clothes, his guitar, and a remarkably positive outlook.

Alvin and Bonnie drove up Georgia Hill's driveway just as Seth and Angel were commandeering one of the family Cadillacs. Richie stormed out the front door carrying a shotgun from his library cabinet. Peeling away in a screech of tires, Angel was in the driver's seat, Seth on his knees on the seat beside her, reaching over to man the wheel because she couldn't see for blood in her eyes. Richie fired into the air after them. The Cadillac roared past Alvin's car and fishtailed down the hill. Richie fired again. Angel mashed the gas pedal. Bonnie and Alvin watched in dismay. The Cadillac was doing forty when it rammed the live oak at the base of the driveway, killing Angel instantly and sending Seth through the windshield into the tree.

THE UPSHOT OF all this was multifold. Frank Billodeau was dead, likewise Angel Bainard. Richie, ravaged by guilt, became obsessive in caring for his now handicapped younger son, who despised him for obvious reasons. R.J. was hiding in exile somewhere. Bonnie took over running Block's with Alvin's able assistance. Abe Percy and Hollis Jenks, bit players so far, were alive and keeping well.

Then there was Mary Billodeau. Her life was never so good

as after her husband killed himself. She kept her management position at Block's while enjoying a peaceful home life now that misfortune had chastened her daughter into utter subservience. Her daughter, interestingly, changed her name. Nothing major, just "Delly" instead of Adele. It seemed she preferred the feeling, when called by that, of being someone else.

$$=== \text{T W O} ===$$

Bonnie, R.J., Alvin

December 1956. Two and a half years have passed since that bad day at Georgia Hill. A '55 pickup turns off the coast highway outside Hancock Bayou and bounces down a seashell road overlooking the winter-brown marsh. The air is cold and dry. Twigs on the scrub trees are brittle as ice, the clouds crystal filaments high in the sky. Houses scattered about are erected on pillars in case tidewaters crest the levee, a rare event that occurs mostly in summer but is remembered all year round.

Sallie Hooker's house was at the end of the road. It was roofed with corrugated tin and had two smaller structures behind it, a work shed and an insulated cold locker. With rice cultivation shut down this time of year, Sallie, as her late mother had done all her life, dressed game to bring in money, anything from deer to mourning dove. In duck season she and her niece cleaned the birds, wrapped them in wax paper and set them on shelves in the cold locker. Out-of-town hunters would drop them off bloody with birdshot and collect them pristine as grocery chicken on the way home from weekends spent at lodges on the marsh, home to Lake Charles or Shreveport usually, though some hailed from Texas or farther away, that's how renowned was the hunting in these vast wetlands.

Sallie's niece's son, eight years old, helped pluck the birds whenever the women got behind. He dunked them in boiling water and fed them into the plucker. The machine took the big feathers but left the down to pick off with your fingers. The feathers went into burlap sacks to be ground into feed and fertilizer; the guts, heads, and feet into barrels hog farmers collected twice a week. The smell was strong even when the temperature fell below freezing, as it often does in December in southwest Louisiana.

The man who got out of the pickup was one of Sallie's clients. A professional guide, bearded and lanky, he looked the part in a woolen watch cap and boots, the laces dragging same as any hunter who's just removed his waders. But the boy had noticed that the boots were high quality, not the cheap knockoffs most guides wore, and his shotgun, propped on the seat inside his truck, was a Holland & Holland over-and-under, its receiver engraved with floral scroll and its two triggers plated in gold. You never saw guides with custom guns—too much wear from the elements and from doubling as push-poles to nudge their flat-bottomed pirogues through the winter marshes, the barrels pitted, the once gleaming stocks dull with an accretion of blood and grime you could scrape off with a fingernail. But it was the man's dog, which leaped from the truck into the boy's arms, that gave the biggest hint. A Chesapeake Bay retriever, burly and sleek, it was too fine a specimen for any local to afford.

The man's ducks were teals, small and drab but for a blazon of color on the wing, like a soldier's combat patch. The boy loosened the thong from around their limp necks. He asked the man if he'd taken out a party this morning. "Just me and the cur," came the answer.

The boy scratched the dog under its ear. With its owner it acted trained beyond personality. With the boy it was puppylike, lapping any skin its tongue could find. "Tarzy!" His great-aunt came out of the plucking shed. Sallie's apron was bloody and her hands were shiny and dripping. "Fetch them birds here 'fore they rot in your grip."

"Tarzy?" The man had never asked his name.

"For Tazwell," he said, embarrassed.

"Tazwell Hooker. Very goddamn fancy."

Sallie straightened. "Now come on, you. No swears round the boy."

Tarzy was watchful in the moment that followed, thinking the man would scold her for talking uppity. But he gave a respectful nod. "My mistake."

Sallie took the ducks. "Only four?"

"No kinda cover out there. Nutria ate every stick."

Nutria is the giant muskrat that infests Louisiana marshes like roaches in a New York apartment. With fur prices low and few people inclined to eat the gamy meat, the creatures were spawning in record numbers. Litters of baby nutria, pink and squinty, would nestle in every bog come summer, feeding an equal surge in the population of their main predator, cotton-mouth moccasins.

The man told Sallie to keep the ducks. "Sell 'em, cook 'em, they're yours." Weekend shooters might not eat what they killed, but professionals rarely gave up their birds, even the rat-like *pule d'eaus* or the fishy-tasting spoonbills. Each was a meal, part of the wages. Nope, Tarzy thought as he listened, there's something going on here.

The man made to depart. "Here, boy." The dog snuggled in Tarzy's arms. "I guess he likes you better'n me."

"Wanna give'm over?"

"What would I do then, clean birdshit like you?"

This stung—Tarzy hadn't meant to be wise. The man called again for his dog, which obeyed at once.

Tarzy went to rejoin his great-aunt. In the lowlands beyond the levee there were glints of iced-over ponds at the base of bare trees spearing upward from the muck. The boy preferred the swamp this time of year, crisp as a frozen planet. Spring turned it fetid, summer turned it creepy, made the night throb with the calling of bugs and bullfrogs and the boggy thatch under your feet crawl with gators and snakes.

"Hey."

Turning to the voice, Tarzy snared a coin arching toward him through the air. A quarter—enough for a matinee movie in Hancock Bayou or a plate of garfish balls at the town lun-cheonette. He gripped it pensively as the guy climbed into his truck. The cold locker's compressor revved up with a diesel hum. As the pickup crunched away down the road, Tarzy thought to himself with certainty, that man there is a criminal.

SETH BAINARD NOW went by Seth *Hooker,* his mother's maiden name. He hadn't done it through lawyers or registered the change with city hall. It was a private protest against all things Bainard, though not including, as yet, the money.

From the front seat of a limousine bringing him to Georgia Hill, he watched the swim of light and shadow from passing trees and buildings. He felt the vehicle turn into the front gate and wondered if the live oak was scarred from when his mother had hit it. He hadn't been back here since that day almost three years ago. Nor had there been any contact with his father, though Seth knew Richie kept tabs on his welfare and made big donations to Lake Charles Hospital where Seth had been treated after the accident and where he now worked as an inpatient aide.

The limo came to a halt and the driver turned off the motor. The sudden silence jarred Seth with the noise of his pulse. Told his father was desperate to reconcile, he should have been calm with moral triumph. Richie was ill. Seth had gathered from Bonnie's message that his condition was critical. The stage was set and the power in hand to deny his father all pardon. Seth's eyesight, damaged in the accident, could discern bright-lighted text with a magnifying glass. The book he most practiced on was a red-letter Bible he'd found at the hospital. It had made him expert in the pronouncements from Jesus on sin and punishment, which is to say, being just past seventeen, he'd fallen prone to mistaking the Savior's job for his own. Deeming himself his father's judge came naturally as a result.

The passenger door opened. "Mr. Seth."

He recognized the voice. "Alvin. I thought it might be you to drive me here."

"Drive only Miss Bonnie nowadays."

Seth asked for his cane from the backseat. Alvin passed it to him handle first, like a knife. He swung his legs out and down to the ground. His gaze swept too smoothly, like a drunkard faking acuity, across Alvin and the shadows beyond. From a distance he could tell light and broad movement. The world was otherwise murk.

His agenda today was to meet with his father and afterward sit down with his sister to preview Richie's will. Chilly as ever, she'd explained on the phone that Seth would receive no inheritance without first making peace. He would have refused on the spot but for recalling from John 15 that Jesus felt obliged to tell sinners they'd sinned lest they not realize they were sinners at all. "Now they have no cloak for their sin," said the red-letter words in Seth's Bible. The instruction made plain his sacred duty to get over to Georgia Hill and lay some terminal blame on his father.

He and Alvin passed through the foyer. Alvin explained that Richie had been moved to the sewing room. "Ground floor. Easier."

"Where's Bonnie?"

"In her office upstairs. Waitin' on you."

"The queen in her chamber."

"Carried the load when others didn't." Alvin's tone irked Seth almost snobbishly. The guy was the help, after all.

The sewing room was off the breezeway between the main house and a bank of detached garages. Its auction antiques had been replaced with hospital furniture now that Richie was too weak to climb the stairs to the master suite. He walked little these days—to the john, the terrace. Instead of a canopied king he slept on a hospital bed. To receive Seth today he'd been dressed by his nurse and propped in a sitting position on a stuffed chair before the window.

Seth couldn't make out the droop of his father's face or his hair lying limp as grass cuttings on his scalp. But he sensed Richie's infirmity from his ragged breathing and the unmistakable scent of a body breaking down. When Richie reached out his hand, fingers fluttering like fronds in a river current, Seth detected the movement and shook in a craven reflex.

Alvin asked the nurse to leave and to close the door behind her. Seth protested that the meeting was private. "He stays," Richie rasped. Seth felt for a nearby chair, Alvin a palpable presence off to one side, a guard to keep intruders out, Seth in. Richie inhaled as if before a deep dive. "Been wantin' this."

"I heard."

"Been hard, thinkin' o' you still ticked off. Was hopin' . . ." Richie swallowed, started over. "You and me might . . ."

"Be happy again?" Seth was angry to feel himself moved by the scene, upset at the injustice of confronting this hurtful man only to find him already broken.

"Be friends, I's gonna say. But happy's good."

"After what you did?"

"Hopin' you outgrowed that."

"Outgrowed?"

"Wrong word maybe."

Seth held up his cane. "Got this to remind me."

Like an injured duelist forced to flail, Richie lashed out, "Goddamn crutch is all that is."

Seth almost laughed. "I guess you're not gonna beg my for-giveness."

"Said I'm sorry. Said it a thousand times, sayin' it now."

"My mother died. It was your fault."

Richie's shoulders caved as if he'd been punched. He cleared his throat. Seth couldn't see the bubble that formed on his lip, only heard the confession that popped it. "I loved your mother. More'n she did me, no surprise there. Why I don't complain what I got now."

"Man's reachin' out," Alvin said. "Oughta 'cept his apology."

Seth turned. "You've come up in the world."

"Still a workin' stiff."

"But working on who?"

"Doin' my job for folks I admire."

Richie had slumped in his chair, groggy from medication. "How long?" Seth asked quietly.

"He got it spread everywhere," Alvin said.

"Strange not to care." The statement was harsher than Seth felt.

Something snagged in Richie's chest. His breaths became coughs that cascaded into wet hacks. Alvin held a steel bowl under his mouth to receive what came out. "Better you go," he said.

"To see Bonnie?"

"Why her?"

"Talk about money, I guess."

"Ain't no money without no shake-hands 'tween you and him."

"And how is that your business?"

"'Cause Miss Bonnie say it is." Richie's cough worsened, tissues tearing inside with the sound of ripped paper bags. "Car's out front. Come back when you're a mind to do proper." Alvin's voice was taut with feeling. "Just know the clock's tickin'."

"He shot my mother!"

"Shot *at* your mother. To put a scare in her only, and for cause she brung on herself."

Seth remembered the cause. "I should've kept my mouth shut."

Me too, Alvin didn't say, though he did offer the young man a prescription that worked for him: "Only way now's to put it behind."

Seth took up his cane and, swinging it before him like a scythe, squinted his way out of the room. He felt robbed. His father was beyond even curses now, his past as out of reach as his future. At the end of the breezeway, he heard a voice call from the top of the front stairs:

"You and Daddy talk?" Bonnie had been waiting.

Seth groped for the banister. "So I can get my cut, right?"

"It's how Daddy wants it. To set things right by his family."

"Was my mother family?"

Bonnie was ready for this. "A good man made a bad mistake." Unwed and unworldly, she excelled at ruling the land she inhabited. "If you can't let bygones be, we've prepared an alternate will that drops you altogether."

"We?"

"Daddy. And me." She spoke with measured empathy, what a competitive player feels for a crushed opponent.

"If R.J. ever shows, he'll tell you to go to hell."

"Doubtful."

"You talk?"

"I don't know where he is, I don't care. That's been Alvin's department for years."

Seth had heard nothing of his brother since his disappearance. By now he knew the seamy details of R.J.'s attraction to Seth's mother; they'd been leaked to the press by prosecutors furious that the accused had got away. But he resented R.J. more for the shabby business with Adele Billodeau. Angel had been everyone's fixation. Adele, he imagined, was his alone.

Bonnie went on, "You need to fix things with Daddy or those checks to your hospital stop."

"Him and me are all good," Seth heard himself say.

"Alvin was witness. Don't try to lie."

"He'll testify."

"Then come on up."

One hand on the bannister, he ascended the stairs to Bonnie's office overlooking the courtyard. He perceived her as a shape backlit by the window, a body floating in a shimmering pool. "Five percent," she said without preamble, "of the company's annual net revenue."

"Translate, please."

"You'll never be rich but you'll never be poor."

Seth nodded, knowing the deal would be rescinded once Alvin told her what had transpired downstairs. "My thirty pieces of silver."

"Five. The thirty's for R.J."

"He's taking your money?"

"Man's gotta eat."

Pity and letdown came over Seth. R.J. had been his hero once, possessing a rebel integrity made immaculate by his absence. "And the rest? Who gets that?"

Bonnie didn't reply. The winner doesn't have to.

ADELE "DELLY" BILLODEAU got married in 1955. Arthur Franklin was fifteen years older than she, an eternal salesman for a succession of manufacturing companies that he swore never treated him fair. His first wife had left him for an old flame she met at a high school reunion. Delly was her replacement to keep house and raise their daughter.

She was nowhere near the same feisty chick she'd been before R.J.'s assault and her father's suicide. Those blows had made her receptive to Arthur's proposal on logical grounds that he was the best she could hope for. Echoes of her rape recurred as an anxiety dream triggered by stress. That stress usually concerned Fiona Franklin, Arthur's fourteen-year-old daughter from his first marriage. Delly was twenty-one now, an age better suited to be Fiona's big sister rather than parent, yet she smothered the girl with the vigilance of a Mother Superior. She couldn't help thinking that only when Fiona was safely launched would Delly too be safe from her bad dream.

In the dream, a canopy made of feathers obscures the sky. It follows her everywhere, like a rain cloud over an unlucky man. Sometimes it's overhead at the high school gym, sometimes at the barroom where she gets drunk and flirty with a man whose face never shows. Feathers blot the moon out his car window and stream like moths from his radio as he fiddles with the dial after they park. Her hands turn to feathers as they struggle and clutch. Like a burn, the pain worsens when he stops.

The dream occurred again on the eve of a weekend excursion she and Fiona took with a cousin of Delly's in December 1956. The cousin, Corinne Meers, loved people with problems, leaping into meddlesome overdrive whenever anyone she knew encountered compelling misfortune. She'd first descended on Delly after Delly's crisis three years ago. Their friendship had since taken a high school dynamic whereby the prom queen, with an eye toward rescue, restyles the frump to the height of Hollywood fashion. As a result, Delly's hair was now dyed red as Rita Hayworth's and permed tighter than Pearl Bailey's, a clownish transformation she relished as completely appropriate.

Regret for agreeing to accompany Corinne and her family no doubt had brought on the dream. Delly would have preferred to stay home washing clothes and making toast. She woke sweaty, heart racing, but settled herself by thinking okay, I had it again, but it's over, it's past, I'm fine. The feathers haunted her—how they swarmed suffocatingly like a pillow pressed over her face. *Feather* and *Heather* were the connection, she supposed. Heather Lane near the high school was where it had happened, a link so pedestrian it embarrassed her, as if even her terrors were dumb.

The Meers excursion was to a hunting lodge in Cameron Parish. Drive time from Lake Charles was just under two hours. As everyone piled in, Delly warned Corinne's husband that she got carsick unless she was at the wheel. Donald Meers said she could ride up front but that he didn't allow females to drive his Lincoln. "This baby requires a man's touch."

"This baby," Delly said, "don't know a man's touch from a hog's."

"Says you. From experience, I guess."

"Donald!" Corinne said. "That's vicious."

"Didn't mean nothin'."

"Called her a hog!"

"No," Delly said. "He said I've experienced *the touch* of a hog."

Corinne stared. "Ain't that kinda almost worse?"

Delly's stepdaughter giggled in the backseat, further irritating Donald because Fiona was a pretty thing whom he considered a prime target for his boyish charm. "Can't believe how y'all jumpin' on the guy payin' for this trip," he said.

"You mean your daddy?" Corinne said.

"Now dammit that's enough! I'm a mind to leave you home."

"Fine," Corinne said. "Why the hell I'm goin' duck huntin' anyhow?"

"Me and Joey's huntin'." Joey was the Meerses' teenage son, the premarital mistake that had turned out handsome as his father but with less hair tonic. "You and Marjorie gonna eat chocolate pie and swim in the indoor heated swim pool." Marjorie was the Meerses' younger child. "It's a resort, this place," Donald said to Delly. "High tone."

"Donald's daddy built it," Corinne explained. "Section Eight Gun Club. We been lotsa times."

Delly took the front seat and soon began to get queasy. She cranked down her window for some outside air. Passengers in back screamed for her to close it, though scrunching together in the frigid blast was welcome in some quarters. Delly stole a backward glance at her stepdaughter, who'd been way too blasé squeezing in next to Joey at the start of the trip. Fiona's sweater had popped open two eyelets down, revealing a contour of pale skin curving into shadow. Might as well wear a sign saying *easy lay*, Delly fumed to herself.

Donald tapped her knee, startling her. "Things're better now?"

She took the question to refer less to her car nausea than to troubles with her husband that she'd recently confided to Donald's wife. Divorcing Arthur Franklin seemed an impossible hope, but the protracted freeze she'd willed on the marriage at least had brought about his exit to a boarding house in town. He'd let his daughter continue to live with Delly because work often took him away for long periods. It also gave him an excuse to phone the house at all hours, peek through the windows, hatch nutty plans to win back Delly's heart. "Only thing ever makes me feel better is a nap," she said.

"I'm with you on that," Donald said, annoying her with his attempt to be nice. Everyone knew her past, was the problem. They ascribed the mess of her life to what had happened in high school and to the years of vain wait for her attacker—her *supposed* attacker, people prudently put it—to be caught and brought to justice.

Stomach fluttering again, she pressed her cheek to the cold window. The car was traveling on an imperceptible decline, the terrain a few feet above sea level at most. The region's famed wetlands extended from the roadside to the southern horizon. Twisty channels of peat-colored water wound among islets of vegetation that from a far distance appeared to bob on the water like moldy bread, unpretty nature at its most lovely.

Donald lit a Camel. Delly rolled down her window to be sick. Vomit sprayed down the side of the speeding car like flames down the side of a hot rod. Threads of it laced across the back window, causing Donald almost to drive off the road when he turned in horror to look. Inside the car, outbursts came according to age, disgust from the grown-ups and hilarity from the kids. Delly was the exception. To hear Marjorie Meers declare that the stuff had frozen to the glass and then to see Donald's aghast expression, well, it struck her as pretty damn perfect.

THE SECTION EIGHT Gun Club was probably the only hunting lodge in Louisiana with an indoor pool. It wasn't glamorous—a small cement rectangle edged at the waterline with mustard tiles that changed back to cement for the pool surround and back to mustard up three sides of the enclosure, the fourth side featuring a broke-down sauna and a long set of windows overlooking a patch of dead cornstalks and the misty brown marsh beyond. The water was heated by a boiler through piping that left rust streaks down the walls and made the muggy air inside taste of chorine and fuel oil. Including a pool and sauna in Section Eight's design had been a grandiose whim by two of the club's original partners, Richie Bainard and Burt Meers. Neither would have been caught dead using either one.

The pool was deserted on Saturday afternoon but for Delly and little Marjorie. Fluorescent ceiling lights made Delly's skin look fish-belly white. Reclining on a chaise made of pink rubber tubes, she put on her dark glasses to create a private cave where she might hibernate maybe forever. The sound of a splash alarmed her. Marjorie had done a backward dive off the side of the pool. Fearing she'd land wrong and never have babies as a result, Delly ran to the ladder with a towel and ordered her out of the water. Somehow the notion had taken hold that she was the girl's babysitter. After Joey had disappointed his father by announcing at the last minute that he'd rather not hunt, Corinne had gamely replaced him on this morning's expedition. They'd returned a few hours ago and now were resting in their room.

Time was upended here. Hunters convened at four A.M. for breakfast, donned their waders and Barbour coats and with the sky still dark thundered on flat-bottom powerboats out to the marsh with guides, decoys, and retrievers. Delly rose early to observe them in full safari style. The club had seven guest rooms. Members were businessmen, boisterous and affable. Their wives and girlfriends carried themselves like Hemingway mistresses in web belts and tailored khakis. They returned in early afternoon to a gourmet repast of game and seafood sloshed down with selections from the club's alcohol armory. Naps followed, later a light buffet and cards or billiards before everyone retired early in order to do it again tomorrow. Even Delly, who was generally intolerant of mindless good times, conceded that it'd be fun if it suited your taste. It didn't suit hers. So here she was at the pool—which, she'd noticed, featured a small bar in one corner of the enclosure. "Time to go back to your room," she told Marjorie.

"Boring."

"Read a book. They got 'em on loan by the front desk."

"Go like this?" Marjorie wore a crinkly blue one-piece with ruffled leg openings. "Can I wear your top?"

Delly's top was a thigh-length jersey she'd bought at a dress shop during the half a day she'd spent searching for a passable swimsuit. It was designed to serve as a modest cover within which you needn't suck in your stomach or constantly tug the elastic at your rear. She needed this garment. It gave warmth in the lodge's drafty corridors, and when wearing it, she could eat a full lunch and afterward go around in her bathing suit without entirely wishing to kill herself. No one else was here, however, so pulling it off briskly she pressed it into Marjorie's hand like the last ticket out of town.

The girl padded out the exit door. Delly headed for the bar. The older kids, Fiona and Joey, were off exploring on their own, something she usually wouldn't have tolerated but was too tired to question now. The bar was self-serve. She went behind the counter and mixed a bourbon and Coke, marking the chit with Donald's name. Leaning on her elbows like a saloon regular, she pondered turns her life might have taken to land her anywhere but here. The alternatives were scant. It was hard to see herself rejecting Arthur Franklin's prim devotion in the wake of her toxic past. She'd been one of the cool girls once. Stacked. Not stupid. A little loose, and why not? She'd had a pretty face and a bodacious build. Inherited wealth ought to be spent.

She noticed her reflection in the mirror behind the bar. Encased in floral fabric, her breasts impended downward like unpicked fruit below her plump arms. Her suit was cut low under her armpit, revealing a crevice of flesh where the flank of her breast rose off her ribs, a pillowy peep she hadn't noticed in the dressing room mirror when she'd tried on the suit. Lulled by whiskey and solitude, she bent forward to study herself. Within her suit's central V her breasts were dotted with moles. Sexy, she thought, and shimmied her shoulders to ripple her bosom in a sour version of vamp.

She fixed another drink. Yawning, she looked forward to

lounging in her room before dinner. She wanted to lie naked under the ceiling light and pretend a listening bug was hidden there; she wanted to give it something to listen to. She rolled her drink across her forehead, clinking it against her dark glasses. Shutting her eyes, she felt as bodiless as a wish.

"Was a greenhead mallard, I'm tellin' you." The voice punctured her reverie. "Not my fault your damn dog couldn't find it." Two hunters had entered the pool enclosure and were approaching the bar, peeling off gear as they came.

Delly froze, a floozy drinking alone in the afternoon—in a swimsuit no less, tits and ass spilling out like cake dough overflowing the pan. She crossed her arms and shrank into herself. Behind her sunglasses she lowered her eyes, as if not seeing the men meant they couldn't see her. She'd noticed a little, however—black hair and brown, large body and lean, a broad clean-shaven face and a narrow bearded one. The big fellow took a stool in front of her. His palms flattened on the bar. Wedding band, gold watch. "Tom Collins," he said. "Mixer, no booze."

She turned from the front of the bar to the glittery shelves behind. A tremor of self-consciousness disoriented her as her gaze climbed the rows of bottles.

"Higher, sweetheart. Way up top."

A bottle of Collins mix was just within reach as she stretched on tiptoes. The pull of her suit riding up her behind told her she was being played. The mirror held a distorted image of the guy ogling her ass. She dropped her hands to her sides and adjusted her suit with the grace of an Olympic diver. She thought of smashing a bottle and twisting it into his face. She thought of daring him that he could have her for ten dollars.

"There's one open right here," the other man said. Clearly

the younger of the two despite his full beard, he joined Delly behind the bar, handing her a bottle of Collins mix and helping himself to a beer from the ice chest on the floor. She felt silly and grateful for what seemed his deliberate rescue attempt. Intent on making a getaway, she tried to slide past him in the tight space, her eyes still averted. He turned abruptly and spilled beer down her front. The icy liquid splashed her thighs and she recoiled with a squeal, tits bouncing like a tavern wench. He stammered an apology.

"It's okay," she mumbled to his legs. "Happens all the time." She wished she was dead. Nothing was worth another second of her pathetic skulk through life.

"No harm done," said the other man. "I'll lick it off."

"Whoa, cowboy," said the guy beside Delly. "Mind your manners."

She regarded the one across the bar—gorilla shoulders and a face childlike in its mildness. "*Dog!* I oughta be horsewhipped for that."

She wanted out of there, forget the retorts she could have launched on a better day. She sidestepped from behind the bar and started for the exit.

"Make him buy you a drink, at least."

This, from the younger one, seemed even coarser than the other's "lick it off" comment. Sure, share a drink with the swine after what he'd said, throw *all* self-respect out the window. Summoning a sneer, Delly looked directly at the bearded man for the first time. A quake shuddered through her, scalp to knees.

It was him.

———

R.J. HADN'T LEARNED of his stepmother's death until many days
after it happened. Like everyone who wasn't there, he believed
it a blameless accident. He knew his father's grief would be
bitter; the passions Angel had provoked in Richie would go as
dark as they'd burned bright. For himself, he'd come to terms
with his absurd infatuation if not with all its consequences. His
drunken tangle with Frank Billodeau's daughter was harder to
process. Nothing about that night made sense then or now.

Public sympathy for the death of Richie Bainard's wife had
benefited R.J. in that few were inclined to mount a serious
manhunt. Prosecutors vowed to pursue the fugitive to the ends
of the earth but the police dragged their feet from the start. R.J.
remained at large with minimal effort. Rumor put him in
Canada, Mexico, on an oil rig off Corpus Christi, and behind the
counter at a Baton Rouge gun shop. Now here he was sipping
beer in his father's hunting lodge two hours' drive from where
his accuser claimed he'd raped her like a beast.

Delly gathered her wits. Clearly he didn't recognize her
behind her curly red hair, sunglasses, and extra pounds. When
he asked her to let him and his friend make amends for their ill
manners by buying her a drink, curiosity trumped fear and she
said okay. She gave her name as Ethel, after Lucy's sidekick.
We're Richard and Alvin, they said.

R.J.'s eyes were electric blue. It was a detail she'd worked
hard to forget. The image of his downturned mouth likewise
returned despite the beard now concealing it. Sitting at the
table across from him, she forced herself to look square at his
face. He'd hit her that night to shut her up, a rap on the temple
that had seemed to burst her eardrum like a jabbed stick. Let-

ting the memory wash through her and keeping calm in its wake emboldened her to press on. "How was the hunting?" she asked.

"Fair," R.J. said. "Do you hunt, Ethel?"

"I wouldn't care to kill living things."

He laughed. "Me neither, come to think of it. I shoulda stayed home and got a normal job."

His friend shot him a look.

Delly asked, "Where's home?"

"Wherever anybody else is buyin'," Alvin cut in. "Another round?"

Delly knew she should get out of there for the good of her soul. R.J. tapped a cigarette out of his pack and offered it to her. She shook her head more to clear her mind than decline a smoke. He lit up and laid his Ronson on the table, its chrome shiniest where his thumb touched. He wagged his empty bottle and asked her to get him another beer. She did.

Returning, she joked about getting tipped as a waitress, drawing a smile from R.J. that cut lines around his eyes, gratifying her with the promise that even he would get old and die someday. She threw her head back and drained her drink. R.J.'s friend Alvin used the moment to put his hand inside her thigh.

R.J.'s conversation turned to babble at once. His smile turned leering and foul, a jack-o'-lantern let rot on a doorstep. She glanced down sluggishly to check if the table was glass-topped and therefore could let him see this pig feeling her up below the ashtray and coasters. His seeing would make it worse. The violation. The way she didn't react when Alvin's hand moved higher.

The table was cloth-covered. R.J. couldn't see. Seconds passed while the room spun. Alvin's hand caressed her, its try at seduction more repulsive than had he just clamped her flesh like a starfish engulfing a clam. Did R.J. detect what was happening from her frozen expression, a glaze of stunned submission that he'd observed before on this girl whose face he'd forgotten? I'm yours, did it mean? Come ahead? Please stop? He'd been the mature one that night on Heather Lane, the one with strength and experience. She'd depended on him to tell her what she wanted. She'd depended on him to be kind.

Disgust welled up in her. She stood, said incoherent good-byes, and stumbled in a daze out of the pool area and down the hall to her room. She was shaken but not tearful. She'd pushed the game to its limit, by choice. That made all the difference.

SHE COLLAPSED ON her bed in her bathing suit. A sort of sleep came. She woke in panic over Marjorie's whereabouts. The room's walls were painted dark brown to help guests fall asleep early. There were twin beds side by side, and for a doorstop a heavy kiln-fired jug that probably once held homemade liquor. She heard her stepdaughter singing in the bathroom and fell back with a groan on the mattress. "Fiona, time please?"

"Almost cocktail hour. Live it up."

"Not funny. Um, did you see Marjorie anywhere?"

"She's fine." Fiona poked her head around the door. "I never saw you drunk before. You were goofy."

"I had two drinks."

"You wobbled."

"Possibly."

"Better get ready if you're comin' to eat. The dining room has a jukebox and it's not all square either. It has Elvis Presley. Joey loves Elvis."

"The devil's music."

"Don't be a spaz," Fiona said. "Everyone knows you love it."

Delly had wine with dinner but couldn't face her food. It was just her and the youngsters tonight. Corinne and Donald stopped by the table. They'd come in from the marsh at two, slept till sundown, now would skip dinner in favor of a local gin joint. "Behave," Corinne told her kids. "Delly needs to relax this weekend."

The menu was hand-printed on little cards. Fiona complained about the selections and Joey razzed her, their banter grating on Delly with its pretend bickering and cutesy gibes. At least Fiona wasn't dressed like a whore tonight. And Joey? Delly studied him through the candlelight. Eyes avid, head cocked intently to the pretty girl beside him—for an instant he resembled R. J. Bainard the night she'd first met him. The vision incensed her. She leaped to her feet but quickly reoriented herself as a spinster nanny, forlornly soused, dining with adorable children.

"You okay, Miz Franklin?"

"A little seasick, Joey."

"We're on land," Fiona said.

"Barely." Delly's chair creaked under her weight as she sat back down, more cause to feel just great.

Someone cued up the jukebox and "The Great Pretender"

came on. The dance floor filled. Fiona and Joey got up and soon were whispering mouth to ear as they swayed. His hand rode low on Fiona's back, fingers tapping her rump in rhythm. Delly's husband, the few times she'd straddled him, used to press down on her tailbone like a jockey pressing a horse's withers to drive it to peak performance. She'd told him it felt good after the first time he did it. It became his foremost sex technique, wheeled out like a reliable casserole, making her wish she'd never mentioned it.

She reached for her wineglass. She'd drunk more today than in years. Tipsy in the afternoon, passed out at sundown, tipsy again at night. "Me and you, what say?" She froze at the voice at her ear, knowing at once it was R.J.'s friend. The man turned to Marjorie. "Help me out. Tell your mama don't be shy."

"She's not my mama."

"Don't talk to him!"

"*Dog,*" he said. "Gimme a chance. My own children think the world of me."

"And your wife?"

"In heaven, poor thing."

"Still with the ring."

"Sentimental. Woman was dear to me."

"Don't Be Cruel" came on the jukebox. Marjorie urged Delly to dance with the man.

"All three of us," Alvin proposed. "We'll start a conga line." Somehow Delly wound up on the dance floor with him while Marjorie bopped in reassuring proximity. "Don't be mad, Ethel," he said to her over the music. Ethel? The alias threw her briefly. "Only way I know is head-on." He towered over her, moving to the music like a football lineman, swaybacked and muscle-bound.

"You were disgusting this afternoon," she said.

"You gave me fever."

"I'm gonna sit down now."

"Please. I'm a nice man. Don't know a soul around here, is all."

"What about your guide?" She gathered her nerve. "He's a friend, looked like."

"He's nobody's friend." The song ended. "Good-bye, Ethel." Alvin bowed to her. "I leave tomorrow."

"A pity." The words popped out like a goose bump. Delly saw Marjorie return to their table and Fiona and Joey slip out of the dining room. Little registered beyond the heat in her face. She managed a question. "Whatsa matter, hunting no good?"

"It's all right for mallard and pintail. No canvasback, though."

"How is killing one bird different from killing another?"

"Canvasbacks are rare. Rare makes it special." Her focus retracted from distant points to the curious figure before her. He seemed more gnomish than apelike now, a lackey whose cardboard gentility was a clue to the company he kept. "Special," he said, "means I'll cherish it forever."

They were alone on the dance floor. The clatter of busboys created an insulation in which the couple lingered unguardedly. She thought to herself that this man was a widower doomed to pick-up lines and lame come-ons. Yet he knew things about R. J. Bainard that Delly wanted also to know. *Nobody's friend?* It was music to her ears. She said to him, "A man oughta take time if he's after special birds."

"I got time. Till tomorrow mornin', anyway."

"Lucky me," she said. "Lucky you."

———

THE SCARIEST PART about what followed was that she saw it coming and still couldn't stop it. If anything, the apprehension of danger sharpened the shock when it hit, a faint foreboding preceding the blow like a whisper preceding a scythe.

The kids had gone to their rooms. Delly and Alvin strolled to the pool enclosure to get a drink at the bar. Its moisture-smeared windows framed a night view of the marsh, a soupy blackness under a sky riddled with icy stars. She felt as if she were with an uncle she didn't know well, a fellow black sheep with whom she shared a dislike of the rest of the family. There were some empty chairs outside the sauna. He pulled two close together. "You're pretty."

"Don't start."

"You're my ideal, I can't help it."

"Oh?" That syllable sealed it. A sliver of need.

" 'Cause I do like a plump girl. Smooth'n round, and all that softness everywhere." He reached down and took hold of her wrist. "So relax."

When you touch a flame, the reflex to pull away precedes the sensation of pain. That was the effect of Alvin's hand on her wrist. She wrenched it free before any parallel memory of the time with R.J. came back. She strode toward the exit until what felt like steel bands seized her in a bear-trap embrace.

Alvin kicked open the sauna door and shoved her to the wooden bench inside. Her mind screamed. He squatted on her chest and pinned her arms under his knees, his crotch inches from her face. When she tried to buck away he pressed his thumbs into the glands under her jaw. "I thought we was friends here." The ceiling spun overhead. The sauna door swung shut like a coffin lid.

She inhaled through her nose, preparing a mighty scream.

As if reading her thoughts, he reached inside his blazer and withdrew a ring of keys clipped to a jackknife. He unclasped the blade and displayed it between his face and hers, turning it to catch the light from the bulb in the sauna room ceiling. "I never cut nothin' but a toenail with this before, but I will cut you if you interrupt me here."

She nodded. His face was a blur beyond the glinting blade.

"Don't wanna hurt you. Don't wanna fuck you neither, not now, even if it did fire my mind the second I seen you today." Sweat from his face dripped onto hers. He touched the knife to her windpipe. "You put that idea in my head, Ethel."

The knife's point was like a bee sting or a sharp pencil. The pulse in her neck fluttered beneath it.

"Teasy cunt like you, what I'm s'posed to think? Tell me you sorry at least."

Silence.

"Talk to me, girl."

"Sorry."

There was a pause as he gauged her sincerity. He tapped the knife against her throat like a pointer against a bulletin board. "I forgive you." He climbed off her, closed the jackknife, brushed his pants clean. He warned her not to call the police. "I get hauled outta bed for this, I'll see to it you watch your pretty daughter die." His tone was genial. "Go back to your room, go to bed, sleep late. I'll be long gone time you wake up."

Silence.

"Let's hear it, Ethel. Say you'll be good."

"I'll be good."

When he delayed in responding, she thought for a moment she'd done something wrong. "That's nice," he said. "No chance we can start over here, is there?"

She tensed as if electrocuted.

"Ah." He sounded disappointed. "Got it."

She tried to keep as still as roadside litter until he left, but a sob broke from her that to her horror made him turn around in the sauna doorway. Clamping shut her eyes, she felt him lean over her, his face looming close, his exhalations in her nostrils. With supreme courage no one was there to applaud she opened her eyes to confront what she expected would be his knife coming down in a scorpion strike. But instead he said gently, "I lied before, Ethel. I would never hurt you or your child. And my bad language before was plain gross. Just talked outta upset, you know?" His jaw muscles throbbed and he looked about to cry.

She nodded, more terrified now than ever. *Please go,* she prayed over and over.

He went. In the doorway his silhouette slumped at the shoulders as he gave a last heavy sigh. *"Dog."*

FIONA. SHE HAD to find Fiona.

Alvin's threat propelled Delly down the hallway. The room numbers blurred as she ran. Outside her door she got her key and turned the lock with iron calm. Fiona's bed was empty.

She went to the Meerses' suite. Their door was unlocked and the interior pitch dark. She entered. The felt presence of the room's unfamiliar furniture gave a sense of trip wires and booby traps.

She heard voices in the bedroom. A man's voice in low tones—then Fiona's voice giving timid replies to questions Delly barely heard but understood perfectly.

"You said."

"I know."

"At least do that, come on."

A zipper unzipped. "I don't know."

"You said no stopping."

"Ssh."

"Not gonna stop."

"No. No stopping."

"No?"

"No. I said no."

Delly's foot grazed one of the lodge's kiln-fired jug door-stops. She knelt and took hold of its neck. A natural weapon, heavy as a log. She raised it over her head and went at Fiona's assailant with vengeance years in the making.

She slammed the jug down with all her power. It didn't shatter. It hit his skull with a thunk that dropped him to the floor like a dead man. The jug broke apart on her second swing, but its neck stayed intact in her grip. She swung down again, the damage done this time by a ceramic edge jagged as flint. And finally once more, when the last of it shattered and left only her fist to strike over and over.

Fiona was screaming somewhere. The man lay limp on the floor, his slime warm around Delly's fingers.

Voices sounded. Lights came on. Donald and Corinne, returning from their night out, ran to their son. Joey was curled in a ball with his arms over his face like a child found under a cave-in. Roused from bed in the adjacent room, Marjorie stumbled in with drowsy whimpers that turned to a screech. Fiona crawled across the room and huddled against the far wall. Blood streaked her face like war paint. She glared at her stepmother with hate in her eyes.

Delly realized whom she'd attacked by now, but didn't yet grasp that she'd made a terrible mistake. She'd distinctly heard Fiona say no. She was sure she'd heard Fiona say no.

CHIEF HOLLIS JENKS of the Lake Charles Police Department had coordinated the search after R.J. jumped bail ahead of his trial in 1953. Failure to catch him hadn't hurt the Chief's reputation; people were satisfied that Richie Bainard's agony over the death of his wife was ample retribution for any crimes of his son. Chief Jenks took early retirement three years later with an engraved plaque and a surprisingly comfortable pension. He bought a big house in Lake Charles's tony Charpentier District and a bass boat for the lake. He always had cash for his grandchildren's birthdays and for the collection plate at church.

This good life was disturbed by a telephone call in January 1957. Jenks recognized the voice, its theatrical drawl, but couldn't match it to a face. As he and the man spoke, an image formed of the waddling fop who'd been R. J. Bainard's attorney. Like Jenks, Abe Percy had retired soon after R.J. fled, though without the nest egg Jenks had accumulated. He asked to meet Jenks somewhere out of the way. "My house no good?" the Chief asked.

"If that's an invitation, why thank you. But it's a little too posh for me."

The comment, laden with what Jenks remembered was

Percy's tiresome innuendo, put him on guard when they met at a roadside diner. Abe wore a linen suit that Jenks swore was one he'd sported three years ago, though now there was no chance of buttoning the jacket over his girth. Abe walked with a cane, his face swollen and veiny. "You look well," Jenks said. "Stay active, do you?"

"I do not. It was all I could do to mobilize and drive here today. Coffee, Miss," Abe said to the waitress. "And the brisket barbecue, greens on the side, with cornbread and a Coca-Cola."

"It's ten o'clock in the mornin'," Jenks said.

"I rise at four. This is lunch."

"Big meal, even so."

"Eating brings me solace. My gluttony is a cry to heaven."

The food arrived. Jenks sipped black coffee while Abe ate. In the weeks before R.J.'s trial they'd communicated regularly. Now they sat in separate silence like an old couple on New Year's Eve. "An early riser, you say?" Jenks asked.

"Devils hound my sleep. I'm sure you sympathize." The lawyer wiped his mouth. "I had a visitor yesterday. Miss Adele Billodeau."

"There's one from way back."

"She came to my home. Which is to say, my one-room garret above Alderson's Bait Shop. You see," Abe said, "I've yet to secure a retirement situation as pleasant as yours." His eyes narrowed in their pouches. "And she had, did Miss Adele, the most extraordinary news."

Jenks was impassive. This fruit is waltzing me, he thought.

Abe explained that Adele had encountered R. J. Bainard recently. "Our own dear boy, discovered at last."

"Where?"

"Not far, not far. Yet off the beaten path."

"Where?"

"I'm not going to tell you, Hollis. May I call you Hollis?"

"Fine."

"Fine. But no, I'll not be telling you where."

Chief Jenks sighed. His plan for today had been to buy a set of wrenches at Block's Home Supply, let his wife fix him lunch, assemble the tricycle he'd bought for his grandson—then dinner, TV, and bedtime with no lovelier dream than that tomorrow pass the same way.

"But honestly," Abe went on, "R. J. Bainard does not interest me. We know he did something to that girl, or *with* her. And we know why."

"'Cause his mother and Coach Billodeau."

"His *step*mother, Hollis. Don't be gross."

"Why she come to you? You were against her, those days."

"I was always a gentleman to Adele. She knew I pitied her for her mistreatment."

"Mistreatment? Charge was rape."

"Verdict dubious."

"We don't know that."

"Nor do we care," Abe said, his tone sharpening. "Do we, Hollis?"

"Gotta say, you're losin' me."

Abe leaned forward. "You're on the payroll. R.J. is living free under everyone's nose. Bainard money makes it happen."

"I'm retired, case you hadn't noticed."

"As am I. Jobs equally well done, if not equally remunerated."

"You're way off here. Way off." Jenks was lying, of course—
except in one respect. He indeed had been Richie Bainard's mole
inside the hunt for R.J., keeping him informed of any develop-
ments that might lead to finding the fugitive. Where Abe's accu-
sation was wrong was in Jenks's incentive. The money came
second, a carrot to take the sting off the stick. The main thing
that had made the Chief comply was Richie's threat to expose
him for his part in Walter Dopsie's death almost thirty years
ago. No matter that Jenks was a better man today, that he'd
since renounced his youthful enthrallment with the Klan at any
number of church testimonials. Such allegations from someone
as admired as Richie Bainard would have ruined Jenks in this
town where he'd been reborn.

It had taken Richie, on first meeting the Chief after R.J.'s ar-
rest in 1953, about five seconds to recognize him from that ugly
night in Pinefield. Jenks's globular head and cornmuffin face
emerged from buried memory like a demon emerging from
smoke. Still reeling from Seth and Angel's car crash, seeing the
leader of the gang that had beat Walter to death standing before him in the uniform of the Lake Charles chief of police had
overwhelmed Richie. He went dizzy and fell into the arms of
Bonnie and the family chauffeur, Alvin Dupree. They got him
some water. Like a madman's babbled last words, his breathless
account of Jenks's terrible deed sounded nuts to Bonnie. But
Alvin took it in thoughtfully. He leaned to Richie's ear and suggested he say nothing more, that the leverage against Jenks
might be useful. Bonnie had been impressed.

Abe dabbed his lips with a napkin. "I want what you have,
Hollis."

Jenks summoned his blankest look.

"Money. From Richie Bainard. For my silence. About his son." Abe was pleased how tough he sounded.

"You worked for him. Ask him yourself."

"They fired me after all that. Richie out of longstanding spite, his daughter because she thought one country lawyer would never do for the great Block's corporation."

"Guess you're outta luck."

"Ten thousand dollars." The number seemed not too small, not too big. "I expect a prompt reply. Otherwise it's not R.J. who'll suffer, Hollis. It's you."

Jenks stayed to finish his coffee after Abe left. Before coming today, he'd had an inkling that the lawyer would accuse him of taking bribes and threaten to blow the whistle. It would have been unpleasant but still a penalty in keeping with Jenks's belief that we all pay for our sins eventually. His own disgrace he could handle, but to think of it touching his family, his grandkids, was more than a little annoying.

It had been a while. He hoped he could still reach his Bainard contact. A man named Alvin, it was—no last name. Jenks smiled, remembering the guy's mania about insulating the family from scandal. As if anyone cared that the mighty Bainards were as scummy as everyone else.

DRIVING BACK INTO town, Abe pictured couriers in trench coats leaving bags of cash at obscure drop points and shivered to think of participating in such hijinks. Adele Billodeau's visit yesterday had aroused similar excitement that he might yet find fulfillment by ruining Richie Bainard at last.

She'd looked a fright, unrecognizable as a onetime hot ticket. Her mad tale had poured out in a monotone. Imagine almost killing a teenage boy! Warped by depression and booze, she'd bludgeoned the kid to protect her stepdaughter—totally in error, it turned out. "No one knows I saw R. J. Bainard that afternoon," she'd explained. "They think I'm just a time bomb that blew. I'm only telling you, Mr. Percy—"

"Abe, please. You're a grown woman now."

"—because I don't trust the cops and because you were nice to me back then. About what R.J. did." She looked at him straight. "People still don't believe me."

"It's hard for them, Adele, to speak of a white girl raped."

"Delly. I go by Delly now."

"Delly." It sounded like an Irish harridan with ten kids. "Precious."

In the course of deposing her before the trial, Abe had cloaked their sessions in kindness. She'd seemed to forget that she was the prime witness for the prosecution and therefore the target he must destroy. Her isolation had made it so easy. She couldn't confide in her mother, who'd pulled an ostrich act over the whole seedy episode; nor in her father, who'd offered only useless remorse before opting out altogether.

Abe had told Delly yesterday that he would need time to work up a plan to bring R.J. to justice now that they knew where he was hiding. His mind was already swirling with plans first to shake down the Bainards for money and afterward to demolish Richie's reputation as a self-made success whose public spirit derived from private sorrow. Shaking Delly's hand good-bye, he'd promised he would help her.

"Not me. Help my father."

"Your father?"

"He shot himself."

"I do remember."

"For letting me down, I think." Her composure in speaking of her father's suicide intimidated Abe. He'd met Frank Billodeau once, when Frank had come in to testify that R.J.'s assault on his daughter was for jealous payback against him. "My life's finished," Delly went on. "Catching R. J. Bainard won't change that. So don't do it for my sake."

"For your father's sake then," Abe said. "And my own."

BONNIE BAINARD SAT at her father's bedside holding his hand in hers. "Hey, Daddy."

"Oh. Hi." His voice was slurred with morphine.

"It's Bonnie."

"I know who it is." For a moment he hadn't known. It filled her with irksome pity. In the early stages of his illness Bonnie used to look forward to these chats for their reprise of the collaboration they'd shared. It was mostly blankness now. She'd grown impatient, discouraged by his insistence despite his debility to review business matters she ably could handle. She wanted him to let go, wanted him, as he'd long promised, to entrust her with all he'd created. "Seth come back?" he said.

"Daddy, please. He's not worth it."

Richie's filmy eyes closed out his daughter's frown. "Your opinion."

She had no sympathy for his continued concern for her half brother. He'd fretted miserably over Seth's recovery from the car accident, supported him, took pains to include him in his will only to have Seth, as Alvin had told Bonnie afterward, reject Richie's plea to reconcile. The kid would inherit nothing as a result.

"When I getta see R.J.?" he asked.

"R.J.? You can't be serious."

"One time. All I want."

"Christ, Daddy. Why?"

"Things to say."

"Say them to me."

"Not the same. You're my strong one. He's . . . not strong."

His thin hand groped for hers. Bonnie patted it distractedly, like a doctor with more than one terminal patient. She'd always admired her father's grit; it testified to her growth as his daughter and colleague that in his present infirmity she admired him rather less. She was Richie's equal that way, having yet to prove, when the need arose, to be insufficiently heartless.

It maddened her that he now wanted to reconcile with R.J. as well as with Seth—she pictured them all blubbering at Richie's bedside and tasted bile at the back of her throat. Alvin had been smuggling money to R.J. on Richie's order for years. Bonnie didn't care to know the details. But she was loyal. She would never terminate the payments. She expected to fund R.J.'s worthless life until the day it ended.

Her brothers were weak. One exploited old wounds to make his betters feel guilty, the other had run away in cowardice rather than confront an accuser he'd sworn was lying. Now her father was weakening, too. Make your bed and lie in it, Bonnie thought. Even if its sheets are shrouds.

"Bon?"

"I'm here."

Her father's eyes—brown pupils, yellow whites—stared as if off a cliff. "Want my boys back."

"I know, Daddy." She squeezed his hand slightly too hard. "And I'll get it done like I always do."

It could have been any night in early 1957 that Alvin had his hands in Bonnie's unpinned hair and was massaging her scalp like a spa professional. They were in her upstairs suite, lights low, shades drawn, her father asleep downstairs.

Alvin worked from behind a love seat on which she reclined. Her bathrobe was loosely tied at the waist. Her long toes curled and uncurled in a flex of feline unwinding. He was in his street clothes and she, just out of the tub, was imperially naked under her robe. Opportunistic by nature, he explored alternate drives with Bonnie; his resulting peace of mind signaled a balance of aggression and servitude. He liked that she was queen and he the rug under her feet, that he could mean nothing to her and yet tend to her welfare like no other. "You're sayin' you want me to fetch R.J. home?" he said idly.

"It's what Daddy wants. Do you think it's risky?"

"Not long as it's temporary."

"I don't like it. He's my brother, okay—doesn't mean I care to see him."

He glided his hands down her front under her robe. He watched her body arch and was filled with awe at Bonnie's ignorance of her own gratification. She preferred to be impregnable, to let down her armor only in condescension to the pleas of a lesser being—of Alvin, that is; or, say, the girl inside her who liked this more than she knew. The robe loosened. He saw between her small breasts the vague dents in her sternum resembling baby thumbprints in clay. Their dialog skimmed above these things like blue sky above a tornado. "He's lookin' well, gotta say."

"R.J.? Why not? Been on the tit all his life."

"Speakin' o' which."

"*Nosir.*" She slapped his hand. Her nipples had perked. They were long—longer than a whole segment of his pinkie finger. The sight of them exposed and erect, when she permitted it, excited yet also embarrassed him, which offered then a twisty thrill when in exasperation she thrust them in his face like bugs she was making him eat. She demanded a story. "That girl at the hotel," she prompted. "The slutty one you met."

"Ethel? What about her?"

"You were hard on her?"

"She was hard on me."

"A tease?"

"Flashin' me skin all day, and them wide-mouth smiles that you know was born to suck. Girl like that's gotta learn."

"You taught her?"

"I did."

"And?"

"And what, Bonnie?"

She shifted a little. "Did she learn?"

"Couple times. Couple ways." He bent to her ear. "Had her beggin' like a baby."

"Tell me . . ." Her tone yielded to whispery wonder. ". . . how she begged."

Alvin talked while continuing to massage her, spinning a

tale of rough seduction as schematically plotted as a Hollywood thriller. His hands roamed as he spoke, sliding further under her robe, parting it slowly until it lay open like two terrycloth wings with her body larval pale inside. She drifted to the sound of his story, his amorous poetry. Her legs were pronged open totally beautifully and her hand moved between them with the spacy concentration of a genius chewing a pencil. He pressed his crotch against the back of the love seat and stroked her arms with his tenderest touch.

He was in love with Bonnie Bainard. A large factor in his feelings was his conviction that she could never love him. Her indifference was commendable in his view. He wasn't worthy of her except as a personal implement along the lines of a fork or hairbrush. His fondest dream was that she would never tire of using him. Of the wedding band he wore, he told strangers that he was a widower and told people who knew otherwise that pretending to be married helped him better to savor his sins. He wore the ring in honor of his secret crush. Bonnie never asked him about it, though he liked to think she knew.

He spent a lot of time plotting ways to put his love to her best use. She was unaware of his tireless considerations; he hoped to keep it that way to spare her any unpleasantness he might perform to promote her ambitions. It spoke to the depth of his affection that he knew better than she what her ambitions were, how she longed to bloom in a garden free of dreary reminders of family failing and scandal.

Recently Alvin had learned, through Hollis Jenks, that some skunk lawyer out of the Bainards' past wanted a cash bribe to keep R.J.'s whereabouts secret. It was exactly the sort of collateral crap that Alvin couldn't let touch his beloved. More than he blamed the lawyer, who was only trying to turn a buck, he blamed R.J. for smearing Bonnie with the muck of his life just as her time to shine was nigh. He felt loyal to his old lieutenant, *semper fi* and whatnot. But it was nothing compared to this.

With wonder in his eyes he gripped Bonnie's shoulders as she rubbed herself. Her teeth were clenched but sounds escaped. She possessed a stubborn sexuality. Inhibition and pride made for a torrent when the floodwaters broke; the sounds went from grudging to grateful. In a moment she would dismiss him crossly with no acknowledgment of what had just passed. He adored her all the more for her odd ways, adored taking care of her and fulfilling desires such a lady deserves but need never admit.

AFTER THE EMERGENCY passed of cranial fracture and swelling, Joey Meers was transferred from critical care to the Lake Charles Hospital's Angela Bainard Convalescent Wing, one of several philanthropic town projects Richie Bainard had bankrolled in his late wife's name. Joey remembered nothing of Delly Franklin's attack. His speech remained halting, his limbs rubbery. His hair, shaved for surgery, had regrown to a boot-camp buzz. His face was slack on one side, with a sleepy eye that made his mother weep when she visited and made Delly's stepdaughter Fiona not want to visit at all. His parents deemed it proof of his brain damage that he bore no grudge against Delly. Corinne and Donald Meers had cursed her at first. Lately they were saying forgiving things to make it look better when they flushed her from their lives.

A varsity basketball star, Joey missed his teammates more

than the game, missed the easy popularity that had carried him like a wave through his schooldays. That was gone now, a fact people's solicitude confirmed every day. Only his cousin Delly was honest. A frequent visitor, she told him when he looked improved and when he looked like shit. She regularly tidied his room and took his dirty clothes home to wash. "How's about we dump the flowerpot?" she asked one afternoon, holding it up for his verdict.

"Dump. Incinerate. Do what you want."

"What I want is for you to buck up."

That was the tone, insufficiently abject, that annoyed and amused him by turns. How dare she act snippy when she ought to bow and scrape? His parents by contrast would grab both his hands and talk slowly. His words trailed his thoughts and he needed a walker to get around, still he didn't like being treated like a foreigner.

"I'm here if it helps and I'll go if it don't," Delly said.

He yielded out of exhaustion. "Don't go. I know I'm a jerk sometimes."

"I can stay till your counselor gets here. Better you're a jerk with me than him." She bent down and hugged him in his chair. "Least I deserve it."

"Oh. Beg pardon."

They looked up. "Afternoon, Mr. Hooker," Delly said.

"Didn't I say call me Seth, Mrs. Franklin?" The young man in the doorway had an earnest manner conveyed in fidgets and squinty stares.

"Then time you call me Delly." She didn't remember him from high school, just another faceless supplicant who'd cleared out of her way as she cruised down the hall. She'd heard from

hospital staff that he'd been a long-term patient and now coun-
seled others in the same boat.

"You were having a private moment," Seth said. "I didn't
mean to intrude." How he leaned one-handed on his cane
seemed an attempt to look suave.

"You can see us?" Joey asked.

"Against the light of the window, a little." Along with impaired vision, Seth's injuries had left him with a gawky ungain-
liness that wasn't helped by his hatchet haircut. He lived at the
hospital and liked it—which in itself, he would have been the
first to say, argued for keeping him here.

"I gotta go," Delly said.

"How's Fiona?" Joey slipped the question in quickly, like a
card into a house made out of them.

"Still hates me." Bad subject. "See you tomorrow."

"My folks'll be here around noon."

"I'll come at suppertime."

Seth listened with an avid expression, trying to picture what
Delly looked like, her voice rich with self-disgust. "You and his
parents don't get along?"

"No," she and Joey said together.

Seth laughed before realizing it wasn't funny. When Delly
asked him how Joey's therapy was progressing, he answered,
"Doing well. Learn to walk, learn to read. Then run for Congress."

"I can read," Joey protested.

"In bits. I struggled, too. Practice makes perfect," Seth added
pointedly.

Joey explained to his cousin, "He wants me to read the
Bible. You'd think," he went on, pausing to arrange the words

in his mouth, "that I'd rate a real headshrinker instead of a Holy Roller."

"I'm neither," Seth said. "I'm just someone who's been through stuff, too."

"Car accident, was it?" Delly asked him.

"Yes." His tone said no more questions.

A hospital orderly tapped the doorjamb. "Mista Seth? Visitor down front."

"For me?"

"Sister, I think. Waitin' outside."

"Probably come to disown me in person." Seth felt his way across the room to the window overlooking the parking lot. He motioned Delly over. "Tell me what you see."

A black sedan idled before the building's entrance. "Is that a Cadillac?" There'd been a time when the word felt luscious on Delly's tongue, like *Paris* or *caviar*. But now whenever she saw cars of that make she remembered the last time she'd sat in one.

"No doubt," he said.

They stood near each other at the window. There were scars, little divots linked by threadlike lines, across the upper half of his face. She peeked at his eyes. Rather than fishy or dull, they had a pale green brightness flawed only by aiming at nothing.

"She there?" he asked.

A tall young woman in a tweed jacket and slacks stood arms crossed at the top of the steps. Her thick hair had the sheen of a hundred brush strokes and its silver barrette flashed in the sun. "That's one mean-looking girl," Delly said.

"Amen to that."

"Your sister?" She studied his scarred face and wondered if it hurt to be touched.

"Half," he said. "Thank God."

EACH DAY BEFORE sunup, itinerant laborers gathered at the Esso station on the state highway heading west from Lake Charles. They sought a day's wages and maybe a sack lunch for sweat-work on farms and construction sites. Alvin scouted the group for weeks, discreetly asking various candidates what they would do for five hundred dollars. An ex-convict out of Okla-homa named Freddy Baez gave the correct answer. "Anything." The task Alvin preferred to avoid would get done after all.

In his late twenties, Freddy had a beard and good teeth and a slick way with barmaids that belied unreasonable passions when it came to money. Alvin might have been of easier mind in soliciting him had he known that Freddy had done time at the Oklahoma State Penitentiary for an incident of armed rob-bery that unbeknownst to the judge included Freddy's dis-memberment and burial of his cohort in the desert near Fort Sill. This part of Freddy's personal story never came up. Alvin asked only if he would kill someone for pay. Freddy said maybe. Alvin repeated the offer of five hundred dollars. Freddy said six or I walk. Alvin knew he'd found the right man.

He spent his own money to outfit Freddy in premium field gear. It had to be top shelf if he was to pass as the sort of wealthy sportsman that might patronize the Section Eight Gun Club as a guest of the Bainard family. Since there was no way the ruse could survive Freddy opening his mouth, Alvin told him to act hungover and say *nada* when they met their hunting guide. Freddy gave thumbs-up.

Alvin asked R.J. to take them to a duck blind out on Finney Pond, on the lee side of a natural berm between the marsh and the Sabine Preserve. The pond, windswept and isolated, had lately produced nothing to shoot but coots and songbirds. R.J. suggested they try elsewhere, but after Alvin's passionate spiel about contemplative scenery and healthful air, it was to Finney Pond they headed in R.J.'s mudboat.

It was the last day of duck season, 1957. The predawn dark was razor cold. Panes of ice buckled as the mudboat's wake rolled through the shallows along the weedy banks of the channel. In the glow of R.J.'s running lights hundreds of *pule d'eaus* skittered and took flight, black wings beating like bats pouring out of a cave. The roar of the mudboat's tunnel drive solved any issues of conversation. Freddy turned his face from the wind and hugged R.J.'s retriever for warmth. Alvin stared stoically rearward, watching R.J.'s pirogue, tied on a line thirty feet aft, shimmy and bounce in the mudboat's wake like a hypnotist's watch gone mad.

R.J.'s favorite part of any marsh run was to slalom among the islets so fast that he couldn't think. He'd moved around often since fleeing home. Except for loneliness and occasional mortal panic, life had passed tolerably well. Sometimes he'd pretended he was fleeing injustice or that he was a spy eluding assassins; more often he'd played guitar, drunk beer, and waited for Alvin to bring him money. Settling in Cameron Parish had led him to settle in other ways also. He'd injured a girl once—the sexual encounter on Heather Lane dogged his memory like an old massacre in the mind of a veteran—but he'd strived since then to be decent. Redemption never occurred to him. He sought only to do no more harm.

The morning sky went from black to brown. R.J. eased his mudboat alongside the duck blind and killed the engine. A wooden box embedded in the muck and fringed with papery reeds, the blind was covered with a sheet of green-painted tin whose edge he gripped with icy fingers and hauled into the mudboat. The hewn bench inside the blind accommodated three men shoulder to shoulder. He told the others to climb in; he'd join them after he beached the boat a distance away and paddled out in his pirogue to set the decoys. His dog leaped ashore in anticipation of sport to come. Alvin and Freddy stretched their frozen limbs and prepared to disembark while R.J., his back turned, held the boat steady with a push-pole.

Freddy inserted two shells into his shotgun and banged the barrel closed. "No need to load up yet," R.J. said before recoiling in surprise from the weapon aimed at his face.

"Don't shoot!" Alvin said, as if shocked by what was happening.

Freddy glared at him. "The fuck. I coulda done him inna back and we'd be goin' home now."

Too dismayed to be scared, R.J. asked Alvin, "What the hell you got goin' here?"

Alvin said to Freddy, whose face was scarlet with cold and perplexity, "'Member what I told you? Boy first needsa hear who and what for. *Then* he gets it."

R.J.'s eyes darted back and forth between Alvin's face and the barrels of Freddy's shotgun, which resembled a figure eight around two wells of bottomless black.

"Don't be scared," Alvin said. "When's time, I'll tell you."

R.J.'s thoughts began to accelerate. Options occurred to him—leap overboard, attack, give a winning smile—but were so jumbled that his brain locked like an overheated engine and became completely still.

"Tell him," Alvin said to Freddy, "who hired you."

"You hired me."

"Who beyond me?"

"Um . . ."

Alvin cut him off. "Fact is," he said to R.J., "your brother hired Freddy and me to kill you here this mornin'."

The information took a moment to penetrate. "Seth? Did that?"

"Your daddy ain't well. An' comes to splittin' up money, two ways beats three any day."

"Gee." R.J. slumped on the mudboat seat with a vacant look, like a prophet who got it all wrong. "If you told me Bonnie wants me gone, I'd believe it. Or my father. Christ knows, Richie Bainard's capable of about anything."

"Richie Bainard?" Freddy said. "The hardware king?"

Alvin's expression stayed placid, but for Freddy to hear much less speak the name "Bainard" had not been part of the plan. He unzipped his gun case and withdrew a side-by-side twelve gauge, loading its shells with indefinite purpose.

"Guess I shoulda charged more," Freddy laughed.

Alvin raised his weapon. With two guns aimed at him, R.J. would have appeared to any onlookers, of which there were none, like a very important dead man. "It's time," Alvin said.

"Alvin. Jesus."

Freddy asked R.J., "You wanna turn around like he said?"

The flick of R.J.'s eyes between the guns became frantic.

"Have it your way." Freddy leveled his weapon at R.J.'s chest.

"One thing first," Alvin said.

Freddy turned just as the sergeant, with a delicate movement, swung the barrel of the shotgun he was cradling to within inches of Freddy's forehead. He pulled the trigger. The earsplitting report carried no echo, dispersing across the marsh like spooked birds. The picture imprinted R.J.'s retina like a flashbulb burst. He saw it happen, didn't comprehend it, saw it again in afterimage with a plume of skull material spouting over the water and fading into smoke and pink mist.

Freddy pitched across the gunwale as if clocked by a prizefighter. The back of his head emptied into the water, forming a blood cloud laced with stringy bits like spoiled milk in tea. With infant wonder R.J. studied the flow, enamel red with steam coming off it, till his reverie was broken by Alvin's voice. "You're welcome."

R.J. tried to swallow. Couldn't.

"I done this for you. So you'll see things clear."

Long pause. "What?"

"You heard me before. Seth asked me to arrange this undertakin' against you."

R.J.'s thoughts groped back to moments ago. "Me and him always got on okay."

Alvin spat onto the boat deck. "Hear me again: it's for the money. And his mama besides."

"Angel?"

"Puts her death on you, he does."

"I wasn't even there."

"You know what happened."

"I know what you told me. She drove into a tree."

"Runnin' away, same day as you. Big coincidence."

"I have no idea what you're saying."

"Runnin' to each other. You and her. Lovers." Alvin shrugged. "It's what he thinks—and not for no reason, you gotta admit."

R.J. surveyed the marsh. In the usual way of shock, his mind was empty throughout this display of contemplation. He indicated Freddy. "Why kill him?"

"I shoulda let him proceed?"

"Shouldna got started in the first place!"

"'Cept you wouldna bought it otherwise. *Dog,* I only let him get close to show the level of feelin' against you. You got lucky," Alvin said, "thanks to me. Now let's bury this garbage and get home. 'Less you wanna keep huntin'."

R.J. wasn't hearing. "Think he'll try again?"

"Seth? No question. Crash messed him up, made him mean as dirt. Best bet? Get far away and never come back."

"I'm not scared of him."

"Your daddy's dyin', and there's a lotta dough on the line. Boy won't miss twice."

"He's dying?"

"Tumor in the head. Down to weeks."

R.J. absorbed this. "He dies, Bonnie takes over."

"Seth right beside her, he hopes."

R.J. regarded Freddy's body. He took out his lighter and cigarettes and smoked for a bit. At length he said, "Is it my imagination, or does he look like me?"

"It's there. With the beard especially."

"I've thought about it, you know? Killing myself. Thought

about it for real, thought about faking it. Close the book. Make a new start." R.J. spoke as if alone, as if to his face in a mirror. He told Alvin to hand him his shotgun.

It was a nervous moment for the sergeant. Their marine past prevailed and the order was obeyed.

"C'mere, boy." Since hearing the shot earlier, R.J.'s dog had been scanning the water for something to retrieve. It padded down the embankment and bounded into the boat. "Such a good boy you are," R.J. cooed. He raised Alvin's gun. The dog wagged its tail. It sniffed a gunpowder scent at the mouth of the barrel and was starting to lick the metal when R.J. pulled the trigger.

He set down the shotgun and patted Freddy's pockets. He began to strip the body. "Help me get off his clothes."

"You shot your dog."

"You blew a man's head off! Now do like I tell you and give me his clothes."

From there the pattern was Alvin squeamish and R.J. deliberate till at last R.J., shivering in the cold from having undressed to don Freddy's gear, pushed the corpse—now dressed as R.J.—to the deck of the mudboat between the fore and aft seats where it lay in a grievous splay. He placed Alvin's gun in Freddy's hands, its barrel directed at the charred ravine that was the top of Freddy's face. Blood from the dog pooled under both corpses.

"I killed myself today," R.J. said to Alvin.

"Say what?"

"Sat in my boat and shot my dog, then me."

"We're leavin' him here?"

"We paddle home in my pirogue. Someone'll find him, and that'll be that for R. J. Bainard and the shitty life he led."

"They'll know it ain't you."

"You saw we look alike. And critters'll work him over." R.J. slowed down his thoughts to explain. "I want it ended. I want to be gone in the ground."

Alvin looked unwell. R.J., by contrast, apparently possessed a knack for this stuff. He took out another cigarette but thought better of it. He stuck the pack and his Ronson into the pocket of the canvas jacket on Freddy. "Good time to quit," he said.

What had been an hour's ride here in the mudboat this morning took five hours in the pirogue going home. Paddling away from the scene, Alvin's last vision was of Freddy's body sprawled beside R.J.'s dog, poor dog, on the bloody deck of the mudboat. No one saw three hunters head out this morning, no one saw two return. Thus did R. J. Bainard's life conclude—alone in the wild, poor man.

THE GRAVITY OF what had happened at Finney Pond wasn't lost on Alvin. The only thing that could have made him feel worse would have been if Freddy Baez's body were somehow traced to him. To stain the Bainard name even by association would have put him into torment. He slept poorly, unable to keep from picturing a man on the marsh with R.J.'s clothes on his back and Alvin's birdshot in his brain. It didn't help that he heard nothing from R.J. for weeks afterward. They'd parted at the boat dock and hadn't spoken since. Terrified that these loose ends would disturb his good thing with Bonnie, he hid his anxiety beneath chirpy high spirits that were driving her up the wall. That was the state of things when at last the phone call came.

A trapper had found the bodies. The contents of the dead man's wallet provided identification and the location of R.J.'s rented room in Hancock Bayou. Alvin stood by as Bonnie took the call from the Cameron Parish sheriff in Richie's office, her feet propped on the desk in fixed repose as she received the grim details. She'd never been close to her brother and hadn't seen him in more than three years. But knowing he was out there alive had made their father's imminent passing seem less lonesome to her. "Was he depressed when you saw him last?" she asked Alvin after she hung up.

"He was never too cheerful."

"Gotta feel sorry for him." She sounded as if she did. "I guess a funeral's in order."

"After you go down to ID him."

"Excuse me?"

"Next o' kin. I believe that's policy."

"Body has no head, the man said."

"It's got a head."

"How do you know?"

He caught himself. "I seen stuff. Hardly ever a shot takes off the whole thing."

"And his face and hands all chewed? Jesus God."

It can't be overstated how distressed Alvin was. He dreaded that Bonnie, on viewing the corpse, would realize it wasn't R.J. and deduce that her brother had murdered a man to stage his own suicide. Believing him a killer would, Alvin worried, further spook her skittish heart. His one hope was that the resemblance between Freddy and R.J. had been improved by exposure outdoors, leaving Alvin and Bonnie's love affair to continue its upward course.

SALLIE HOOKER HAD had no contact with her daughter after Angel left Hancock Bayou with Richie Bainard in 1938. She'd learned they were married only after chancing on a copy of *The Lake Charles American* with a photo of the couple as honorary king and queen of the Calcasieu-Cameron Fair in 1948. She guessed right away that the little boy in the picture was Angel and Richie's child. To not know her grandson or have any hope of meeting him didn't depress her as much as you'd think. She was pleased for Angel and grateful for God's miracle that a child of her blood could have so brilliant a future.

She was saddened by R.J.'s suicide. He'd come by her facility at the start of duck season last fall and declared right away who he was. Her memory of him as a child was entirely warm and she saw no reason to pretend otherwise. She'd asked about Angel, which took him aback since he had no idea of the women's connection. Thus it was R.J. who first gave her the news, as Alvin Dupree had given it to him, that her daughter, his stepmother, had died in a car crash. "An' the child?" Sallie had asked.

"They call him Seth. He got hurt but is okay, what I hear."

Her closed eyes indicated she was thanking the Lord. "My grandson a Bainard. Ain't that a thing."

R.J. had put his hand on Sallie's shoulder. "We're related now, you and me."

"Now you jus' silly," she'd said. She'd begun to cry, remembering her daughter, still you could tell his words had pleased her.

Those had been their first exchanges. There'd come a subsequent moment when he confessed he was on the run from the law.

"Hadda wonder why you here, actin' poor," Sallie said.

He'd felt relieved that she didn't ask what crime he'd committed. Robbery or fighting she could probably accept, but to think that the little boy she'd raised could have harmed a girl would have been a sore disappointment.

And now that boy was dead, his remains found on the marsh in condition that would have been worse if not for chill winter temperatures. Muskrats and carrion birds had consumed much of the face and fingers, but insects, gators, and rot weren't a factor this time of year; the body was decently preserved inside layered hunting clothes. The trapper had brought it in his flatbed to Sallie's cold locker for storage pending collection by the sheriff. Men lugged it in like a sack of grain and laid it on a worktable in the middle of the locker. Though the upper skull was gone, Sallie didn't hesitate to touch the stringy hair at the temple, remembering its lovely chestnut color when R.J. was a baby.

She was preparing to spread a tarp over him when her niece's son came in from outside, where he'd been listening to the trapper describe his big find. Tarzy studied the body with chagrin. "Why you gone kilt your dog, too?"

"Who you talkin' to, child?" Sallie said. The locker's open front door had let out cold air and the compressor came on with a diesel cough. "That man he can't hear you."

"Kilt his dog."

"His name was R. J. Bainard, and jus' you remember times he nice to you. Not for us to understan' what make a soul go down."

Tarzy studied the remaining face. What was his great-aunt talking about? He'd never seen this guy before.

Sallie covered the body and stepped back. "God's will not ours be done." She shut her eyes. "Tarzy?"

"Yes, ma'am?"

"Give a prayer. Even 'bout his dog's okay. Good Lord love His creatures, too."

Tarzy closed his eyes. "I'm sorry you dead," he said aloud, adding in his mind, whoever you are.

THE LAKE CHARLES *American* reported R. J. Bainard's suicide the day after his body was found. The next afternoon a sputtering brown Oldsmobile pulled up at Sallie's place. A fat man in a linen suit clambered out looking like a food critic lost in Provence. The rest of the world might buy the suicide story, but Abe Percy dearly hoped it was wrong. He'd come to Hancock Bayou to investigate.

Tarzy was there alone, his mother and great-aunt doing errands in town. His chore today was to clean the plucking machine behind the cold locker. He pulled feathers by the fistful from the exhaust vent and stuffed them into burlap sacks, the feathers itching to his elbow and clinging like a furry rash. The locker loomed nearby with the loaded presence of a room someone died in, presence conferred by an actual corpse. Tarzy was curious for another peek. When the visitor waved a dollar

bill and asked if he might look inside, the boy led him around
back with an air of authority.

Abe walked with a cane and breathed in a musical wheeze.
He grimaced at the smell of feathers and offal and held a handkerchief over his nose. Tarzy unbolted the door and swung it
open. The locker was an eight-by-eight box with a six-foot ceiling. Entering, Abe started to shut the door behind them to keep
cold air from escaping. Tarzy leaped to prevent it from closing.
"Of course," Abe said. "No light."

"No air!" Tarzy said. "No gettin' out either." He indicated
the locker's latch mechanism—it opened only from the outside.

"Good heavens! That's a frightful hazard."

"Ready see'm now?" Like a magician unveiling his show-
stopper, Tarzy yanked off the tarp with flourish.

There were bloodstains on the collar of the canvas jacket;
otherwise it wasn't as gruesome as Abe had feared. Weeks outdoors under freezing rain had cleansed the gore. The blast had
penetrated the forehead above and slightly to one side of the
bridge of the nose, suggesting R.J. had faltered at the last instant before leaning on the trigger. Abe examined the result.
"Grew a beard, I see."

" 'Kay," the boy said.

"Yes?"

"Gotta go."

"My time is up?"

"Family comin' today. Take him home."

"Really?"

"My aunt said. She be mad we in here."

Abe sighed. For this he'd paid a dollar? "Pity the beard. It hides a man's finer features, which I suppose was the intent."

"He had a beard, same."

Abe regarded the boy. "Who had a beard?"

Tarzy went quiet.

"Did you know R. J. Bainard?"

"He brung his birds."

"And this is he?"

Tarzy sensed snares being set. "Who else?"

"Indeed."

"Kilt his dog."

"I heard. Perfectly vile."

"I like dogs."

"So do I."

The boy drew the tarp back over the dead man's face out of respect for this sacred new topic. "Never had m'own."

"Never had a dog? Every little boy should have a dog."

Tarzy nodded. The old lawyer said to him gently, "I believe you and I are in sympathy, young fellow. I believe if you gave full vent to your distress at the death of this man's dog, you might consent to help me catch the animal's true murderer."

"Help how?"

"Just leave me alone with this . . . *evidence* for a moment. Guard the door, and take care I'm not entombed by that latch."

Tarzy hesitated. "Man kilt his dog. Then hisself."

"As you say. I wish merely to confirm the fact so that no dogs will suffer from our negligence in the future."

Tarzy stepped outside the locker, leaving the door partway open to let in light. Abe, with the lofty disdain of an English butler confronting a clogged toilet, unbuttoned the fly of the dead man's woolen trousers. He then fished out the penis with a charcoal pencil and examined it, poking it with the pencil as if separating mushrooms from peas on a dinner plate. He looked up to see Tarzy gaping at him through the doorway.

"Oughtn't be spying, boy!" He had another thought. "Come. Your testimony could prove useful."

Tarzy entered, his expression full of misgiving.

Abe lifted the penis, pale as pasta but intact thanks to its frigid confinement in the man's undershorts. "Are you familiar with term *circumcision?*"

Tarzy was not.

Abe unzipped his pants. "Circumcised." He indicated the table. "*Un*circumcised. Do you understand?"

Tarzy's eyes went back and forth. He nodded.

Abe put himself in order, repositioned the dead man's organ and buttoned the fly. He put his pencil back in his pocket. "I realize that was nasty," he said to the boy. "Just remember, I'm an attorney."

ABE WATCHED FROM a distance up the road when Bonnie Bainard and her chauffeur arrived at Sallie Hooker's later that day in the company of two Cameron Parish sheriff's deputies and a Lake Charles hearse. The chauffeur, an imposing fellow with hands like slabs of meat, opened Bonnie's door, glaring at the deputies when their vehicle splashed through a puddle and almost soiled her.

Alvin had seen the original damage done, so inside the cold locker knew to hold his breath and tighten his anus before the tarp was removed. But how could Bonnie have prepared for the ravaged thing she was expected to call her kin? She didn't flinch. She sniffled once before instructing the funeral parlor attendants to load the body. "Cremate," she added. "Tonight."

From there, the deputies escorted her and Alvin to the single room above a saloon that their investigation had turned up as R.J.'s hideout in Hancock Bayou. Bonnie wanted none of her brother's effects but Alvin said take his guitar at least, the old steel resonator that Richie had bought from Joe Falcon. "It'll be sentimental one day, you watch."

"Sentimental? Me?" The quip was high humor for Bonnie. "Sure, throw it in the car." Thus did Alvin fulfill R.J.'s one order when they'd parted ways after Freddy—don't forget the National.

R.J.'s burial urn was interred at Orange Grove near his mother, stepmother, and grandfather. Reporters had been advised that Richie Bainard was unable to attend due to extreme grief. In reality, Bonnie had told him nothing about her brother's death; she wanted to limit to one at a time the family traumas she had to juggle. A photographer got some distant shots of her bending to the earth in white gloves as the pastor and a stocky attendant looked on. The pictures ran in the Sunday paper and were condemned by many as invasive of the Bainards' bereavement. Rumors circulated that the photographer worked for a publicity firm in the family employ.

The limousine windows were dark-tinted, denying snoopers at the graveyard gate any glimpse of the passengers inside. One of the snoopers was Abe Percy. He would have been intrigued by Bonnie's look of pinched amusement as the limo pulled away, though what conclusion he might have drawn is debatable. Everyone mourns in his own way.

CORINNE MEERS VISITED her son Joey at the hospital annex every other day. She dressed smartly for these outings—today, a camel waistcoat and skirt with a matching pillbox hat—on the chance that she might meet a young medical man who would ask her to join him for coffee. She'd never been unfaithful to her husband, but her discontent with Donald had carved a hollow inside her that rather than fill with PTA or charity work Corinne had left optimistically empty.

She was annoyed to find her son absent. There came a tap on the door as she stood in the empty room. "If you want Joey, he's out," she griped.

The visitor entered. "I'm looking for Mr. Hooker."

"He's out walkin' with my son evidently."

"Ah. Taking advantage of our warm spell."

"Mus' be a sight, coupla gimps on a sidewalk."

"At least they won't get far."

She laughed. "I shouldn't laugh."

"Got to sometimes, in a hospital."

"You a medical man?"

"Lord, no. Too dumb."

"Business with Mr. Hooker, then?" She saw the man's reaction. "Was that nosy?"

"I'd say."

Corinne blushed, more perturbed than embarrassed now that he'd confessed he was no doctor.

"But since you ask," he went on, "I'm here to beat his brains in."

"A fistfight?"

"Was thinking a boot or a chair."

"The man is blind."

"Didn't say I'd fight fair."

Next, to her surprise, she said what she felt. "You got a scary way, kinda."

"Not once you know me." He arched an eyebrow. "Cuppa coffee?"

"I beg your pardon?"

"Seeing as how you've been stood up."

"I have not been stood up! I am waitin' on my son."

"And I'm waiting on you. Coffee or no? It's not gonna change the world either way."

He wore loafers, chinos, and a pinstripe fedora cocked to one side like a salesman who loves his job. His beard was crisply sculpted, giving him the look of an evil duke. Extending her hand, she realized it was damp with nerves. "My name's Corinne Meers. *Mrs*. Corinne Meers."

"Freddy Baez."

"Oh, is that . . . Portuguese?"

"Mexican. My mother's name. She was a famous whore, I'm told."

She yanked her hand away. "That's no way to talk to me!"

With no little presumption he took her chin in his fingers and drew her face toward him. His blue eyes were vibrant but their low-slung lids looked woeful as a bloodhound's. "Don't lie, Corinne," he said. "You like it just fine."

———

JOEY AND SETH hobbled along a tree-lined road at the outskirts of the hospital grounds, testing Joey's upgrade from walker to cane. Joey had healed enough in mind and body to question his prospects for further improvement. Was this it? The sag in his face, the hitch in his gait—was this his life from now on? "Could be," Seth said.

"Jeez. Can't you just lie like my mother?"

"I can be honest because I believe you'll recover completely. I'm afraid your mother doesn't."

"You noticed."

"Your cousin, on the other hand, believes it, too. She'd make a good counselor."

"Delly? Why, 'cause she's rude as you?"

Seth grabbed Joey's arm with an awkward flail. "Don't be calling her rude. That girl's got spirit to burn."

"She's stone crazy."

"She's red hot."

Joey began in singsong, *"Se-eth likes Del-lee / Se-eth likes Del-lee . . ."*

Seth took a playful swipe at the boy with his cane. A car approached. They moved to the shoulder to let it pass. A bearded man was at the wheel.

The car, a red convertible, braked and U-turned, holding crossways in the road. Joey felt idiotic standing there, as if his and Seth's lame conditions were mocked by the vigor of the vehicle and the man driving it. In a cocky gesture befitting the athlete he'd been, he gave his new cane a whirl, as if he had no idea how he'd come to be holding it. The car gunned forward, zooming past them with a wallop of wind. "Loser," Joey muttered.

"Who?"

"*Me*. For bein' a goddamn cripple."

"Don't blaspheme."

"That a joke?"

"Yes and no."

"You and Delly, who knows what you're thinkin' half the time?"

"You're a little spotty yourself."

"Only since she busted my skull."

"I'm warning you. Criticize her, you're gonna have a fight on your hands."

"From you? There's a joke."

"You don't know chivalry? You don't know honor?" Seth raised his fists like a bare-knuckle boxer and punched comically at the air.

Joey forced up a scowl. "Shit. I knew you and her was made for each other."

DELLY WAS HOME at the little ranch house she shared with Fiona when Abe Percy called. She wasn't surprised to hear from him, what with R.J.'s name in all the papers for his universally praised suicide. "Guess that ends the case," she said.

"Maybe not." Abe then asked an unusual question.

She didn't hang up. "It was a long time ago. And dark."

"I realize it's distasteful."

"Why do you care? They already buried him."

"Which must have been welcome news."

"That he's dead? I have my doubts. Would've liked to seen the body."

"I saw it. And I have doubts."

"So your question—"

"Pertains. Please don't think I'm enjoying this." But Abe *was* enjoying it. He hadn't spoken to any women other than phone operators and waitresses for years. He used to enjoy their company more than was proper. He liked trashy ones best, ones like Delly, though at twenty-two she was older than his preference. He asked why she was still skeptical.

"The timing. Like when my father shot himself. I didn't want to believe it was suicide."

"Well, if not that—"

"Murder, okay? Not logical, but that's what I thought. Because I loved him and couldn't picture him giving up that way."

"But who?"

"He admitted to you about him and Angel Bainard. And then R.J. going wild when he found out."

"You think R. J. Bainard killed your father?"

"Did then. I blamed R.J. for everything bad there was, because of what he did to me. But Daddy was just trying to set things right in his own mind, I know that now."

They chatted. Delly's cousin Joey was recovering from his injuries, she said; her stepdaughter Fiona was still so mad at her that she was spending, of all things, more time with her father, from whom Delly was now separated. Abe was moved by this outpouring. It was reminiscent of the trust Delly had shown him in the run-up to R.J.'s trial, and trust always attracted him powerfully. "Would you join me for dinner sometime?" he asked.

"Like a date?"

"Oh no," he stammered. "Just to talk. I'm far too ancient for you." The comment begged her rebuttal. He despised himself for hoping she would.

"I'm seeing someone pretty regular."

"Wonderful! Who?" *Who?* His pushiness shamed him.

"Um," she improvised, "a doctor at Joey's hospital. Loadsa class."

"And not an old fat man like me."

Sharply she said, "Mr. Percy, I don't mind fat and I don't mind old. It's just I'm involved." She offered some consolation. "What you asked before? About R.J.'s thing?"

"I shouldn't have put you through that."

"It was . . ." She took a breath. "I know because my husband's isn't—it was circumcised."

"You're certain?"

"He made me get close, okay?"

There it was: The dead man wasn't R. J. Bainard. "That's helpful to know."

"Gonna tell me why?"

"No." It was Abe's surest assertion today. "It's for your safety. And mine."

ABE'S NEXT STOP was the neatly kept and pricey home of Lake Charles's former police chief, Hollis Jenks. The old lawman was sloshing gasoline down mole holes along his front walk when Abe pulled up. "You got balls comin' here," Jenks said.

"On the contrary," Abe said from his car. "I've acted with forbearance by not going straight to the authorities. But what use would that serve? To see you disgraced and myself empaupered? Surely there's a better way."

"Lord, I hate a man talks like that."

"I'm raising my price." The rattle of Abe's car motor proclaimed the wretchedness he sought to disguise. "Twenty thousand dollars. Inform the Bainards."

"Got nothin' to do with me."

"You're a fraud, Chief Jenks. A wanted man thrived thanks to you. Now an innocent man has been murdered."

"Gobbledygook."

"Expect a visit from the sheriff in that case."

Jenks shook his head. "I did some homework. The big-hearted lawyer with a bedroom to spare? All them poor little children and you."

Abe's face blanched only a little—his scandal in New Orleans had happened so long ago, it seemed another man's life, another man's shame. Jenks noticed it anyway:

"Ring a bell, does it?"

"A grave error on my part. But as well-meaning as it was inappropriate."

"Still pretty spicy. Front page, I'd say. Even now."

"They had nowhere to go, nowhere to sleep! I gave them a home."

"And got what back?"

Abe saw the futility here. "I say again: ten thousand dollars cash . . ." He'd dropped the price without realizing it. ". . . or all this . . ." He waggled his finger to delineate Bo's retirement haven. ". . . will be *gone*."

"Your shit against mine," Jenks said.

"Possibly. Or it could be the basis for mutual benefit." The proposition disgusted Abe, though he prayed it might be accepted. Jenks did:

"I want half whatever they give you. I'll push for the twenty."

"Partners, then."

"Partners." But after Abe drove away Jenks said aloud, "Guess again, freak."

A HALLWAY LED to Bonnie's bedroom suite at the opposite end of the Georgia Hill house from where her father lay in drugged slumber. Alvin had skipped down it on many past evenings in anticipation of serving his lady, but since her brother's funeral she'd all but ignored him. He paced the house flipping coins or blowing his mouth harp—softly, so as not to disturb her— while praying that she would assign him a task he might perform to her satisfaction.

Bonnie spent her days in her upstairs office. Though she complained of the business duties that burdened her, she liked being hands-on in running Block's, preferring to type her correspondence and take her own calls rather than hire a secretary. When things were good between them, Alvin stood by to sort her mail, change her typewriter ribbon, refill her fountain pen. One glance from her and he'd know to bring the car around to head off to a Block's locale perhaps hundreds of miles away. The trips were his favorite times with her, their valises in the trunk, separate rooms booked at modest hotels. She used to ride in back, Alvin up front like a proper chauffeur. But on the excuse of needing to be nearer the heater or to share sips of his orange pop she increasingly wound up beside him, a voice in the dark if they were driving at night, a fragrant weight against his shoulder if the miles had lulled her to sleep.

The hesitance with which she'd invited his advances stirred his utter gratitude. Lying unclothed before him, she showed no concern for his pleasure or his feelings. The understanding that these intimate perks could be cut off at any time carried, for him, an erotic component that he'd quite enjoyed until they actually were. Her office and bedroom were off-limits now. Tension crusted the air when they crossed paths in the hall or at Richie's bedside. Alvin wondered how things had gone so awry. He should have let Freddy Baez do his work. With R.J. dead for real and Seth cut out of his father's will, all Alvin's problems—which is to say, all Bonnie's problems—would have been solved.

In the depths of one of his morose afternoons he found a folded note under a paperweight on the foyer table. His heart leaped to see his name written on it in Bonnie's schoolhouse cursive. When leaving him memos, she kept an odd protocol whereby work instructions were addressed to "Alvin" and personal ones to "Sgt. Dupree." She was so ill at ease with affection that she masked it in formality. Thus "Sgt. Dupree" gave a foretaste of sweet reunion. His knock was timid, his eyes downcast in expectation of blinding radiance when she opened her bedroom door.

He hoped she'd be wearing her robe; it represented as bold an invitation as she could permit herself. A shoulder or foot massage would lead to the robe falling open as he performed in priestly obliviousness for the willowy nude unveiled before him.

His stories would come next. Dirty ones, her enjoyment of which, once piqued, far exceeded Alvin's experience or imagination. In constant quest of new material, he memorized passages from pornographic literature and spent his pay to interview prostitutes rather than to fornicate with them. For purposes of research he sometimes pursued cheap pieces like that Ethel at the Section Eight Gun Club. A girl like that had no better use, and Bonnie did enjoy hearing about it afterward. To conjure an arousing story was to be the diligent lover she deserved.

But Bonnie wasn't wearing her robe. She had on a gray skirt and sweater, her hair was bunned, and her face was stern as a boxer's at the opening bell. "You got my note."

"I did." There'd be no stories today.

She beckoned him inside. A tidy arrangement of chair and love seat took up much of the sitting room. Last time they were together here, she'd been sprawled naked on the love seat like a body thrown from a truck. She was all business now. "My brother's funeral the other day?"

"Yes . . ."

"You cried."

"I did?"

"At the graveside, Alvin. You cried when I put the urn in."

"Me and him went back a ways. Korea an' all."

"It's why I was surprised," she said. "Since obviously you knew it wasn't R.J. we were laying to rest."

"Well, yeah, the real R.J.'s with Jesus."

"Don't hand me that crap." Her sacrilege shocked him. "That body was someone else. Tell me I'm right," she said, "and let's get to the consequences."

Alvin surrendered. "Man was some acquaintance o' his."

"You didn't know him?"

"Never got a name."

She asked him how and where.

"Three of us huntin', R.J. goes bang. I 'bout wet my pants." Cowed by Bonnie's anger, he'd kept his eyes down. He raised them contritely. She was grinning with wolfish glee, like a goody-goody who's turned a new leaf. "*Dog?* You knew?"

"Hell yes, I knew. The second I saw him in that icebox." Her exhilarated movements released her hair, unpinned apparently, in an uncoiling snake down her back. "I was just waiting to make sure no suspicions."

Alvin felt behind him for a chair to collapse in.

"I'm evil, huh?" she said.

"R.J.'s the one gotta carry it. You done nothin' wrong."

"In my mind, Alvin. *In my mind.*" She began to pace, ruffling her shoulders and working her neck beneath the burden of dastardly thoughts.

There was no way Alvin could give voice to what was blooming before him. Bonnie's sinewy wildness was thrilling to behold. All he could do was sit back and gaze up in wonder, like Jack watching his beanstalk rise.

She unbuttoned her cardigan and yanked it down off her shoulders and arms. Her black brassiere, at his eye level, fronted her torso like a reveler's mask made raunchier for its mock modesty. His heart beat so fast it hurt. She propped one foot on the arm of his chair and he knew without looking that she was wearing nothing under her skirt. Her inner thigh pressed the side of his face. "You said you kissed a girl there once," she said.

"Done it lotsa times." He'd done it never. He'd recited descriptions from *Fanny Hill* with himself substituted for the lead role.

"Will you for me?"

"Okay. Sure." His eyes dropped to where her skirt had ridden up. Yup. Nothing but her. He took a moment to gather himself. "Ready?"

Her answer was muffled but clear enough. "Fuck yeah."

He was at it a while. Kissing wasn't possible with her hands pulling hard on his head; it was mostly wetness and licks in multi-directions and breathing through his nose. He had no awareness of enjoying the act beyond the fact that Bonnie seemed to, and even that came into question when he heard her growl, "Get it out." He stopped at once, thinking he'd hurt her. She stepped away from the chair, further shook out her hair, and reached behind to unhook her bra. "Get it out," she repeated, whereupon, looking down to his lap, he discovered that indeed he'd been enjoying himself.

"This?" It was an honest question.

Her arms were folded across her bare chest. She unfolded them. Hands to her side, she met him eye to eye for the first time today and for the first time ever with something other than command in her gaze. "Yes, please."

He got it out. She never did say "please" again, though it echoed in his head during much of what followed, along with "thank you," of course.

LOVE WAS MADE between them that day, and of an ease and fulfillment far better than most people's first time together. But Bonnie being Bonnie, her thoughts returned to practical matters moments afterward. "The dead guy. Did he deserve it?" They lay entwined on the love seat.

"World's a better place without him."

"So you knew him?"

"By type. Jailbird all the way."

She shivered. The idea of mortal violence made her feel like royalty, when royalty took guts and wielded real power. "Hard to picture my brother a killer."

"He was no slouch in Korea."

"He killed people there?"

"Part o' the job."

"Bit different this time. Head all split open."

"No different," Alvin said.

The phone rang across the room. Naked, he went over to pick it up with a brisk hello. Bonnie, like any woman who'd just lost her virginity, was alert to the occasion's details and would never forget how anger flushed his body as he listened. "Don't call here again!" he barked before hanging up. When she asked who it was he didn't reply at first, bending to pick up his shirt and drape it over his lower half. Sensitive to her innocence or merely shy himself, he didn't want to offend her with lamplight illuminating his dangling self. "You remember Chief Jenks?" he said.

"Daddy's old snitch? Practically an imbecile, I always thought."

"Wants to come visit."

"For that you yell at him?"

"I shoulda said yes?"

"God no." She laughed. "My hero."

Distractedly, his mind still on the call, he collected his clothes to leave.

"Don't be a stranger," she said.

"Jus' leave me a note."

"Oh, and Alvin?"

He turned.

"Happy Valentine's Day."

Again his body blushed. "That today?"

"Didn't get you a card."

"I won't complain."

She gave a smile the likes of which he'd never seen on her.

"You okay?" he asked.

"Little sore. Little . . . surprised. Funny," she began.

"What is?"

"Valentine's Day. Makes it memorable. Not that I'd need it."

Alvin swayed at the ankles, adrift in wondering if she'd just paid him a compliment. "Me neither," he said.

"Why, thank you, Alvin. That's sweet of you to say."

In a full swoon now, the naked man absently dropped his bundled clothes, stooping to pick them up as color flooded his face and cheeks. He was now in love as deeply as a person can get. This was good and bad news—good in that the world is always improved by love, bad in that henceforth he would go about working on Bonnie's behalf with fresh and ruthless vigor.

THE DATE OF Alvin and Bonnie's first occasion of intercourse— Valentine's Day, 1957—preceded by one day an event verifiable by Lake Charles town records or by taking a walk through Orange Grove cemetery. The event occurred in the waters of the lake and involved Hollis Jenks.

The lake is cold that time of year, but Chief Jenks prided himself on catching largemouth bass under any conditions.

Towing his boat on a trailer to the public ramp, he drove his truck into the parking area at dawn. He wasn't adept at backing the trailer and preferred an empty lot in which to maneuver. After several tries he got lined up and began inching down the ramp until the trailer wheels submerged and the boat lifted off its cradle on the water rising beneath it. He put his clutch in neutral, set the emergency brake, and got out to loosen the cable attaching the boat to the trailer. Straddling the trailer hitch, he grunted over the winch to gain slack in order to float the boat free. He would then tie it to the dock beside the ramp, go park the truck, and be the first one to the best fishing spots on the lake.

Something unusual happened. The emergency brake let go and the truck and trailer swooshed down the ramp into the water like a new-launched battleship, taking Jenks under and pinning him there between the winch and tailgate.

His face was upturned not two inches below the water's surface when boaters found him later. No one doubted that it was an accident, not even the person who'd crept up and released the brake. He'd only meant to give Jenks a scare—to which end, mission accomplished.

None of the Jenks family at Hollis's wake recognized the fat man who entered the viewing area with a deeply mournful visage. When he placed an envelope presumably containing a cash gift in the basket of cards at the foot of the coffin, they received him as a dear friend. He tearfully shook every hand in the condolence line, took a seat in the back of the funeral parlor, and prayed for strength in this difficult time. Someone tapped his shoulder. "Surprised to see you here."

Alvin slid into the pew next to Abe Percy. Brown suit stretched across his frame and black hair slickly sculpted, he resembled a gangster at Easter mass. Abe realized it was the man he'd spied with Bonnie Bainard in Hancock Bayou and again later at R.J.'s funeral. "You work for Richie," Abe said.

"For Mr. Bainard, yes."

"I've been hoping to speak to him personally."

Alvin indicated the candlelit casket at the head of the viewing room. "You stand a better chance with Chief Jenks over there."

"I know his son is alive."

"Thought Jenks had only daughters."

"Don't mock me!" Heads turned to shush Abe. "I'm talking about R.J."

"We buried that boy last month."

"You buried someone. And I can prove it." Abe's reason was not at its best. He was spouting off to a stranger without heed to decorum or prudence; worse, he embraced it as a heaven-sent opportunity to make something positive happen at last. "I want thirty thousand dollars from the Bainards within one week. Stick it here." He handed Alvin a yellowed business card embossed with his name and a post office box.

Alvin studied the card. "They won't never oblige you on this."

"Think not?" Abe was mimicking movie talk now, trusting that any danger would likewise be pretend. "Then they'll find they have cause for worry."

"Way I see it, I know your name, what you look like, and where you pick up your mail. The worry might be yours."

"Is that a threat?"

"Pretty much."

"Well, in that case . . ." Abe struggled to keep up his bravado. "I'm not the only one who knows. Silencing me won't make a difference."

Alvin was disappointed but not surprised. "I suppose you won't tell me who."

"It's my insurance policy." Abe had in mind Tarzy, the colored boy in Hancock Bayou, and Delly Franklin. "To corroborate that whoever you and Bonnie Bainard buried in much haste was *not* her brother. Hence the question, who was the dead man? Who killed him? And where is R.J. now?" Proud of the points his summation had struck, Abe was taken aback by Alvin's response:

"How much you leave in the kitty?"

"Excuse me?"

"By the coffin there. You donated to the family, right?"

"I did what's proper."

"How much? I'm curious what a man will pay for a clean conscience. Boat accident? Come on. You and me know better."

"You're saying . . ." Abe realized Alvin was saying a couple things, none of which he could make himself utter.

"Hey, my hat's off to you. Everybody's sold."

"You're implying I drowned Chief Jenks?"

"Somebody did."

"Twenty thousand." Abe licked his damp lip. "I'll be waiting."

With a joyless smile Alvin rose to leave. The smile was hard to maintain. More problems. More chores. For love.

Abe, alone in his pew, surveyed the flowers, candles, and open casket. The morbid spectacle had become almost ordinary in the course of sitting here. He regarded the basket full of envelopes, one of which held his dollar gift to the family of the deceased. The puny sum now seemed as damning as any bad thing he'd ever done, almost.

SETH WASN'T SMOOTH with girls. The best line he could come up with was to beg a favor: Would she give him a lift home from the hospital this weekend? The instant Delly Franklin agreed he began fretting about her reaction to seeing Georgia Hill. He didn't want his connection to Richie Bainard's wealth to influence her view of him. If she liked him more for it, that would be bad. If she liked him less, that would be worse.

Whenever he stood near her at the hospital, Delly's figure was discernible to him as ripe clusters of fruit within fog. Heated thoughts about her had pushed Seth's Bible study to the back burner; perdition and penitence held little attraction compared to someday kissing her breasts. Other obsessions had likewise diminished. His half brother had shot himself dead in some swamp. Case closed. Now his father was dying, another instance of angels working overtime to punish the violence done to Seth's mother. It seemed no longer Seth's mission to tabulate the rights and wrongs and avenge where indicated. Better to dream of winning a woman than get sidetracked by other men's doom.

His and Delly's few exchanges so far had concerned her cousin, Joey. She was vigilant in overseeing his recovery. Recently she'd confessed why. "I'm the one put him in this hospital. Guilt's made me mush, I guess."

"You don't seem mushy to me. More the opposite."

"I've been told that before." She explained how she'd bashed in Joey's skull, attributing it to poor light and much wine. "So if you heard any rumors—"

"I haven't," he lied.

"—now you know the truth. Just me acting crazy."

Anxiety plagued him ahead of their Saturday appointment. His courtship plan involved strategies of picturesque pathos. Showing Delly the mansion whose privilege he'd rejected was step one.

She knew the area of Georgia Hill's address. He asked if she minded taking a detour past the high school. "Kinda outta the way," she said, but turned the wheel as asked.

They sat apart on the front seat of her car. "You smell different," he said.

"Today's my bath day."

"Yeah?"

"Just kidding."

"It's not?"

"Lord, Seth! I bathe every day."

"That's not what I smell," he persisted.

"It's my perm, all right? I got a perm this morning."

"They smell?"

"The chemicals."

"Why would you perm your hair?"

"Why?" She sighed. "I went for a dye job. Get back to my natural color. My stupid hairdresser talked me into a new perm. Now I'm a poodle."

He found this enchanting. "You're not a poodle."

"Ooh, now there's a compliment." She glanced at him across

the seat. His reaction—a baleful expression, as of an old dog kicked by a new owner—told her this cripple with no life was attracted to her. "How much can you see, Seth? I'm never sure."

"With enough light I can see close up. Past that, it's pretty dim."

"Can you see my face?"

"If I got near."

"Then no."

"Correct. You're a shape and a voice. And a smell."

"In movies blind people touch people's faces to tell what they look like."

"Kind of an awkward thing to ask somebody."

"You could touch mine if you want to. Not while I'm driving, but sometime."

Seth touched his own face as if to verify its blush. "Okay."

She studied the road, embarrassed by his embarrassment. "Since I know what you look like, it's only fair."

"What do I look like?"

"Pardon?"

He repeated the question.

"You?" she stalled. "Well, you're tall and kinda thin and—"

"My face."

"You don't know?"

"Not since fifteen, when I got hurt."

"The car accident."

"Yes." He shied from the subject. "I can see myself in a mirror close up. But I don't know how I compare with other guys."

"So what you're asking is are you good-looking?"

"I'm asking am I bad-looking."

This touched her. "You're not. Okay?"

"Not ugly?"

"Not at all."

Seth leaned back and exhaled.

The road wound through Lake Charles's white working-class neighborhood. Carports, clotheslines, vegetable patches in the side yards, tool sheds in back. Some homes had wire-and-plywood coops for chickens and rabbits. "Part of town I grew up in," Delly said. She told Seth the high school was coming up.

"Keep going. Just past, I think it was."

She scanned ahead like a scout expecting an ambush. She avoided this area generally, but had been by enough to know she wouldn't get hysterical revisiting it. "Why don't you tell me what we're looking for."

"A side road called Heather Lane."

She didn't brake or speed up. She didn't jerk the wheel or even waver one bit. She stared straight ahead through the windshield into a landscape hurtling toward her. She pulled over. "Here."

"Heather Lane?" His tentative tone matched Delly's unease like a perfect song on the radio. "Describe it please."

"Same as anywhere." She struggled for more to say. There were fewer houses back then, more trees and empty lots, yet it had always been a neighborhood whose ordinariness only heightened her dismay whenever she returned, that she could have been assaulted where kids play and moms carry groceries and dads push mowers from March to October.

Seth was oblivious. As far as he knew, Heather Lane was part of his story, not Delly's. It was here that the brother he'd admired had verified every slander against him. On this road, under these trees, with a two-bit tramp who doubtless would have given it up freely if he'd shown a little patience. "Heather Lane," he said.

Delly's gaze had fallen to the patch of ground where R.J. had parked that night. She asked, like a hostess chitchatting through agony, "You don't really care what it looks like, do you?"

"This is where some girl once accused my brother of raping her. I want you to know things about me, and that's a big one."

"Your brother?"

"Half brother. Richard Bainard, Jr. From the family that owns Block's."

The information pierced without sensation, like a sharp needle. "I heard he died," she said.

"Shot himself. Down on the coast."

"Your mother was married to Richie Bainard?"

"Till she was killed—in a car crash caused by him. The one where I got hurt."

"Your father did it?"

"He scared her. She ran. She crashed."

"And now you hate the Bainards?" Delly asked hopefully.

"I never hated R.J. He was always fine."

Evenly she said, "No. He wasn't."

"Well, sure. The newspapers had him judged and hanged."

She studied the hub of her steering wheel as if it were the crosshairs of a gun sight. "I was raped."

"Seriously?"

"I was raped," she repeated.

He searched in vain for a response, like a rescuer talking to a man on a ledge with every reason to jump.

"I don't make an issue of it most times." Her voice caught. "But in this case it seems I ought to."

Seth's innocence proved an asset here, sweeping him through a complex moment that would have baffled a wiser man. "That colors your opinion, don't you see?" His voice was full of reason. "Makes total sense that you would condemn someone like R.J. without knowing the facts."

She put the car in gear and started down the main road past Heather Lane. "Your brother. Jesus fucking Christ."

"I can't change what he did. What he was accused of doing."

I accused him. He raped me. The words were there to be howled. But only in silence could she suppress the horrible coincidence of R.J.'s place in their lives. Telling Seth the truth would shatter the fondness forming between them, which itself only dawned on her when she realized it was futile. It made a coward of her. "I am sorry your brother is dead. How's that?"

"Half brother. But thanks."

She turned away from him to the approaching intersection. "Now tell me where to go next."

THEY CAME TO Georgia Hill, pausing in the driveway between the oak trees. Atop the rise, the brick residence, outbuildings, and rolling grounds resembled a small private school. Delly saw nothing, felt everything. "I'll let you out here. You can tap your way up the walk." The belittling was necessary. His brother was R. J. Bainard. He was lucky she didn't spit it in his face.

"I'm not going in. I just wanted you to see it."

"Now I have. And I still think your family rots."

"It's part of who I am. So's my brother. I liked him."

"Do you think I give a shit?"

"He suffered, Delly." To which she scoffed audibly. "Just my opinion," he said. "Sorry."

She was surprised how sad she felt. "I'm sorry, too." She forced a smile all the more absurd for his inability to see it. The smile pushed water over the rims of her eyes. "Now please get outta my car."

"I told you I'm sorry, and that I believe you on your story." His gentle tone confirmed the opposite.

"*Out.*"

He got out. A black Cadillac came up behind, blocking Delly's exit from the driveway. She was rolling down her window to tell the driver to back up when she heard him say from his car, "That you, Seth? Thought it was prowlers. I was fixin' to go for my forty-five."

Seth told the guy sheepishly, "I may need a ride back to the hospital."

Alvin looked over at the other car and glimpsed the back of the head of a poodle-haired woman at the wheel. "Fight with your girl?"

"Just showing her the house."

"Call ahead next time. It not bein' your house no more."

"Hey!" Delly yelled out her window. "Move it!" She banged the horn.

Alvin backed onto the road to let her U-turn out of there.

Seth had found his way to Delly's window. "One thing before you go."

"Make it quick."

"I think you're great."

"Go to hell."

She wheeled around in front of the car behind her. Its window was down. Her window was down. She and the other driver regarded each other. "Ethel?"

Delly hit the gas hard.

SHE FELT BADLY about that "go to hell" and sat down with Seth in the hospital cafeteria the next day. She told him he was nice, she liked him okay, "But your brother was a rapist. That kills it for me." She didn't add that *she* was the victim. She worried that he wouldn't believe her; or worse, that he'd convert it in his mind from an irreparable wedge to some kind of grotesque bond between them.

"The charge was never proved," he said.

"He ran away!"

"From a lynch mob."

"From the truth!" She was stuck. Here she was trying to be a martyr and he was forcing her to get mean. "He attacked a girl. I was attacked."

"A terrible coincidence. It has nothing to do with us."

"*Us?* There is no *us.*"

He felt for her hand across the table. She eluded it easily and fled the room with her head bowed in resignation for the merciful hurt she'd inflicted.

Disconsolate, Seth told his superiors at the hospital that he was ill and needed time off. That message subsequently was given to somebody named Freddy Baez when he later phoned the front desk asking, as an old friend looking to reconnect, if Mr. Hooker would be in working tomorrow.

IMAGINE A MOVIE sex scene where lamps are kicked over and the lovers tumble like drunken cowboys under motel windows grimy with neon light. The camera pans out the window and we see a rain-dappled car across the street with its driver's face distorted in metaphorical meltdown behind the rainy glass. The lovers are R. J. Bainard and Delly's cousin, Corinne, and the car is the big Lincoln driven by Corinne's husband Donald Meers. Thus do we learn that R.J. and Corinne are having an affair and her husband is on the trail.

A lot of adultery results from mere access. Corinne had time on her hands and R.J. was available in everyday ways—meet her for lunch, buy her a hat—that her husband preferred not to be. That she believed R.J. to be a Mexican gangster put further glamor on what was basically commonplace. R.J.'s interest was casual to say the least. Pursuing the first woman who looked his way typified his laziness in love, though it did help that things he'd seen only in banned Chinese picture books Corinne thought up all by herself. Self-destructiveness also figured, an old habit that had found new expression.

It doesn't take a psychiatrist to see that bopping around Lake Charles in a red convertible wearing a beard, a loud hat, and a murdered man's name, let alone showing up at the hospital where his estranged brother worked, suggested that R.J. was ambivalent about his freedom. That he went *back* to the hospital would seem to cement the diagnosis, even if this time it wasn't to confront Seth, but rather, from mischief, to check out Seth's new girlfriend—who was, of all people, Ethel from the Section Eight Gun Club.

Alvin had offered him this gossip about Seth during their roadside rendezvous, routine throughout R.J.'s fugitive exile, to give R.J. his monthly cash. R.J. had confessed in turn that he was seeing the mother of one of Seth's patients. Alvin said this was insane and urged him to get out of town before the Freddy Baez fiasco blew up in their faces. R.J. said that's not my problem since you shot Freddy, not me. Alvin forked over the money with a right-you-are wink that veiled major misgivings. He worried that R.J. might blab to Corinne about Freddy's ashes at Orange Grove cemetery. He worried that Ethel might tell Seth about Alvin's behavior at the Section Eight sauna. Most of all, he worried that Bonnie would find out that things were not going smoothly in her ascension to the top of the Bainard world.

Getting back to that movie scene, our lovers would next be seen emerging from their motel room and kissing good-bye under the bitter gaze of Corinne's husband across the street. Whereupon the camera pivots to show a familiar black Cadillac parked not far away. It's Alvin Dupree. He's tailing the lovers, too. Scratchy blues out of New Orleans plays on his radio till he switches it off to hone his thoughts.

R.J. and Corinne drive off in separate cars. Donald follows his wife. Alvin follows R.J. The soundtrack rises until it changes to knuckles rapping on the door of (cut to) Joey Meers's room at Lake Charles Hospital. R.J. has arrived in his hat and beard with the bounce of a bookie on game day. He nods to Joey, who's alone there. "I'm looking for Miss Ethel. She around?"

JOEY REMEMBERED THE man from when he'd buzzed him and Seth in his roadster the other day. He felt the same wariness he'd felt then, for the visitor had an edgy vitality that seemed to mock anyone sitting inside on his ass in the afternoon. "Ethel?" he said. "Never heard of her."

"Curly hair." R.J. cupped his hands to his chest. "Big."

"Sounds like Delly you're talkin'."

"Who?"

"Delly Franklin. My cousin."

"Went by Ethel last time we met." R.J. indicated Joey's cane. "Still with the stick."

"So it was you in that car. Why you spyin' on me?"

"Not you."

"Well, if it's Mr. Hooker, he ain't here today. Out sick."

R.J. shook his head. "It's his woman I seek."

A protective impulse narrowed Joey's eyes. He knew Delly's history, her very bad luck with men. "She's got a husband."

"Got a daddy, too, looks like."

Joey missed the wit. "Her dad's dead. Shot himself."

"Lotta that going around." R.J. extended his hand. "Freddy Baez."

"Joey Meers."

Delly entered the room. She wore no sunglasses and had lost weight since her encounter with R.J. last winter. His expression gave away nothing. "Ethel?"

She stared at him, her skin suddenly, actually cold. The man who would never be dead to her most definitely wasn't dead now.

"*Delly*," Joey corrected. He proceeded with introductions. "This here's—"

R.J. cut him off. "You probably remember me as Richard,"

he said to her. "From Section Eight when we met?" He moved toward her, his face scorching her eyes. The teeth in his smile looked predatory, like dentures on a mummy.

"Thought you said your name was Freddy," Joey said.

"It is," R.J. said to him. " 'Richard' was temporary, same as 'Ethel' I bet."

"I told you it was *Delly*," Joey insisted, annoyed at being squeezed out of the dialog like an underage pest. He sensed that there was more going on here than former acquaintances meeting. His ignorance of all else didn't stop him from trying to help. "Delly Franklin, say hello to—"

"Freddy Baez." The mummy's grin widened. "Honest."

She shook his hand. She was fairly sure she shook his hand.

"What's with this 'Ethel'?" Joey asked her.

R.J. turned to him. "How old are you, kid? Been around a little? You know what I mean."

"I do all right."

"Then here it is: me and Delly had a flirtation. Her being married, turns out she had to hide her real name—same for me. It happens with grown-ups sometimes."

This was mad babble to Delly. The one fact that anchored her was that R.J. seemed again not to recognize that she was Adele Billodeau, his girl from Heather Lane.

"A flirtation?" Joey said to her. "With him?"

She couldn't find words. The men looked allied in malice toward her, deceptions crisscrossing the room like sabers hacking and stabbing.

R.J. offered in a teacherly tone, "It was innocent. A few drinks, a few laughs."

"I gotta go," she said to no one.

"Nice to see you again," R.J. said.

It was too much. She faced him head-on and held it for three heartbeats. He *must* remember! Yet his expression stayed affable, his manner courtly. She left the room with a mumbled apology that she kept repeating all the way down the hall.

Alone again with Joey, R.J. observed that Delly was an unusual name.

"It's short for Adele."

"Ah." R.J.'s shoulders fell, relieved of the strain of staying upright for so long. "I was afraid of that."

DELLY DEFIED ALL good sense by not going straight to the police from the hospital. Instead she drove to the little ranch she shared with her stepdaughter. She pounded the steering wheel and cursed herself for retreating in a fluster while R.J. had stood there smug as a dictator's son. She told herself that she would have him arrested tomorrow. She'd be Delly Franklin one more day, and Adele Billodeau ever after.

She was surprised to find her husband's car parked trunk-open in front of the house. Arthur Franklin came out lugging a bedsheet stuffed with clothes and tied at the corners like Santa's bag. Fiona followed him, popping gum. Delly got the picture at once and pleaded with her not to do this. The girl twisted past her and slid into her father's car. "It's not forever," she said.

Delly glared at Arthur. "Happy?"

"She's been beggin' me to take her." He was wearing the

same suspenders with which he'd hung those same trousers on the shower rod the day he and Delly got married, to steam the wrinkles smooth; a trivial failing, it encapsulated all the reasons she couldn't stand the sight of him. He stuffed the sack of clothes into his trunk. "You think I got room for this at my dump?"

"Fiona belongs with me. I'm her mother."

"Not technically."

"This is her home."

"She's got her reasons."

Delly knew what they were. Tensions had been high between her and Fiona, who resented her stepmother for a long list of routine affronts capped by, in an ultimate teenage grounding, Delly smashing the skull of her boyfriend. "I'm sorry," she said as she knelt by Fiona's car window.

Fiona rolled it down partway. "I don't sleep good here. I'm mad at you all the time."

"Be mad. I can take it."

"Practically my first kiss, and you come flyin' outta the dark like a monster."

"All true. But don't go."

"I wanna hate you—which I hate, 'cause I know you care about me. It's why I'm goin' to Daddy's. To think. To sleep." Fiona's face behind the car window looked twenty-five instead of fifteen, saddening her stepmother deeply. "I know what's best for me."

"Believe me, you don't. Now please get out of the car."

"Daddy, can we go?" Fiona rolled up the window and reached for the radio.

"Delly," Arthur said from the other side of the car. "There's a letter inside for you. A man dropped it off." His affected disinterest was clearly a strain.

"Did you frisk him? Get his name?"

"I would never. I want you to be happy any way you can."

"I'm going for that divorce, Arthur. Don't care what people say."

"I wasn't jealous," he went on. "I knew he wasn't a rival."

"There is no rival."

"Almost worse. Thrown over for naught." He tried to catch her eye. "You look pretty, by the way."

She scowled. "So I been told."

Arthur, by his expression, didn't like the sound of that.

THE SEALED ENVELOPE printed with "Mrs. Franklin" was on her kitchen table.

> Adele,
>
> There is an old colored woman in Hancock Bayou in Cameron Parish whose little nephew knows it was not R. J. Bainard who died. Her name is Sally something and everyone knows her in the town. Keep it in your head. Pardon the mystery. Everything is well. I will contact you soon.
>
> Your friend, Abe

Delly returned the note to the envelope and put it in the drawer of her bedside table. Headspun from seeing R.J. earlier and her husband just now, she didn't even try to decipher its meaning. It seemed more kooky than serious, like Abe himself.

That night she had the old nightmare again, gobs of feathers spiky in her mouth like the bodies of dead insects. Waking with a start, she lay still as her pulse slowed and her perspiration dried. She remembered that she was alone in the house, Fiona gone away. Headlights swept her window. It was nothing—people come home late all the time. But Delly got out of bed composed in the certainty that this could only be bad.

Peering out from behind her curtain, she saw a car up the street creeping forward mailbox to mailbox, a darker shape within the dark night like a shadow moving under a lake. It came to a stop three houses down and extinguished its lights. The driver emerged and looked around briefly before heading her way in a slow trot. Fear slithered down her arms.

She lost sight of the person in the darkness and crouched to the floor in certainty that he was outside her door. Seconds passed. She peeked out her window again. When the car's headlights came on she recoiled as if electrocuted—the man had looped back unseen. As he drove away, stockpiles of fright suppressed inside her all day blasted outward. She slumped against the bedroom wall and sobbed, her arms clasped over her head as if under the jeers of a hostile crowd.

The man who'd assaulted her four years ago was alive and in Lake Charles. The beast who'd put a knife to her throat last winter was likewise here. And now this strange old lawyer was passing cryptic notes saying everything was fine when it wasn't. Shaken by fear that in daylight had been bearable, she resolved to call the police right now.

But she didn't—and the reason was Seth. He was a puppy she'd dismissed with a kick. Yet he was so earnest and kind, his heart groping before him like that damn walking stick, that she told herself it would be cruel at this point to revive her charge against his brother. She'd made it through the ordeal. She'd survived. She would put her trauma behind her and let events take their course. Humility and smallness were her natural state. She wouldn't recognize herself without an unfair burden to bear.

The logic appalled her even as she embraced it; there was a lie in there somewhere that she feared to unearth. She returned to bed not even wondering who might have been casing her home after midnight. She set her mind to the different puzzle of when exactly she'd lost her mind, and fell into dreamless sleep.

R.J. HAD DRIVEN around town after encountering Delly at the hospital. By pretending not to recognize her, he'd given himself time to address the challenge she posed or to hit the road again. It wasn't a hard choice. He'd lived for years at others' discretion. No way would he do it again.

Adele Billodeau.

He remembered her. He remembered that night. Certainly he'd rushed her, especially after she'd removed her jeans and placed his hand on her pussy only to pull it away in anxious apology. She turned hysterical with self-reproach for leading him on. She couldn't breathe through her tears and said she was suffocating. He'd hit her then, a cuff on the temple to snap her to. She'd quieted, and he'd realized there was pleasure to be had, like a swift runner lapping a slow one, in asserting power over someone without it. Desire had nothing to do with it. He recalled the scene as grueling. Her body went limp once she realized what was going to happen. He pushed her knees wide and got into position. He'd needed his hand to harden himself but only a little spit to get in. He'd closed his eyes in concentration and willed himself to conclusion. His mouth against her throat had left her slick with saliva, and afterward, in the car's charged darkness, he'd dabbed her frantically with his shirt to try and make her clean again.

Sweat ran down his sides as he drove. He was sure that if the right person were beside him in the car he could have drawn his pistol and shot that person dead. He fished the weapon from under his seat. It had belonged to Freddy Baez, found in Freddy's pants with a wad of cash—blood money from Seth, no doubt—when R.J. had switched clothes in the marsh. Heeding Alvin's warning that Seth wanted him dead, he'd been keeping it handy in case. He fingered the trigger. R.J. had done it before, in Korea. A bang, a recoil, and behold the wonder you've wrought, like turning in all your cards for a new poker hand that can only be an improvement.

He was disappointed not to have been able to attend his own funeral. He wondered if seeing Freddy's ashes interred might have made the man's murder more real to him, more deplorable. R.J. owed his rebirth to an act of violence for which, truth be told, he was grateful. It's why so far he'd done nothing against Seth for hiring someone to kill him. His spirits were frankly better now. The little bastard had done him a favor.

———

He was lying in bed with Corinne Meers when their post-coital dialog stumbled onto matters of import. R.J. told her he'd met "someone named Delly" in Joey's hospital room. Corinne launched into details about her cousin's crumbling marriage and cracked personality that R.J. found unexpectedly compelling.

Corinne was displeased by his interest. It provoked her suspicion that "Freddy," as she knew him, was just another horny Latin after every woman alive. He laughed off her jealousy and confessed that he wasn't a Mexican gigolo but rather was Richard Bainard, Jr.—fugitive, dead man, Block's heir, all of it. She gave a yip as if poked with a stick. "Did you really do my cousin like she said?"

"Some booze went by, but yeah. We fucked."

"*We?* I knew it! She weren't no damn virgin."

"That's what she said?"

"No one believed her. She had a cheap reputation."

R.J. didn't like Corinne saying this. Judging Delly was the opposite of judging himself—nobody's right in her case, everyone's in his. "You don't look too upset about what I just told you," he said.

"That you ain't Freddy Baez?"

"For starters."

"My husband's gonna be a lot less mad I'm leavin' him for a Bainard instead of a Mexican."

He absorbed this. "Glad to oblige." She gave him a big kiss, arms around his neck, bare leg slung over his hip. He told her there were complications, namely that the wealthy scion "R. J. Bainard" was ashes in Orange Grove cemetery. "If I turn up alive, I'm back to my fugitive self. Stay dead, and I'm free and all yours—but broke."

"Then you got to come clean, baby. 'Cause you a Bainard, and Bainards ain't broke by a damn sight." She reached down her hand. "And you sure as hell ain't dead."

"I do that, I go to prison."

"Not if my cousin drops the charge, it bein' a big lie anyway." She kissed him again. "I'll talk to her. Tell her you regret any misunderstandin'."

"Then she'll know I'm alive. Be the end of me."

"She knows already."

"You think?"

"She saw you, right? At Joey's?"

"Stood two feet away."

"Trust me. A girl don't forget."

"She hasn't said anything, far as I know. To the cops, I mean."

"Maybe she gonna hunt you down herself."

"Maybe she likes me."

"I tell her you think that, she'll kill you for sure."

He warned her, "She's liable to hate you for even saying you know me."

Corinne shook her head. "For hurtin' Joey she's in my debt deep. And that young fella from the hospital oughta softened her some." She snuggled to R.J., warmed by these racy initiatives. "How bad could it a been, anyway? Lord knows I'd forgive you a roll in the backseat."

R.J. saw no chance of gaining Delly's cooperation. It was vile, that night. He'd been drunk; her too. He'd screwed her partly to shut her up, her prattling on about high school and boys with no sense of the world's real problems. But he shouldn't have forced her, shouldn't have hit her. That more than anything else—the smack of his hand on the side of her head, the awful look of defeat in her face—made him want to scratch out his eyes to take the vision away.

"That young hospital guy?" he said at length. "Seth? He's my brother."

Corinne sat up. "He goes by Hooker, not Bainard."

"Even so."

"*Your* brother, likes *my* cousin, who *you*—"

"Yes," R.J. said.

"And we ain't even talkin' about me and Donald."

R.J. definitely didn't want to talk about that. "I'd make it up to her if I could. Your cousin. Meet her face-to-face if she wanted."

Corinne stopped stroking his shoulder. "That's just stupid."

"Somewhere public. Safe, tell her."

"Why?"

"Make my case." He studied the bedside wall beyond where Corinne lay. "Make my regrets."

"She'd throw a fit. Pull a gun, shoot you dead. You don't know her."

"Be her right."

Corinne considered. Seeking Delly's help could go a couple ways. She might run to the police. It would force R.J. to flee and Corinne to join him in penniless exile, a romantic scenario that wouldn't last a month. But if Delly could be persuaded to retract the rape charge, he could emerge from hiding, claim his fortune, and Corinne's life would really get wonderful. "I'll give it a shot," she told R.J.

His whimsical proposition had become real. He liked that it terrified him.

Corinne asked how he'd come to take "Freddy Baez" for an alias.

"Name of a man I killed. Who's now buried under my headstone."

If R.J. had hoped this confession would make her rethink her ardor, he was talking to the wrong person. In rapid sequence it sparked Corinne's disbelief, amusement, arousal, and dirty Chinese pictures. She dug him, was the problem; virtue wasn't a factor. And it might have worked out for her if she hadn't overestimated Delly and underestimated R.J. in terms of their moral character—and too, if she hadn't misjudged her husband's capacity for entering the story in a big way.

≡ THREE ≡

Seth, Delly, Audrey

Lake Charles, late spring, 1957. Weeks have passed since Delly first got the feeling that someone was spying on her house. It's happened several times since, a car on her street late at night, and still she hasn't told the police. She worries that once she starts talking she'll be unable to keep quiet about R. J. Bainard being in town. She doesn't want to add to the hurt she's done to his brother. Better that she hurt instead.

Delly wasn't alone in delaying to do the right thing. It seemed everyone was awaiting the hand of God to sweep down and make it all better. The exception was Alvin Dupree. He remained a busy bee in his labors on Bonnie's behalf. She was in poor spirits. Her father clung to life, but with such piteous bouts of pain and dementia her most loving reaction was to contemplate smothering him with a pillow. When lucid, he continued to ask about seeing R.J. once more. She was tempted to lie and say that R.J. had committed suicide. It might put an end to his delusions. It might also end him, she feared.

Such calculations were ingrained in Bonnie, a reflection, no doubt, of her mother's precision with numbers. It was therefore inevitable that she acknowledge the potential upside of R.J. actually being dead. Alvin, sensitive to her ponderings, considered doing the black deed himself. R.J. was a wild card, bound to throw more slime on the Bainard name if no one moved to stop him. And there were Alvin's own interests at risk. He'd hired Freddy Baez to put a scare into R.J. that would send him out of Louisiana and maybe even the country. A change of plan—that is, waxing Freddy—had become necessary after the Bainard name passed his lips. R.J.'s witness of the unfortunate episode threatened Alvin's future with Bonnie like a serpent asleep in a toy box. Alvin had killed his nation's enemies in the Pacific and Korea. Could he do the same to an old comrade?

R.J. himself helped answer the question. After weeks of waiting for Corinne to set up a meeting with Delly, his impatience for action led him to drive his car to Georgia Hill as routinely as if the last years hadn't happened, as if he still lived at home like any unemployed heir. He trotted up the front steps and banged the knocker. Freddy's pistol was jammed under his shirt. He felt proud to be launching this frontal attack, though he knew that cowards sometimes leap into the fray simply to end the suspense.

A maid answered the door. Her cry of protest when he shoved past her carried down the breezeway to the sewing room where Bonnie sat in vigil at her father's bedside. Stepping out to the hall, she recognized her brother at once despite his beard and middleweight gauntness. "Surprised?" he said with a twisted smile that went far to conceal his fear.

"Never." She smiled back.

Aware of the maid observing them, Bonnie stepped warily into his embrace. Feeling against her abdomen the pistol under his shirt, she mouthed something to the maid over his shoulder. "Please what?" the maid said.

He looked behind him. "You talking to her?"

"Miz Bonnie say 'please' to me, but she no say what for."

He realized his sister had tried to signal the woman to get help. "Please fetch my brother a whiskey, how about?"

"Yes," Bonnie said, her smile still holding. "Two."

The siblings eyed each other with the mutual suspicion of strangers dressed exactly alike. Not for them the proverbial bond of twins. Their one shared personality trait was needing only the voice in their head for company.

She pointed to the pistol bulge. "I know you shot that man we buried."

He blinked but once. "Now where'd you hear such a thing?"

"From Alvin. And I saw him, too—face all gone."

R.J. processed the information into columns of allegiance and treachery. "Daddy thinks it, too?"

"Daddy's ill. Right down the hall, but might as well be a million miles. Ah," she said to the approaching maid. "Drinks. Shall we take them to the sewing room?"

———

RICHIE BAINARD HAD many positive qualities. But he did beat his wives from time to time, and that fact alone doubtless condemns him in most people's minds. R.J., in no small paradox, fell into that category. His first thought on seeing his father withered and frail was of his mother, Esther. His second thought was *Good*.

The nurse discreetly stepped out. Sister and brother stood at opposite sides of Richie's bed, leaning inward like competing priests. The pistol in R.J.'s trousers felt redundant and juvenile. His father's breathing, soft as tidewater under a pier, made the scene feel timeless. "Son?"

"Daddy?"

"That you?"

"I came home."

"R.J.?" The question became an oath. "*R.J.!*"

"What? What!" He looked vainly to Bonnie to clarify.

Richie arched off the mattress as if hit with high voltage. He gave a cry that was plain if not clear. "*Say sorry.*"

It confused R.J. He'd planned to bombard his father with end-of-life insults before leaving his presence forever. He hadn't planned to say sorry. He found that he very much wanted to.

But what appeared to him like an offer of absolution from a father to a wayward son looked otherwise to Bonnie. It offended her to see her brother fill with emotion as he formulated some plea for their father's forgiveness. She issued an opposite order. "Go on. Tell Daddy you forgive him."

R.J. took this in sluggishly. "I thought he wants *me* to say sorry."

"Why would he? He cares about his soul, not yours. He's saying sorry. Tell him okay and let him pass peaceful."

"Forgive him why?"

"Because of Mama. Because of Angel. He's always felt terrible about how he treated them, and you and Seth just spit on his tries to make amends."

"He hit Mama."

"Yes, he did."

"More than once."

"Yes, he did."

"Angel too?"

"Of course." She told him about that last day when their stepmother, bloody and frightened, sped down the driveway into the oak tree. He'd known only what the public had been told, what the papers said—that accidents just happen sometimes. "Daddy was the one made her crash. He beat her up and she ran away and I guess he scared her from steering right."

"Scared how?"

"He liked his guns." She shrugged, not flippantly—it meant the worst was now out and there was no more to tell. She stroked her father's arm with fretful devotion, like a miser polishing silverware.

"I was fond of Angel," R.J. said.

"You and every other man."

"More than fond."

"Like I said."

Their father yanked his arm from her grip and raised it as if hailing a taxi. R.J. and Bonnie looked down at him. His eyes were fixed on things not there, like a dog that peers down an empty hallway where floorboards have inexplicably creaked.

R.J. drew his pistol from under his shirt. He studied it scornfully, as children do when they discover that something supposedly dangerous is not. With an air of attempting a casual experiment, he pointed the barrel at his father's face.

What can Richie have made of this? There wasn't much going on inside anymore, no reflections sorry or bitter, no thoughts beyond a dull animal sense that he was caged with no way out. His children's agitation around his bed must have seemed like a television playing snowily across the room or a weird flutter in the room's flowered wallpaper. Something hard and cold touched his lips. Like a baby tonguing a sharp pencil, he recoiled in reflex as it was pushed inside his mouth.

Bonnie watched aghast as R.J. bent over their father and stared into his wide eyes from inches away. Gagging on the pistol barrel at the back of his throat, Richie clutched at his son's wrist. R.J. cocked the hammer back. Bonnie lunged across the bed and shoved her brother off.

"Relax. Little scare, is all." Of himself, R.J. meant.

"Daddy?" Her rubbing of Richie's arm became frenzied, as if scouring a hole to retrieve something inside. "Daddy!"

"He's asleep."

He looked *too* asleep. The thought that he was dead struck them simultaneously. Bonnie's face took a classic *pietá* expression while R.J.'s had the aspect of child's after committing a hurtful prank, disbelieving the very bad thing he's done.

Richie stirred. His son strode from the room in relief he disguised with a smirk. Bonnie had seen enough. Her appalling brother could not be trusted to stay dead and out of trouble. She must end this once and for all.

ON THE WARPATH now, she subjected Alvin Dupree to such a grilling about R.J.'s activities in exile that he cracked like a sorority snitch. Alvin did his best to mix in believable lies with the unbelievable truth. His biggest lie was to reassert that R.J., not he, had shot Freddy Baez; the next biggest lie was that R.J. had assaulted another girl recently, Ethel Somebody at the Section Eight Gun Club. On the true side of the ledger, Alvin told her that R.J. was using the dead man's name as an alias and was dating the daughter-in-law of one of Richie's former business partners. Lastly he informed her of Abe Percy's extortion attempt on the family. Bonnie accepted Alvin's excuse that he'd deceived her out of protectiveness. She would take charge from here.

On her order, Alvin arranged to meet Abe at the same diner where, by coincidence, Abe had met Hollis Jenks three months earlier; the old lawyer, desperate for straws to grab, took it as a positive omen. "Thirty thousand dollars," he said as they slid into the booth across from each other, "is all I require to go away happy. My word is gold on that."

"It can be done," Alvin said, "providin' you come through for us."

"*Us.* Aha!" Alvin's insinuation, at Hollis Jenks's wake, about drowning the Chief had filled the lawyer with dread of the Bainards doing him likewise. Leaving the note with Delly about Tarzy Hooker had been an attempt to establish a failsafe.

"You're right," Alvin conceded. "R. J. Bainard is alive." Still smarting from Bonnie's tongue-lashing, he was antsy with the nervousness that comes when a dream so near resists coming true. "You told me there's another person out there could confirm the fact."

"There are, yes."

"More than one?"

Abe was mortified by his loose mouth. "I shouldn't say."

"I shouldn't give you a pile of money."

"If I tell, what's left to protect me?"

"Honor. Yours and mine."

"We may have a problem in that case."

Alvin glanced around as if to summon a waitress. It was a signal. A young woman with the presence of an Amazon queen joined them from two booths away. "May I introduce Miss Bonnie Bainard," Alvin said with formality.

She extended her hand. "It's been a long time, Mr. Percy."

"You know him?" Alvin asked her.

"My mother's best friend."

"Dear Esther," Abe said.

Bonnie's smile was sweet. Alvin, from experience, knew the lawyer was in for it now. "If you're broke," she told Abe, "I wish you'd have come to us. You're practically family."

"Please. Your father never liked me."

"He never liked anyone, so what? I decide things."

"A lady of stature now?"

"I always had stature. Shame no one noticed before."

"I noticed," Alvin said. Her cutting glance said don't be pathetic.

Abe ventured, "I saw you at your brother's funeral."

"Yet here in my grief you're blackmailing me?"

Abe winced at the change in tone. "But your brother isn't dead—rather the point of this meeting, I'd thought. You want him protected, right?"

"I want him incarcerated, Mr. Percy."

Abe's dream of a windfall vaporized. "Then why am I here?"

"To earn your reward for helping me bring him to justice."

"Your own brother?"

"Are you passing judgment?"

"It's just for years you obstructed the search at every turn."

"My father did, not me. Now you'll get paid for catching a crook instead of protecting one."

Abe already was spending the thousands in his head when Bonnie asked for the names of others who could testify to R.J.'s being alive; she would pass the names to the police and demand they reopen the case. Abe named Delly Franklin and Tarzy Hooker. He almost expected to get his cash right there. "I gave her a note about the boy's importance to the case."

"I want that note," Bonnie said. "Does she keep it with her? This . . ."

"Delly's her name." Abe elaborated, "The former Adele Billodeau."

"From my brother?"

"The same."

"Little troublemaker, that one."

Alvin said to Abe, "You'll take me to this Tarzy?"

"Why?"

"I want to know what he knows."

"Sure." Spoken with barely a twitch.

Alvin nodded. He was more comfortable now that matters had moved to the A-B-C stage, when steps proceed one at a time to their destination. "Might gain you your first install-ment."

Abe's mouth had gone dry with the inkling that he'd just sold his soul. He didn't know what Bonnie and Alvin would do with the information he'd given them. He didn't want to know. He would get his money and they'd get whatever; later he could contact the authorities and turn in the Bainards for their foul ways. The rationalization helped him slide out of the booth with an air of confidence despite the table edge creasing his gut.

Bonnie fished a hand into Alvin's lap as they watched the lawyer leave. Her manipulations weren't for his pleasure. She was piggybacking one stirring event on another. Had she been fond of tobacco or alcohol, now would have been the moment to light up or pour. Alvin was the only vice she'd ever known, until today's little caper. She mused, "He would've taken less." Her hand stayed busy under the table.

"Man won't get a dime."

"You have a plan?"

"Don't ask."

"My clever Sergeant Dupree."

"At your service."

"Oh, I know."

"We should go now."

"Maybe not yet."

She withdrew her hand after a moment and he looked down at his tented trousers. "Lordy."

Bonnie stood with aplomb that to Alvin signified genetic refinement and supreme femininity. She was bright but provincial, hence clumsy in her quest to catch up with the fast life she'd missed. He indulged her quaint notions whatever they were, so gamely rose and followed her out of the diner. Patrons and waitresses regarded him with a range of reactions. He kept his eyes ahead, a sentry at his post.

CORINNE MEERS'S SCHEME to get her cousin to drop the charges against R.J. was a long shot to say the least. Beyond the legal release, she wanted Delly's blessing on her and R.J.'s affair. Seth Hooker was the key. Corinne thought if she could fix up him and Delly together it would soften the sting to her cousin of watching Corinne become happy and rich on the arm of her nemesis.

It was her son's last day at the hospital. Seth had kept his distance since being snubbed by Delly outside Georgia Hill, but Corinne pressured him to come say good-bye. She and Delly were packing Joey's things, the boy lying sullen on the bed as they worked, when they heard Seth's cane clacking in the hall. Entering, he put on a front of ignoring Delly and handed Joey a leather-bound Bible. "The Jesus words are in red. Easier to follow that way."

Joey, though much improved, was anxious about returning to home and school. "Did you mark the dirty parts at least?"

"Don't be pissy," Delly said. "It's a nice gift." Protecting Seth's feelings was a sisterly reflex that he, still hoping for more, didn't appreciate.

"This place gets comfortable," he said to her. "It can be scary to leave."

"You know from experience?"

"As someone who stayed, yes."

"You'll go someday."

"I just need a reason."

"Christ!" Joey said. "Get married you two and be done with it."

"He's too good for me," Delly said, being nice if accidentally candid.

Corinne made her move. "Well, I think he's perfect." Like a matchmaking aunt, she insisted that Delly and Seth immediately come have coffee with her in the hospital's basement cafeteria. "Now tell me why," she said once the three of them were situated around a table, "you two lovebirds can't get together like everyone wants?"

"Like who wants?" Delly said.

"Like anyone with half an eye for love and fate and shit."

Seth was humiliated—also heartened. "Suits me."

Delly shook her head. "I can't look at you and not see your brother."

"He's dead. Not even a ghost anymore."

Delly wondered if he could really not know the truth. "Might prefer if he wasn't. So I can kill him myself."

"Maybe just cuss him a little," Corinne said. "Clear the air once and for all."

"He's a monster, you stupid ass."

"Just tryin' to be helpful."

"It'll take a miracle to help me."

"And dammit I got one in mind." Corinne whapped the table. "I'm in love with R. J. Bainard and we're gonna get married."

"You know him?" Seth said. He remembered R.J.'s burial at Orange Grove. "Wait, what?"

Delly's hand was already reaching for Corinne's throat. "You will never—"

"We're in love."

"He's evil!"

"He'd dead," Seth said. "Isn't he?"

"No, he ain't dead!" Delly snapped. "It's all been a big goddamn trick."

Seth accepted this. It confirmed his belief that he was always the last to know anything. "Why didn't you tell me?"

" 'Cause I'm a fucking saint who only knows to bear the whole load. I felt crappy enough about you as it was."

"You felt crappy?" A positive sign.

Corinne jumped in. "Please oh please, Del. R.J. hates what happened, really he does."

"Hates what?" Seth said, embarrassed by his ignorance.

"She accused him of rapin' her."

"She did?" He turned to Delly. "You did?"

Delly's glare hadn't left Corinne. "Please oh please what?"

"Please let him please say he's sorry, okay?"

"Say sorry. To me?"

"To us," Seth said.

"Us?"

"He owes me as much as you."

"What the fuck are you talking about?"

"I see better than you on this one." His brother was alive and Delly the one he'd assaulted. That she'd hid all this from Seth made him angry; it also made him adore her, for surely she'd done it for his sake. He wanted to shake her by the shoulders and tell her he'd got the picture at last—and how could they run from the coincidence that had blasted their lives if that same coincidence brought them together? "R.J. is why my mother died," he told her. "My father thought they were having an affair."

"Not true!" Corinne wasn't sure, but when you're in love . . .

"It's what he thought." Seth's voice was firm. "And it wasn't completely off base."

Delly sneered. "I thought you liked R.J."

"I did. I do. Doesn't mean he can't be an idiot."

Indignant at how the conversation had gone off track, Corinne launched her last best bid. "R.J. wants to meet you face-to-face."

Delly didn't look shocked. "It'll cost."

"Money?"

"Something he'll miss, Corinne. *You*. End it."

"We're in love, honey."

"Not if he wants to meet me."

Corinne exploded. "Who're you to give demands? You're a woman with nothing."

"You're a woman with a wife and kids."

"You don't even like Donald."

"I like Joey. I don't want him hurt."

"Coulda fooled me."

Seth assured Delly, "Joey will be fine whatever his mother does. He's pretty clear on that score." Translation: Joey knew his mom was shallow as paper and counted on her for nothing that mattered.

"Listen to him, Del," Corinne urged. "He's a doctor."

"He's no such thing. He's one notch from the man with the mop."

Seth's spirits had risen at the prospect that this mess might shake out in his favor. "I think," he told Delly in a measured tone, "that you ought to sit down with my brother."

"*Half,*" Corrine corrected.

"I also think," Seth went on, "you should postpone any demand about him and Mrs. Meers breaking up. If your meeting with R.J. doesn't satisfy, I'll help you call the police."

"Maybe I'll call them ahead of time, set me an ambush."

"R.J.'d come anyways," Corinne said, "goofy way he talks about you."

"Goofy how?"

"Halfway nice, I suppose."

The tidbit hit Delly with unlikely impact. It introduced a new angle into this three-way debate whose meaning Corinne could never have fathomed and whose repercussions, as indicated by Delly's imperceptible shudder, Seth could not have imagined.

On June 24, 1957, a mass of cool air in the western Gulf undercut a pocket depression of humid, warmer air and set the outer winds whipping in a classic cyclone style. It was in the Bay of Campeche off the Yucatán Peninsula—where the asteroid that killed the dinosaurs hit 65 million years ago, its crater now a vast undersea teacup whose crosscurrents of water and wind have spawned storms for countless millennia.

The first sign of trouble was a radio message from a Mexican shrimp boat that described heavy swells and wind gusts top-ping fifty miles per hour. After half a day fighting the elements, the men on shipboard bid exhausted good riddance to the storm plowing north to the gringos. People in southwest Louisiana were relieved when the Weather Bureau advised that it was four hundred miles away and veering toward the Texas coast. Somewhere else, that is.

On that same Monday, Donald Meers bought a Smith & Wesson revolver at Block's Home Supply. Donald was the son of the Lake Charles construction magnate, Burt Meers. Neither bright or accomplished in his own right, his ego rested entirely on faith in his virility—faith shattered, needless to say, by his wife's affair with a Mexican vagrant. His purchase of a hand-gun was equivalent to buying a Porsche or a hairpiece in re-sponse to some similar setback.

The next day, Tuesday, June 25, he returned to the store to buy a box of ammunition. It was about the same time that a government reconnaissance aircraft reported that winds of the Gulf storm were approaching a hundred miles per hour. The newly named Hurricane Audrey was projected to make land-fall late Thursday near Corpus Christi. The Weather Bureau advised area residents to secure their homes and businesses and to think about moseying inland.

ALVIN DUPREE AND Abe Percy headed for Hancock Bayou early Wednesday morning with a plan to be back before the weather turned. Breezes were freshening ahead of the hurricane that the radio said would hit Texas about a hundred miles west of Cameron Parish tomorrow evening. Warm rain fell in a drizzle. Roads were decent. Alvin drove, Abe the passenger in more ways than he knew. They bore southward toward graying skies like storm-chasers after a funnel cloud.

Conversation was spare but useful in sharpening Alvin's dislike of the lawyer. "So desolate," Abe said of R.J.'s choice of Cameron Parish as his hideout. Thinking Alvin wouldn't know the word, he added, "Nothing to do for entertainment, I mean."

"Lieutenant Bainard ain't about entertainment," Alvin said.

"Everyone needs a little."

"Entertainment done him with that girl. Entertainment done him with Angel."

Abe cackled. "His father's wife. Classic."

"All in his mind."

"I doubt that. And I told his father as much when I telephoned him after Frank Billodeau came forward."

"So you the one set Richie off that day?"

"He needed no help."

"But you gave it anyway."

Abe smartly stopped talking for a while. Then he got stupid again: "Where are you from originally, Alvin?"

"New Orleans."

"No kidding? I was born in the Garden District. I used to practice—"

"In the Ninth Ward."

"How did you know?"

"When I was a boy you put me up after my father got convicted, before they moved me to the foster home."

"Where was your mother?"

"Was a murder conviction."

"Oh." Abe hesitated. "I don't recall prosecuting such a case."

"He confessed, got life. You came around only after."

"After."

Alvin shifted in the driver's seat. Abe thought the conversation was making him uncomfortable; along with the .45 automatic under Alvin's coat at the small of his back, it was. "Gave me a bed for a time," Alvin said. "Tide me over. Guess you did that a lot."

"I wouldn't say a lot."

"I recognized you first time we met."

Abe wondered why Alvin hadn't mentioned this before. He was afraid to ask why he was mentioning it now. A question had to be asked: "Was I nice to you?"

"One word for it."

Alvin switched on the radio and turned up the volume to play over the raindrops drumming the Cadillac roof. It was WJBW out of New Orleans. The song was "St. James Infirmary Blues." Alvin hummed to the middle verse:

> Seventeen coal black horses, hitched to a rubber-tired hack,
> Seven girls goin' to the graveyard, only six of them are comin'
>   back . . .

Abe did not like the song.

WINDS WERE PICKING up. Tarzy Hooker was tying down gear outside the tool shed when the Cadillac pulled up at his aunt Sallie's place. She'd taken the ferry to fetch his mom from her shift at the sugar refinery across the Calcasieu ship channel. Tarzy recognized Abe right away, the lawyer, his dropped pants et cetera having made a strong impression. Because the other man was big, white, and wearing a jacket and tie, the boy guessed he was with the law. The man asked to see the cold locker. "Empty now," Tarzy said.

"What you called, boy?" Alvin asked.

"Tarzy."

"Short for Tazwell, am I right?"

"Yessir."

"*Dog,* I'm good." His cheerful tone notwithstanding, Alvin had begun to feel agitated. The three of them standing in awkward silence under a pouring rain was getting well past absurd. He closed his eyes and gave a robotic nod, as if to instructions only he heard. He opened his eyes on a world unseen since Okinawa. "Now best you show me that cold box."

Tarzy was smart enough to be scared. The men's demeanors matched the slate sky, and the way they stood apart from each other, like rival politicians working the same crowd, suggested that they were here on disagreeable business. He unlatched the door as they watched. Stale air spilled out. The cold locker's refrigeration was off. The table on which Freddy Baez had been laid out was backed against the far wall. There was no window, and a small floor grate at the base of one wall was clogged with feathers and grime.

Rain dappled and reddened Abe's face like an ad for ripe tomatocs. His thoughts reeled from what Alvin had said in the car. He'd touched the children sometimes, boys and girls alike. Never hurt them, never made them touch him, and made up for it always with money and kindness. The balance remained mixed in his mind. He had a feeling it would be clearer after today.

Alvin began quizzing Tarzy about the dead body from months ago, who was it and why hadn't he told the truth right away, all while calling him nigger this and nigger that in behavior pisspoor not least because this was a child with no one to defend him. Abe tried, but Alvin hammered a fist into the crook of his neck that dropped him to the soggy turf with a cracked collarbone at minimum. Abe tried to stand but fell back in the slop with a groan.

Alvin resumed his nasty spew on Tarzy. The interesting thing is that he was faking. He was no more a racist than he was a ladies' man. Like war cries before a suicide charge, he was steeling himself with ancient hatreds to make what came next feel less terrible. He was going to kill Tarzy and he was going to kill Abe, and he would do it for his sake, not Bonnie's. He'd shot Freddy Baez. If it ever came out—beginning with these two— he would lose her. His love had turned selfish. It was a breakthrough of sorts.

Alvin reached into his coat and withdrew his .45. Tarzy shook his head in frantic apology for whatever he must have done to deserve this. He backed into the cold locker. Abe struggled to his feet and swung at Alvin's head with his cane, his miss by a foot not to detract from a commendable try. Alvin threw him into the locker, where Abe collapsed at Tarzy's feet. The boy knelt to see if he was okay. Alvin stood in the rain outside the door and studied them there on the floor. An old man and a little boy, arms around each other, wide eyes looking up. He slammed the door shut to extinguish the image. The latch locked.

"No!" Abe's voice was muffled behind the door. Hands slapped against the wood.

Outside, Alvin retreated a few paces to gather perspective on what he'd wrought, like a painter perusing work at his easel, its messiness possibly art. His mind retained the image of two faces displaying looks of dismay as the locker door closed, their brains not yet absorbing the peril at hand.

Their pounding and muffled shrieks disrupted Alvin's calm. He almost decided to release them. But it would be awkward explaining why he'd shut them inside, after which he'd have to finish them anyway. The better course was to get in the car and drive. Maybe they'd suffocate. Maybe someone would rescue them. Let Jesus decide. He felt rueful in his abdication but glad to be rid of the blame.

The screams faded as he walked through the rain to his Cadillac. He hardly noticed the water soaking his clothes or squishing from his shoes. The trip home was arduous, the rain forming ponds wherever the narrow road dipped. It took Alvin four hours to reach Lake Charles. He looked for a gift shop on the way to buy something for Bonnie. Everything was closed due to weather. It was okay. He'd given her plenty of gifts in the past. Today was strictly for him.

FIONA FRANKLIN HADN'T seen Joey Meers since his first days after surgery. She'd told herself that someone so damaged wouldn't want visitors, but her real reason for avoiding him was that she didn't want to see his parents. In addition to blaming Delly for maiming their son, the Meerses blamed Fiona for dragging Joey down to her trashy level. The girl's only defense was to deflect their contempt onto Delly, clearly the real trash in this tale.

Leaving home to go live with her father had proved a

mistake. Arthur Franklin was a classic wallower. He regaled Fiona with litanies of persecution aimed at forging a father-daughter kinship based on mutual mistreatment by Delly. He sometimes took late-night drives that she suspected were to spy on his wife, casing her house for lovers or for the sound of popular radio songs that might indicate a happy person inside.

At first Delly had begged Fiona to come back but lately had dropped the subject. Fiona wanted to return more than ever as a result. When Delly told her one day that the next evening she'd be transacting "personal business" at Joey's hospital, Fiona saw it as an opportunity to sneak home to inspect it for evidence of her stepmother boozing or bedding strange men, anything that might account for Delly preferring privacy to begging Fiona's forgiveness.

Lest her father likewise go snooping there, Fiona told him, with much innuendo, about Delly's upcoming hospital rendezvous. She knew it would send him on a goose chase and leave the house free to Fiona and . . . *Joey Meers*. Her cousin's name popped into her head as if it had been waiting there all along. It was the perfect excuse to contact him now that he'd been discharged from the hospital and was living back home. She'd say she was worried about her stepmother and would he help her put those worries to rest. All safely formal, no reference whatsoever to the night at the hunting lodge when he'd placed her hand on his penis and got his skull crushed for his trouble.

She feared the ploy was transparent. But wasn't Joey brain-damaged now? It'd be an act of mercy to reach out to him. She dialed his home with steady hands.

———

Hurricane Audrey slammed a seventy-eight-ton fishing vessel into an oil platform and drowned nine men on Wednesday afternoon. Donald Meers just then was tooling in his Lincoln around drizzly Lake Charles with his new pistol in his lap, running stop signs with goofy laughter as if listening, which he wasn't, to a funny radio play. No one saw him. With the rain coming harder, there were few cars in the streets and the cops were keeping dry at the station.

Meanwhile in the basement cafeteria at Lake Charles Hospital, Seth Hooker was preparing to play ringmaster to a small circus assembled at last by Corinne Meers. Delly arrived first. "I smell perfume," he said.

She was defensive. "Sometimes I wear it." The perfume was a mistake she'd tried to wash off. She'd debated how much to attend to her appearance tonight. Wanting to look unbowed and unbroken while wanting also not to care, she'd abandoned her selections and hauled clothes blindly from her closet.

They took a table in the corner. The cafeteria was empty but for some orderlies brewing coffee on the counter between the kitchen and eating area. Seth heard their voices as a gregarious undertone, which increased his self-consciousness at sitting here tongue-tied with the girl of his dreams.

He heard footsteps. Corinne's flowery smell made Delly's perfume seem like the scent of a single petal. "R.J.'s parkin' the car. Rainin' like hell out there. They still say the storm's gonna miss us."

"Be a storm in here pretty quick," Delly said.

"Says you. Who knows what happened for sure."

"*I know.* It's why he's got to stand trial."

"You might lose, Del."

"He got away once. Not again."

Seth hunched in his chair to duck these verbal blows. Corinne said to Delly, "I was thinkin' back on what happened. Weren't your daddy mixed up in it?"

Delly had rehearsed all manner of fireworks with R.J. but hadn't foreseen fighting her cousin. "He shot himself. I'm sure you remember."

"Tell me again why."

"For loving another man's wife. As you goddamn well know."

The two orderlies by the kitchen went quiet. Seth thought back to the memory of his mother and Frank Billodeau in the Block's back room, their mouths and her hand and Frank's buckling knees. "The wife was my mother," he said. "R.J. had a crush on her, too."

"Quite a gal," Corinne said.

"Which is why," Delly said, "I always wondered if he killed my father."

"R.J.?" Corinne laughed. "He's got no such violence in him." She'd either forgotten about Freddy Baez or decided Mexicans don't count.

"You talking about me?" R.J. had entered unnoticed. Corinne jumped up and hugged him as all hers. Delly refused to watch. "Hello, Adele," he said.

"Delly," Seth corrected.

"Adele is fine," she said.

R.J. pulled up a chair. Apprehension showed in his nervous rearranging of silverware on the table. He drummed his fingers before finally looking at Delly, who likewise only just then lifted her eyes to him. He'd shaved off his beard. It made a jar-ring impression, his face as it used to be. She suspected that was the intent.

"I mistreated you, Adele." He let the words sink in, for her understanding and his. "I mistreated you bad. Okay?"

THEY'D BEEN LOCKED inside the cold box all day. It held the blackness of a tomb and, in this fourth week of June, the dank smell of a summer crawlspace. The few words they shared were disembodied and hollow. Yet without them, and without the drape of their arms around each other, the boy and man would have gone insane.

They lay side by side on the plank floor. Their faces, invisible in the dark from inches apart, were inclined to the grated floor vent, about four inches square, where they'd found fresh air after Abe unclogged it with a pencil. Rain pounded the top and sides of the box and wind shook it like a baby's rattle. Water bubbled up through the vent and Tarzy tasted it with his tongue. He felt Abe's arm embracing him and felt his breath on the side of his face. "Why that man do this?" he asked.

"He's sick, honey. Just sick in the head, is all."

"He comin' back?"

"Someone will. Someone soon."

"My aunt s'posed to."

"She's probably delayed somewhere." This was true. Sallie Hooker had been caught on the wrong side of the Calcasieu ferry when Gulf waters surged through the channel and tore away the pier. Abe suggested they pray. He spoke the words and Tarzy listened with eyes shut tight. The words asked for rescue. Tarzy, a wise soul, wondered if it wasn't better to accept the Lord's will and just pray for peaceful passage.

When Abe said "Amen," Tarzy said it too. His mouth was parched and he again dipped his tongue into the puddle spreading from the vent across the locker floor. He didn't know what was different this time until he tasted the water once more. It was salty.

ALVIN WENT STRAIGHT to Delly Franklin's house on returning from Hancock Bayou early that evening. On the slogging drive north, he hadn't thought of Abe and Tarzy locked in the cold box with the storm coming on, hadn't pictured their faces or heard their screams within the rain pelting the top of his car. What kept his mind clear was faith that why he'd done what he did pardoned the fact that he'd done it. As a teenager in 1945 he'd manned a flamethrower that incinerated men at twenty yards. He'd done it out of duty and for marine brothers alive and dead. This latest he'd done for love.

He'd driven by Delly's house several times in the past. Knowing now that "Ethel" from the Section Eight Gun Club was the former Adele Billodeau, he'd been curious about her circumstances and her potential to cause him problems. But today he came with different purpose. Parking around the corner, he dashed through the rain and, guessing from the empty carport that no one was home, broke in through the screened side door.

———

JOEY MEERS, EIGHTEEN years old and no prince of virtue, had inferred from Fiona's telephone call that she would be giving him sex tonight. Like a jewel thief shoplifting chewing gum, he took his mother's car keys from her bureau and drove out into the wet evening for a rendezvous with his cousin.

He wasn't a virgin. A cheerleader many varsity athletes cut their teeth on had provided him the same service. With somewhat nobler aims now, he picked Fiona up at her father's place and drove to her stepmother's. On Fiona's instruction he parked in the open carport. Concealing his car down the street would make it harder to claim innocence if Delly returned early, Fiona explained. "Got it," he said, suddenly skittish in the face of her guile.

Fiona had a door key. The premise that tonight's jaunt was merely to check up on her stepmother's welfare dissolved before the brazen fact of an empty house with empty bedrooms. "We're in," she said.

The question of what to do next was encapsulated by the wall switch inside the front door. Turn it on, and routine acts of teenagers with nothing to hide could commence under unabashed light. Leave it off, and the house would stay as dark as heaven's blind eye and these two could get on with free will. Fiona shook her head no when he reached for the switch. Joey's pulse accelerated as she led him by the hand through the unlit back hall. He almost tripped over the rug, his balance thrown by digging in his pocket for the condom he'd brought. Still unsteady from his injuries, he hobbled after her like an elderly lecher made spry by the power of hope.

Fiona glanced into her stepmother's room across from her own. Something large and dark obscured the closet door. She went over to inspect it, fearing to disturb the mood with electric light. When her eyes adjusted she screamed.

IT WAS PERHAPS an hour earlier when Alvin, not bothering to muffle his footfalls in the empty house, had entered the master bedroom to rifle through the bureau drawers. The closet door had flown open and a man burst out with a squeal.

Alvin had pinned him to the bed and pressed his thumbs into his eye sockets. "State your business. You got three seconds."

"This is my house."

"She lives here alone. Two. One."

"Please! It's my wife's house," Arthur Franklin said weakly. "Steal what you want. I won't look."

Alvin, his knee on Arthur's sternum, reached to where Arthur's hand clenched a small something. He snatched it away and switched on the bedside lamp to see what was written on the paper:

> Adele,
>
> There is an old colored woman in Hancock Bayou in Cameron Parish whose little nephew knows it was not R. J. Bainard who died. Her name is Sally something and everyone knows her in the town. Keep it in your head. Pardon the mystery. Everything is well. I will contact you soon.
>
> Your friend, Abe

Reading it, he felt fortunate to have found the note so easily. This was tempered with knowing that a loose end now had to be cut. He turned the light off in respect for the moment. "It's great you have this," he said in the semi-dark. "And yet sorta not."

Arthur took heart when Alvin climbed off him, thinking they would forgive each other's trespass and slip out like burglars on two different jobs. He sat up and opened his eyes to the black dot of a .45 barrel. "Please no."

Alvin pocketed the note with his free hand. "Name?"

"Arthur Franklin. Sir."

"Good. And since you obviously ain't no thief—"

"I'm her husband. Or used to be."

"To this Adele gal?"

"You know her?"

"A little." Alvin regarded the weapon in his hand. "*Dog,* but I wish you hadn't been here. Or at least you was robbin' the place 'steada . . . what?"

"I wanted a glimpse. Into her life."

"Miss her, do you?"

"So much."

"I understand." Alvin's sympathy brought an eager nod from Arthur, like a patient getting good pills from a doctor. "She got a new boyfriend," Alvin said, improvising now. "They are very in love."

Arthur nodded. He seemed to forget the conversation's fraught conditions in favor of its subject. "My daughter predicted she'd never come back to me."

"You got a daughter. Nice." Alvin placed a fraternal hand on Arthur's shoulder. "This boyfriend of your wife's—he's rich and, you know, just a much better catch than you." Arthur looked about to cry. "Fact is, they're gonna get married."

"Oh God."

Alvin's voice was gentle. "You need to remove yourself."

"Of course. Happy to." Arthur rose to leave.

"No." Alvin leveled the weapon. "Remove yourself."

Arthur was puzzled. Or wanted to be.

"See," Alvin said, "I don't wanna shoot you. And honestly, you got plenty o' cause to go peaceful. Plus you'd be doin' your daughter a favor."

"I don't understand."

"You'll leave her a wealthy woman. Don't ask me how, but it's true. So . . ."

"Remove?"

Alvin surveyed the room. "Light cord, over the door, step off that footstool there."

"You have to be joking."

"How's work goin', Arthur?"

"Fine. Work is fine."

"The truth."

"I was fired."

"Told your daughter yet?"

Arthur shook his head.

"A little ashamed?"

"I want her to be proud of me."

"Do you have life insurance?"

"Not a dime."

"You do now. I'm thinkin' ten thousand dollars."

"Who's got that kind of money?"

"It's there."

"You're lying. You could say anything."

"Again: it's a promise."

"If I . . . now?"

"Lemme show you."

Alvin did, and with such tender solicitousness it could only have come from experience. He'd done it before, making the same pitch to Frank Billodeau four years ago, in Frank's vulnerable hours after he'd confessed to authorities about his affair with Angel Bainard; the bait in that instance had been Alvin's promise that Mary Billodeau would never be fired from Block's. Richie, in jealous fury, had originally ordered a straight execution, but Alvin had urged a gentler course and arranged to meet Frank on a country road. Together they'd leaned on Frank's truck like a pair of old farmers and had a good deep talk about life's ups and downs that concluded with Frank dead from a shot to the temple, Alvin pulling the trigger while Frank nodded in prayerful acquiescence with his eyes serenely closed. Mary had her job to this day.

He guided Arthur to the closet door, reminding him in a voice soft as a hypnotist's of the bounty this would bring to Fiona. Arthur watched with the courage of a queen beholding the block as Alvin strung a lamp cord over the door and looped it around a robe hook on the inside. The footstool made a scaffold. Soon Arthur was teetering on it with the cord around his neck.

Clamping Arthur's arms to his sides in a firm embrace, Alvin was like a cowpoke immobilizing a beloved pony prior to putting it down. He used his weight to pull Arthur down and constrict the noose around his neck. "Steady . . ."

Arthur thrashed weakly. He tried to make sounds but nothing came out. The men looked like lovers against a wall, having relations for the first time or last.

"Steady . . ."

A scream seized in Arthur's chest like stripped gears inside a transmission. His body went rigid. His eyes bulged.

Alvin put his mouth to Arthur's ear. "What I said about your daughter before?"

Arthur listened from the edge of consciousness.

"She'll have a good life, I swear to God."

Alvin kicked the stool clear. Arthur sagged a last inch, the cord disappearing under his jaw. His tongue extruded and his face turned a darker color.

Alvin backed out of the room. He checked his appearance in the hall mirror. As noted, he'd done this before, and no less humanely.

He went out through the carport and cut across lawns to his Cadillac. The rain fell in torrents. His clothes clung like wet bandages as he drove down the road toward Georgia Hill and his ladylove. She was working in her upstairs office, not permitting herself even a glance out the window in worry where her man could be on such a night.

R.J. KEPT HIS eyes on the space between Delly's eyes. She did the same to him, like a contest except for no prize. "I won't go to prison," he said.

"You'll go."

Like fans at a tennis match, Seth and Corinne looked over

to catch R.J.'s reply. He shook his head in lament for bad tidings he couldn't make better.

Delly asked him, "Have you hurt other girls?"

"Never."

Corinne said, "This is goin' nowhere."

R.J. barely heard this. "Any chance you can let this go?" he asked Delly.

"I want you to feel crummy as me."

"I do."

"Why don't I believe that?"

"Because I look good."

The remark was factual. Face clean-shaven and smooth, white teeth, blue eyes flashy as gemstones—the bastard looked too good. Delly protested weakly, "People who hurt people should pay."

"I do. Every day."

Corinne scowled. Let her lover be guilty of anything except frailty.

Seth spoke up. "It's got to be hard, Delly. Always running, always looking over your shoulder."

"I saw it firsthand. Drinks at the hunting lodge? Not exactly Alcatraz."

"I'll beg your forgiveness," R.J. said. "I will cut off a finger. But I'm walking out of here in about one minute and you'll just have to trust that I'm finished as a man. I can't help how it looks from the outside."

"It looks great, is how it looks! Meantime I look like a damn dishrag whose life tanked at eighteen, thanks to you."

"You look beautiful," Seth said.

"How the fuck would you know? You're blind as a bat."
Delly grabbed a table knife and brandished it wildly as if to stab
them all. Stubby and dull, its blade reflected her face in melted
distortion.

Corinne touched her arm. "Give it up, Del. Do you a world
of good."

A dizzying chasm opened beneath Delly that only R.J., in
his first misstep of the evening, could prevent her from falling
into. "My brother's right. You look beautiful."

Clarity returned. She presented the knife. "Okay. A finger."

"Say again?"

"There's many who'd insist on your balls. I'll do with a
finger."

"You're serious?"

"And we'll call it square."

He accepted the knife and held it to the light from the cafeteria ceiling. "Not sure this'll cut through bone."

"Try."

"My finger. You mean it?"

"You offered."

"Enough," Corinne said. The meeting had lost its appeal.
She'd just wanted R.J. pacified so she could call the shots from
now on. "It's way past time—"

"Please shut up," Delly said without looking at her.

R.J. laid down the knife and flattened his hands on the table.
"Lady's choice."

The backs of his hands were flecked with dark hair. She indicated the pointer finger on his left hand, her attention drawn
there by a scar that curled around it like a pink leech. "Cut it off
and I'm good."

"Meaning you accept my apology?"

"Never that."

He picked up the knife and hovered it an inch above the knuckle, like a surgeon blanking out.

Delly's next words surprised both of them. "Did you kill my father?"

He focused. "What?"

"You remember: Coach Billodeau from the high school."

"I met him. We had words."

"Because of Angel Bainard, I know."

Seth, hearing his mother's name, perked up in a negative way.

"I was jealous," R.J. said. Something had changed in his face. Shame makes no one look good. "Over her."

"Pathetic," Delly said.

"It was. For me and your dad both. I felt bad when I heard he shot himself."

"Bullshit. You shot him."

"I swear I did not."

"Who then?"

"Maybe my father. Your dad did fuck his wife."

Delly took this calmly. Truth was fair.

"Any man can kill a woman," R.J. said, "can damn well kill a man."

It startled Seth to hear his brother ascribe crimes to their father just as Seth had done for years. It made the whole notion sound shaky, made him wonder if any fault is ever one hundred percent. "My mother died by accident," he declared with finality. The concession felt smaller once spoken, a deep dark secret now sort of pointless. "Richie did plenty wrong, but not that."

R.J. put the knife down. "So why try and shoot me to death in a swamp? Make me carry this goddamn thing all day long." He took out Freddy Baez's revolver from under his shirt and laid it on the table.

The words were gibberish to Seth—he had no idea of the web Alvin had spun—and the gun of course was invisible. Delly stared at it in disbelief. Corinne thought it was sexy. She attempted to salvage her plan. "Jesus, people. It's about fucking in a car, nothin' more." Her eyes went big. *"R.J.!"*

Knife back in hand, he'd sawed through the base of his pointer finger. Blood speckled the table like ketchup.

Corinne snatched the knife away. "Jesus Lord!"

R.J. pondered his wound as if it were someone else's. "Oops. Cut myself." His gaze jumped to something across the room. He grabbed the pistol, got up from the table, and headed quickly to the cafeteria kitchen and out the back door to the parking lot.

Corinne turned around to see what he'd seen. Two policemen had come in and were conferring with a hospital orderly. They approached the table. "Evenin', officers," she said with a sugary smile.

Seth, lagging the others in realizing what had spooked R.J., heard Delly murmur at his ear, "Cops are here, kid. Time to pick sides."

The policeman was a looming shadow beside Seth's chair. "Officer," he said, "if it's my brother you're lookin' for—"

"No!" Corinne cried.

The cop ignored them. "Are you Miz Franklin, ma'am?"

"Why?"

"There's been a incident at your house. With your girl."

Delly rocketed out of her chair. Corinne crossed herself.

"Your husband," the cop explained, "hung himself in your bedroom. He's dead."

"Arthur?"

"The girl found him."

"Oh no."

"We got people with her. She told us where to find you."

"What was she doing at my house? She lives with—"

"She had a young fella there."

"Joey?" Corinne said.

"You know him?"

"He's my son!"

"Gotta say, he sure frigged the scene. Tried to lift the body, knockin' shit over. Be almos' impossible to establish what happened."

"I thought you said it was suicide," Seth said.

"So it appears," the cop said, with some disappointment.

DONALD MEERS SAT in his Lincoln in the hospital parking lot caressing his pistol like worry beads. He wondered should he charge into the building and gun down his wife and her Mexican lover; rain on his car and wind whipping the trees seemed to urge this course of action. He decided that pumping bullets into the pair would wreck his life almost as much as theirs. Better a clean shot with no witnesses.

He saw the Mexican scurry out of the building and get into his vehicle after ducking from the squad car nearby. He leaped to two conclusions, both wrong. He thought Corinne and her lover had had a fight and ended their affair, and he thought the cops were in chase and the man was making his getaway. He put his motor in gear and pulled onto the road behind the sports car. The gun in his lap made him feel like he was running the wetback out of town. He would chase him to the city limits, yes he would. He'd shake his fist at the taillights and hurl wrathful curses, then go home and forgive his wife after first making her grovel and crawl.

THE POLICE OFFERED to drive Delly to the station but she chose to follow in her car. She asked Seth to accompany her in hopes that he could comfort Fiona with Bible verses. It felt like a lucky break to him even so.

From the station they all—Corinne and Joey; Delly, Fiona, and Seth—drove through the downpour to Corinne's house in the Charpentier District. They went there because Fiona couldn't bear to stay at her father's and more especially at her stepmother's, where she and Joey had found Arthur's body. Questions about what the kids were doing there in the first place could wait. Everyone knew anyway.

Corinne, after they got to her place, voiced sorrow over what had happened but mainly wanted to discuss her own issues. Chirping away as if all bitterness between Delly and R.J. was healed, she speculated on her lover's prospects. "Once R.J. gets his inheritance, I'll give Donald the boot."

Delly assumed her usual role and made tea for Seth and her cousin. A vibrant drift, like caffeine insomnia, gripped her. Hanging himself in her bedroom seemed such a lowdown trick on her husband's part it left her feeling bewildered more than guilty. This had the helpful effect of overshadowing everything else that had bewildered her tonight.

Corinne paused in her chatter. Seth asked to use her telephone to ring his sister at home. Rather than return to the hospital at this late hour, he would sleep at Georgia Hill, his distaste for the place just slightly less than asking Corinne to put him up. "I'll need a lift," he said to no one.

Delly offered to take him.

"You should stay with your daughter."

"She's sleeping." With Joey upstairs, chastely clothed on the bed like Shakespeare's star-crossed lovers. "And I can't."

DONALD MEERS TAILED his rival through empty wet streets to the Bainard estate. After the roadster turned up the driveway, he parked under some wind-blown trees and entered the grounds on foot. Expecting guard dogs and searchlights, he pretended he was a secret commando infiltrating an enemy compound. He carried his gun in his hand because that's what commandoes do.

The windows were lighted irregularly, the main floor dim, rooms upstairs glowing yellow through hazy sheers. Donald crouched in the shrubbery and scanned for movement inside. He knew Corinne's Mexican was in there somewhere. One shot and he'd be on his way, his honor redeemed, a grateful nation indebted.

Headlights swept the house. A car came up the drive and parked in the courtyard. A man and woman got out, talking loud as people do in the rain. "I'm fine," the man said. He had a cane.

"Not in the dark you're not." The woman came around from the driver's side to help him up the front steps.

Donald stepped out from behind a bush. "Delly?"

"Donald?"

The front door opened. "Who's out there?"

Donald raised his pistol. "Freeze, Mex!"

The confusion was slow to dispel even after Donald herded the others inside. Suffice it to say he was now a pivotal figure, though to be candid not for long.

AN OLD DAMP house in southwest Louisiana can get steamy during a summer rainstorm. The thick atmosphere inside Georgia Hill put people more on edge than they might have been in some air-conditioned lobby. And anytime a guest makes wild threats with a loaded handgun you know a household gets tense. Consequently the first moments of everyone gathering in the foyer were neither civil nor informative.

Donald's will to vengeance was iffy; there were moments when he wagged his pistol more like a French fry than a Smith & Wesson. Seth and R.J. meanwhile affected competing versions of calm. All men are boys, goes the saying, and it was surely true of this pair. Had Delly not been present, it's easy to imagine Seth pleading with Donald to calm down and R.J. hightailing it out of there. But Southern manhood has ever measured itself by a lady's esteem, and the lady here was her.

Once Donald was persuaded that R.J. wasn't Mexican, R.J. answered his next question—"Then who the hell are you?"— with weary resignation that suggested he might have preferred to take Donald's bullet than own up to the fact he was R. J. Bainard and this was his father's house. But he did own up to it, after which Donald said to Delly, "He the one? What done you back then?"

She nodded.

"Then damn, let's call the police and end this easy."

"Let's not," Seth said. He turned in his brother's direction. "Please go, R.J. It's the one good thing you can do."

Donald cocked his head. "What's wrong wit' your eyes?"

"They don't work very well."

"Neither's your mouth, judgin' what it said. Now do it, Del. Call the police and tell 'em we got the fugitive."

"She won't," R.J. said.

Delly turned. "No?"

R.J. rocked slightly on his feet. He gave her a deep look, like a poet through the depths of a lily pond. "You like me some, Adele," he said. "That night and this night, you like me more than what's known."

Seth laughed in a not normal way. "Tell him, Delly. Finish it."

She hadn't started breathing again, R.J.'s words having impacted only after he spoke them. How had this happened? She'd left with a guy in the middle of a high school basketball game and insanity had somehow resulted, pouring down from outside her and boiling up from within. She tried a last time to suppress it. "That's just some fantasy. No point to it now, either way."

"Was once," R.J. said.

"We don't know. We can't ever know." It seemed that she and R.J. were the only ones in the room, the only ones anywhere.

"At least let me believe it, okay? It got me this far."

Bonnie came barreling out of the sewing room. She was enraged at the mass intrusion into her house where a man lay mortally ill. Her father's nurse was behind her, bursting with dire excitement that Richie's end was at hand. The ensuing turmoil bonded R.J., Seth, and Bonnie as their father's children at last. They dropped the disputes of the moment and rushed down the hall. Left behind in the foyer, Delly and Donald eyed each other like guests unsure if the party is over. He stuck his gun in his pants as if not to do so would be gauche. Delly fell silent, her head seething with agonized notions that, oddly or not, included none about her late husband.

RICHIE DID LOOK done for. Brief revivals in recent weeks had made predictions of his demise seem like so much crying wolf, but tonight you could feel Death rubbing its hands together like a cannibal at suppertime. The family was reunited, the twins and their half brother joined around their father's bed. They formed a triangle, R.J. and Bonnie at each side by his pillow, Seth at the foot. Seth recited the Lord's Prayer. Bonnie, beyond tears, resented R.J.'s wooden demeanor and asked sarcastically if he'd brought his pistol. He had; since the bloody scene at Finney Pond, he'd kept it always at hand. When he produced it from under his shirt, it was with disgust rather than rancor. He tossed the gun on the bed.

His prayer over, Seth started again at the beginning as Richie's breathing slowed. Bonnie began to tremble, her long preparedness for this event imploding in the face of it. Confronting R.J. as the easiest target, she cursed him for his wasted life, progressing in her list of transgressions from verified crimes to the speculative ones that Alvin had supplied her, namely killing Freddy Baez, assaulting Ethel Somebody, and drowning Hollis Jenks. R.J.'s passive reaction seemed to concede the truth of the charges. Finally moved to defend himself, he told his sister that Alvin was the one who'd killed Freddy Baez and likely done those other things, too.

"Alvin?" Bonnie scoffed. "He never killed anyone."

"There's some ChiCom regulars in Korea would say otherwise. And Frank Billodeau, of course."

She knew the name. "Who?"

"That girl outside—" He meant Delly. "—she thinks *I* did it. But Alvin told me long ago he did it on Daddy's direction."

"Liar!"

"Sure I done it." It was Alvin. His entrance in the room caused Bonnie's face to take the shine of a madwoman greeting a phantom. He went to her side. He was deeply exhausted by today's many labors but did a Lazarus when she kissed him. They stood arm in arm, a public display that was, for them, tantamount to making love in the town square. Alvin said to the room, "And a lot else for this family, no lie."

Bonnie hadn't known. Hearing it now, she knew it was true and she knew it was unforgivable. Alvin, eyes on her, awaited her verdict. She kissed him again. "For which he's got my gratitude," she said, "and whatever more he wants."

Delly appeared in the doorway. She'd been listening outside. *"Hallelujah,"* she said, though the word and her facial expression didn't match. She lunged for Richie's bed.

"I Iey!"

"Grab her!"

Seth, all ears as usual, was confused by the curses and clatter.

"Put it down, Adele. Put it down before someone gets hurt."

Let's catch up. Hearing the ruckus, Alvin had come down-stairs from Bonnie's suite where he'd been resting after his hard day. He was armed, of course. Outside the sewing room he heard the enumeration of his misdeeds and entered pre-pared to accept whatever penalty Bonnie decreed. Delly and Donald saw Alvin come down and followed him to see what was what, on the way passing Richie's nurse who had the good sense to scram after Donald whipped out his pistol like Elliot Ness. Overhearing the conversation around Richie's bedside, Delly, with Donald right behind her, burst into the room and grabbed the pistol that R.J. had thrown on the bed. Thus we have in the sewing room three people with weapons and three not. Everyone is stressed. Everyone is tired. When the storm outside causes the house to lose power and the lights to go out, everyone does the wrong thing.

SIX SHOTS WENT off in the dark, followed by coughs and ragged breathing that accentuated the weirdness of the moment, like giggles at a funeral. A smell of fireworks permeated the air. Seth's voice came from floor level. "Delly? Are you all right?"

"Are you?"

"Thank God."

R.J. spoke next. "Bonnie?"

"I'm here. Crazy bitch."

"I didn't shoot," Delly said. Not true, but in the chaos she honestly wasn't aware. She'd whirled in the dark toward those who'd wronged her and clenched her hand to a fist, settling at least one of her scores. "Musta been Donald."

No answer.

"Donald?"

R.J. continued roll call. "Alvin?"

There came a groan.

Bonnie crawled over. She gasped. "You're wet!"

"M'head."

"Your head? Oh Jesus."

"Love you, girl."

"Alvin, no. Goddamn you Jesus Jesus."

"Please no cursin'. Need prayers this point."

"R.J.! Alvin's hurt."

"Makes two of us, Bonnie."

Seth got to his feet only to trip over a body that would prove to be Donald's. He pitched forward onto Richie's bed, where he landed with a sloshy sound. Shot in the chest by a bullet intended elsewhere, Richie had drained out on the mattress like a crankcase into an oil pan. He'd just passed his fifty-eighth birthday but would have looked much older if the lamp had been on.

Visions adjusted to the dark. Alvin had been hit in the side of his forehead, the bullet piercing his skull and furrowing under the bone from above his eye to above his ear. He was conscious, rambling on with dubious coherence about going straight to hell. His damnation was tied to the word "Tarzy," which caught R.J.'s attention even under the burn of a bullet that had passed through the flesh of his hip.

"What are you saying, Alvin?"

"Icebox in Hancock Bayou."

"What?"

"Where they had Freddy."

"Sallie's place?"

"In the box. Tarzy and the fat man."

"Jesus Christ! Why?"

A pause. "Not sure now."

"Today you did this?"

"Was gonna go back." Alvin remembered the question. "Today."

Whereupon our story gains a hero, for R.J. resolved immediately to drive to Hancock Bayou through the oncoming storm to rescue Tarzy Hooker. But in trying to stand, his leg folded like a broken barstool and he fell into Delly's arms—whereupon *she* declared that she would drive him there, to hell with the weather and all else. She looped her arm under his and they stumbled out the door.

Seth's protests stood no chance. They made their getaway down the dark hallway without a glance behind. He hollered after them, tried to get up, fell down, and floundered on all fours on the blood-wet floor like an ant sprayed with pesticide. He wanted them to come back. He wanted to go with them. He wanted not to be left behind.

Richie's nurse, hiding in the kitchen, had heard the gunshots and tried to call for help but the phone lines were down. Alvin remained conscious for an hour or so, drifting between dread for his soul and thanks to God for giving him Bonnie. His last words before he lost consciousness were "bury me home" or "marry me, hon," Seth hearing one thing and Bonnie another. They would debate it later to no useful purpose.

AUDREY, NOW A Category Four hurricane, turned due north late in the day on June 26 and headed straight for Cameron Parish.

Its track accelerated; landfall would happen early on Thursday, June 27. The news had little effect on local residents. Electric power had been out since midday Wednesday. There were few active radios to receive the Weather Bureau's revised alarm to evacuate *now*. The last reports had said Texas would catch the brunt tomorrow afternoon, so people in Louisiana had hunkered down in their homes as they'd done for countless squalls and tropical storms. They expected to suffer some damage. They expected to survive.

In the last daylight hours on Wednesday, before rains became torrential and winds approaching 150 miles per hour started bending the trees and peeling roofs off the houses like box tops, an interesting natural phenomenon occurred that brought foreboding to any old-timers who recalled it from previous cataclysms. Millions of crayfish scuttled out of the swamps and began streaming through streets and across lawns and schoolyards like a huge green carpet of locusts. Sensing the coming seawater surge, this primordial refugee instinct likewise led creatures such as foxes and rodents and swarms of snakes to make similar breaks for higher ground before the ocean came.

Heavy winds ripped through the night. Telephone poles snapped. Tree trunks cracked, and shutters and sheathing tore off houses to become deadly projectiles hurtling through the air. Yet flooding remained moderate. Warm brackish water pushed out of the bayous and over the lowlands in an ankle-deep flow no worse than what thunderstorms caused now and then. At Sallie Hooker's property, the water pooled like bathwater around the pilings of her house and the base of the cold locker. The two people inside the locker worried at first that it might keep rising. Seepage through the floor vent turned to a spurt. The water rose to a foot high, about halfway up the legs of the table on which Tarzy and Abe sat cross-legged in the dark. Abe held Tarzy's hand and spun tales of memorable meals he'd cooked and brainless dogs he'd owned. He said that someday Tarzy could tell his grandchildren about passing the hurricane with a fat old fool in a cold box. Tarzy laughed more than a few times.

Panic overcame Abe at one point. He told Tarzy about doing bad things for money and bad things with children that Tarzy listened to with incomprehension and dread, for he could tell that Abe was making a final confession. Abe pulled out of his spiral, apologized for his babble and made up a game to play, betting each other on the time between flying debris hitting the sides of the locker. The lags got longer as the wind abated. They noticed that the water inside the locker had leveled off. The storm was subsiding. The promise of morning encouraged them.

It was around eight A.M. when witnesses first saw the wall of seawater about twelve feet high, a brown boil of mud and landscape debris, rolling like a bulldozer from the shorefront over the land. Whole neighborhoods were obliterated by its impact. Sallie's plucking shed already had lost its roof and siding to the wind; the tidal wave took the rest like a matchbox hit by a five iron. It tore her house off its pilings and carried it for miles before the house hit the banks of the Intracoastal Canal and shattered into pieces. The wave knocked the cold locker off its slab and flipped it like a vandalized mailbox. The locker bobbed upside down in the current, its inmates drenched and bruised, terrified yet alive, and, once the shock passed, heartened by the fresh air and patch of daylight visible through the floor vent that now framed a glimpse of morning sky.

The locker began to fill. Abe and Tarzy treaded water alongside broken pieces of table and shelving. Soon there was less than two feet of space between the water and the ceiling, which a moment ago had been floor. They floundered beneath the vent overhead with faces upraised like seals begging for herring. Abe's breathing wheezed and he said "oh God" repeatedly. The boy wedged his fingers into the vent to hoist himself up. The grate broke away, leaving a square hole that gave a view of speeding clouds and sideways rain. He reached his arm through. The air on his skin was a tease of freedom inches away. He yelled for help but his words carried nowhere. Abe, face purple, gripped Tarzy's waist to raise him higher. When his strength failed they splashed back into the water. Coughing for breath, they tried again, and again after that, Abe hoisting Tarzy so he could signal for help through the vent. The effort gave hope. They would try once more. The boy was preparing to launch himself upward when down through the hole tumbled a large black snake.

Tarzy recoiled from the smack of the serpent hitting his forehead. He thrashed screaming under the water with the thing writhing cold in his face. He clawed it away and got clear of the water for an inward breath and outward scream. He and Abe hugged the sides of the locker as the snake slithered to and fro in the sloshing water. It bumped into Abe, who shrieked. In recent months cottonmouth numbers had erupted in the marsh along with the rats and nutria. Tarzy knew the snakes were poisonous.

Another one dropped through the vent. Then another. Abe

splashed and kicked trying to get away from them. His eyes were swollen and his face looked about to explode. He stopped and studied his hand as if he'd broken a fingernail. "I'm bit." He sounded relieved to have it done with.

Tarzy treaded water in the opposite corner. He stayed stone still whenever one of the snakes came near, letting it slide like an eel against him. He kept his eyes down to watch for them in the water and also not to watch Abe, whom he feared would die from the bite right in front of him. But Abe's heart had already stopped. The storm was passing and the sky outside had turned powder gray. Light through the vent illuminated the inside of the locker. Tarzy looked up to see Abe's head flop back with open eyes. Abe's body settled down in the water like a sponge in a tub. A snake slid up his chest and coiled on his upturned face. Its diamond head swayed, its black tongue flicked. Tarzy's terror became extreme.

R.J. AND DELLY left Georgia Hill a little before midnight but didn't reach Hancock Bayou until evening the next day. Driving into the storm, they got as far as Belton, a one-pump village between Hackberry and Holly Beach, before spillover from Calcasieu Lake made the road impassable. Dawn was hours away. Houses were dark, streets were empty. They parked near an abandoned AME chapel that judging from its cinderblock walls and oil-stained floor had once been an auto garage. Raindrops hit like bullets and the wind made a train-whistle sound. The dash from the car to the church left them soaked. It might have been romantic under other circumstances, lovers in the rain and so forth. Not tonight. They'd fled a violent scene

whose scope of injury they could only guess. Their crazy leap
to go rescue a child seemed hopeless now that its adrenaline
rush had subsided over the hours of difficult travel. R.J.'s side
burned where the bullet had passed through the muscle above
his hip—not fatal, not gory, but still painful as a blowtorch. Delly
had driven, letting him sleep or mumble or stare at the wiper
blades. There was nowhere else in the world she wanted to be.

The church door was unlocked. There were four pairs of
rough-hewn benches divided by a narrow aisle they could just
make out in the dimness. They guessed that the narrow windows down each side were made of stained glass because they
were darker than the walls. A small round window above the
altar had been blown out by the wind, yet the storm noise
pouring through seemed strangely far away. R.J. lay back on
one of the benches. Delly sat beside him and studied the hole
where the altar window had been. R.J. shifted in a spasm and
bumped his head on the wood. She slipped her hand under his
head and lifted it onto her lap. The altar window resembled an
eye or some kind of escape hatch. He shifted again. His head
pressed against her belly below her breasts. She looked down.
Her vision had adjusted to the dark. His eyes were open, looking up. He lifted his hand and gripped her upper arm. "Thank
you, Adele," he said.

"You're welcome."

She kissed him then. Not long. Just once. Just right.

It feels like heaven's joke the way skies turn blue and breezes
balmy right after a hurricane passes. Songbirds appear out of
nowhere to serenade families picking through the wreckage.

In the case of Audrey and Cameron Parish, you can't leave hundreds of dead bodies in such a small area without them showing up all over the place. Delly saw dozens, muddy and battered, after she and R.J. switched from car to foot once the ground approaching Hancock Bayou got too boggy to drive. Sand from the beaches clogged the coast highway. Standing water, deep in parts, covered the lowlands to the north. People got around in skiffs and pirogues, calling out names, looking for loved ones. The sound of outboard motors gave a sense of common labor, like homeowners mowing lawns up and down a suburban street. The pervasive shock was somewhat relieved by the sight of people organizing themselves into work crews and search parties. Like survivors emerging squint-eyed from caves, they would swap tales of the holocaust later. Right now there was work to do.

On the drive here from Belton, Delly had spotted a liquor store, broken in and taken a quart of Everclear to douse R.J.'s wound—two holes, entry and exit, about six inches apart and linked by a subcutaneous bruise rapidly turning purple. The bloodstain on his trousers ran to his knee. He grimaced at each step, one hand on Delly's shoulder.

They slogged inland. Channels of seawater encircled mounds of muck, steaming under the summer heat, everything draining toward the mud-colored lake that yesterday had been marsh. The mounds were matted with rain-beaten grass and infested with snakes. Seeing them glisten and glide like worms in a manure pile terrified Delly until she began to think of them as no different from everyone else today, homeless and so tired.

A motor sounded behind them. An old woman maneuvered

her skiff toward the open water, her gaze steady, her face stolid as a wooden Indian's as she worked the outboard tiller. R.J. waved to her. "Sallie!"

Sallie Hooker was much amazed. Even fear for Tarzy, wherever he was, took a momentary backseat to seeing the dead return to life. She veered into the bank and, in one of those moments when massive unlikelihood becomes life's new condition, helped R.J. and Delly into her skiff before continuing her search for the missing child.

Motoring over the flooded land, they saw leafless trees and broken rooftops projecting from the water like the spars of sunken ships. It was getting late. Twilight over wetlands is always lovely; it was enhanced in this case by the absence of intact structures, everything primal and placid. Coming finally to Sallie's property, they saw her house was gone, its pilings sticking up bare. The cold locker too was gone. Sallie cut the engine. The vessel skimmed in silence through the flotsam in the water, the dead animals, weeds, and junk. She didn't bother calling Tarzy's name.

The sky went from orange to cobalt as the sun descended. No one spoke. A flight of ducks pitched down in the distance near a floating platform of wood. Delly gasped to see the platform was covered with snakes. Other snakes swam thickly around it like penguins around an ice floe. To fall overboard would have been a bad way to go, like being eaten by dogs or buried alive. Delly moved to the center of the skiff.

The three of them sat lost in themselves as the skiff's momentum carried it closer to the platform. The snakes were piled in a clumpy mass. From under the pile one of them poked upward like a cobra called by a flute. Delly studied the curious sight. Her gasp came simultaneous with Sallie's. The erect snake was a bare human arm reaching up through the glistening squirm. Alongside the platform now, they saw it was the top of a large submerged box with only a few inches still above water. The upraised arm, thin as a broomstick, wobbled at the elbow before retracting through the pile of snakes and vanishing inside the box.

The skiff almost capsized in the next moments. Sallie batted the snakes away with a paddle and jumped on top of the locker, which bobbed like a leaky canoe. She plunged her hand through the vent and swirled it around till she took grip and hoisted with all her strength. It wasn't Tarzy. The wrist she clasped was wearing white shirtsleeves, the body below as heavy and soggy as a boot pulled from a pond. She let go with a cry of biblical anguish and the arm slid back out of view. Now R.J. too leaped onto the locker, breathing through his teeth, his side on fire from pain. He knelt to the vent and called Tarzy's name. The reply, spoken inches from his face, was a whisper. "Please get me outta here please."

Tarzy, over the long and horrible hours, had grown numb to conditions inside the locker, suspended afloat in the dark with the snakes and Abe's corpse as the locker drifted to deeper water and started to sink. The sound of voices outside had put him into frenzy. He screamed. He clawed at the vent to try and tear it wider, ripping his fingernails bloody. His great-aunt was a vision above him. She fell to her knees and put her face to the vent where his nose and eyes were barely visible above the water rising inside. Her weight and then R.J.'s sunk the locker further. Water spurted from the vent and Tarzy's face submerged. She cried out all kinds of prayers.

Night had fallen. Delly watched from the skiff as R.J. moved to the side of the locker and peered into the black water. Snakes were everywhere, thick and twisty like noodles in a pot. He rocked forward and dove in soundlessly, like a navy frogman mining a harbor. He groped along the side of the locker, sweeping aside the snakes and pulling them off his neck and shoulders, till he found the upside-down door. He took a breath and went under. The next sign of him was Sallie's scream that he was inside, that he'd unlocked the door and was inside with the child. She crawled on all fours to the edge of the locker and stared at the water with the mad intensity of a dog watching kids in a pool. Tarzy surfaced with a gasp. Sallie seized his wrist and hauled him out in one swoop as if sharks were at his heels. She took him in her arms and passed him to Delly in the skiff.

Time moved fast and slow. Sallie climbed in the skiff and yanked the cord of the outboard. Tarzy sobbed. He'd been bitten, he said. Sallie shoved off from the locker.

"No!" Delly screamed.

Sallie circled the locker in the dark. Once. Twice. Delly saw her counting in her mind, gauging how long to search before deeming R.J. gone and rushing Tarzy to shore. It was enough. She swung the tiller homeward and gunned the motor.

Delly launched herself out of the boat and swam the few yards to the locker, splashing wildly to scare off the snakes. She heard Sallie yelling behind her. She got to the locker and pulled herself up. She knocked away the snakes coiled there, grabbing them in her hands and hurling them overboard like wiggling ropes. She waved to Sallie to go and had no reaction when Sallie did so. She crawled along the locker's edge calling R.J.'s name. Like a proud pirate marooned by his shipmates, she didn't bother to turn and watch the skiff depart in the darkness. Soon the motor faded and night sounds of the marsh replaced it.

A GUIDE IN his mudboat found her the next day. She was on her knees atop the locker amid all the snakes she'd killed overnight with her shoe, and she was not in her right mind. She refused to leave there for one thing, clawing the face of her rescuer as he tried to coax her into his boat. She begged him to help her find her friend who'd vanished under the water. The guide realized it was dementia talking and slapped her to calm her down.

Seth would be her savior in the weeks and months ahead. With R.J. dead, Arthur Franklin dead, and Fiona placed in the care of her father's relatives, Delly had nothing left. Seth couldn't pass up the opportunity to make a fresh start that her mental breakdown presented. Once Delly stabilized into more or less her recognizable self, he undertook a supremely patient courtship lasting more than two years. When at last he proposed they get married, she accepted because why not? He was nice, he was good, he loved her—and he never once asked what had possessed her to run off with R.J. that night or what might have passed between them. It was an infinite kindness on his part, since of course there was no good answer.

Money, of which Seth had plenty now that his sister Bonnie was releasing his share of the Block's profits, wasn't a factor in Delly's decision; living in a trailer would have been fine by her for the change of scene alone. But his wealth gave him the means to take her away from Lake Charles and make a new start in New Orleans. He enrolled in the Baptist seminary and was ordained four years later. He joined a parish in Lafayette and became its pastor in 1963. He and Delly had a son they named Francis after her father and lived, thanks to his inheritance, not in the pastor's modest church residence but in a large white house on Sterling Street. Permission to cherish her was Delly's gift for which he never outgrew his gratitude. She was everything to him, did everything for him—ran the household, drove him around, a pastor's perfect helpmate. They were Reverend and Mrs. Seth Bainard, a surname each was proud to claim.

THE SEWING ROOM at Georgia Hill was a mean sight the day after the hurricane. Those alive in the house—Bonnie, Alvin, Seth, and Richie's nurse—were trapped there three days, the power still out and the storm having knocked one of the oak trees across the driveway. They ate crackers and made fitful conversation while two bodies lay at the end of the hall like houseguests sleeping late. Even after electricity and phone lines were restored, news of their ordeal was obscured by Audrey's devastation, more than five hundred dead across two counties being a bigger story than two in a ten-by-twelve room.

Richie Bainard and Donald Meers were buried by people who cared about them. For Donald, that included his parents, two kids, and a number of truly shaken fraternity brothers. His wife Corinne attended the service after initially getting snubbed by Donald's side of the family. Her son Joey negotiated a rapprochement, a nifty act that prefigured his later success as a state politician.

Richie's funeral was a two-phased affair. Phase Two was a memorial celebration held at the Lake Charles High School football field. The W. O. Boston student band—Richie had been a benefactor of the Negro school—paraded together with the girls of the Kiltie marching drum corps in their red plumes and Scottish plaid. Staged by Bonnie and her corporate advisors, the event was attended by state officials and dozens of members, from managers to stock workers, of "our Block's family," as she put it in her amplified eulogy. She gave an air of formalized grief that would have done the House of Windsor proud; the consensus afterward was that under her leadership Block's would become the next Sears Roebuck. Phase One of the funeral, held a week earlier, had been a smaller affair. In the presence of Bonnie, Seth, a preacher, and a shovel crew, Richie's ashes were interred at Orange Grove beside his wives and his father-in-law and his elder son's headstone.

About that headstone: Sallie Hooker's claim that her great-nephew's rescuer had been R. J. Bainard threw an odd light on R.J.'s burial the previous winter. Bonnie's first response was to mock the allegation as a bayou woman's voodoo ravings, but when Tarzy and Delly gave corroboration there was little she could do except wait and see how authorities handled it. Here Hurricane Audrey proved a boon. In its chaotic aftermath, R.J. Bainard was a name whose significance to the parish clerk was overwhelmed by hundreds of other citizens to be certified missing or dead. Like many of the hurricane's casualties, R.J.'s body was never recovered. Sallie, Delly, and Tarzy's testimony that he'd drowned in the storm gave the clerk all he needed to know. Hence today one can find in the Lake Charles historical records two death notices of the same man registered five months apart, a fun fact that few people know.

Seth wept for his father the day they buried him. The shabby way Richie died, shot in bed by a blithering fool, was such a fateful admonishment it seemed to cleanse Richie's slate and open the way for Seth to forgive him. His relationship with Bonnie, on the other hand, remained fraught for many years. In time he began visiting her at Georgia Hill in mutual recognition that they were family no matter what. He knew enough not to wear his minister's collar or to try any kind of preachment. Once, when sitting alone with Alvin Dupree on the terrace, he asked the old sergeant if he would like to pray together. "Most kind," Alvin said with some difficulty. But then Bonnie came outside and Seth had to leave it at that.

Alvin had been left permanently impaired by bullet fragments surgeons were unable to remove from his brain. His gait was unsteady, speech halting. Bonnie kept him home with round-the-clock care. He liked to play harmonica and listen to blues and gospel records. She remained fierce in believing that a miracle would restore him someday. If he said anything halfway coherent or reminiscent of their brief affair she would move heaven and earth to make happen whatever he asked for. That's how she came to partner with Tarzy Hooker's family to buy tens of thousands of acres in Cameron Parish for the cultivation of rice. And it's how Fiona Franklin came to receive a check in the mail from the Block's corporation for twenty thousand dollars in 1959. Alvin had got confused about the amount he'd promised Arthur, a mistake for which he obviously can't be blamed.

Nobody—least of all Bonnie, who carried her regrets with valiant pride, like a stone in her coat pocket—would make the case that such belated good works excused her and Alvin's misdeeds. But nor can we say that whenever she made a charitable donation or broke ground on some new civic project the possibility of redemption didn't occur to her. Hope in someone like Bonnie equals faith in someone like Seth. And she was far from old, after all, leaving open the chance that even many years hence she might start being young.

SEPTEMBER 1964. LAFAYETTE, Louisiana. As she did every evening, Delly Bainard picked Seth up at church in their station wagon to drive him home for dinner. Their son Francis sat in back. She paused by the driveway mailbox to remove the usual bills and this: a small brown-wrapped box postmarked from Cameron Parish with no return address. She opened it. It contained a bundle of tissue paper wrapped around something sticky that since had dried. She pulled the paper apart and studied its contents before tossing it with a screech into her husband's lap. Seth felt for the object. It was slender and knobby, like a twig or a sun-dried pepper. Francis peered over his father's shoulder from the back seat. "Is that somebody's finger?"

It took until breakfast the next morning for Seth to find courage to ask if Delly was leaving. She didn't look up from drying the dishes. Nor did she look at their son. "Will you pray for me if I do?" He thought she was asking his permission to go. Then she added, "I will for you," which told him otherwise.

———

JOE FALCON'S WIFE Cleoma never recovered from injuries she'd suffered getting dragged by a bus in 1938. She died three years later at age thirty-six, leaving Joe to raise their daughter alone. He lost interest in performing after her death and even put aside his beloved accordion. He found love again with a widow named Therese Cormier and in the 1950s began getting back into music, playing with friends on back porches and sitting in at the occasional *fais do-do* near his farm in Acadia Parish. Eventually he formed a group called the Silver Bell String Band with himself as the front man to hook folks into coming to see the once "Famous Columbia Record King" promoted on the publicity flyer.

Joe hadn't recorded since the late 1930s. But in 1964, a year before his death, the Silver Bell String Band performed at the Triangle Dance Hall in Scott, Louisiana, outside Lafayette. The set, with tunes including *"Allons à Lafayette,"* "Lacassine Special," and "Creole Stomp," was captured on audiotape as part of the Smithsonian Institute's Folkways project to preserve American traditional music. There's a photograph in the Smithsonian files of the band backstage. Members listed are Joe Falcon, his wife Therese on drums, Clifford Breaux on fiddle, and Freddy Baez on guitar. Joe holds his black Monarch and Freddy holds a National steel. Aficionados of Louisiana music history will notice that Freddy, a well regarded journeyman player with versatile chops ranging from delta blues to electric zydeco, sports his signature bottleneck slide on his left middle finger, his pointer finger, according to legend, having been bit off by an alligator.

The photographer credited on the back is Adele Baez. Little is known about her. When not touring with such Cajun-Creole headliners as Belton Richard, John Delafose, and Clifton Chenier, she and Freddy farmed a tenant parcel on one of the rice plantations owned by the Hookers of Hancock Bayou. No photo of her exists. Evidently she preferred it that way.

AFTERWORD

Hurricane Audrey hit the southwest coast of Louisiana on June 27, 1957. It left more than five hundred people dead, most from drowning or injury but many, especially children, from snakebite. Lots of books are available on the subject. My favorite is *Hurricane Audrey* by Nola Mae Ross and Susan McFillen Goodson, residents of Cameron Parish, bull's-eye to the storm. Their dedicated compilation of eyewitness accounts is harrowing and uplifting. Audrey's legacy, they write, is "the big picture of life and death—and acceptance, so intertwined in these human hearts."

Amédé Ardoin (1898–1942) was a Creole accordionist and one of Cajun music's pioneers. Like my fictional character, Walter Dopsie, he was brutally assaulted after a performance for wiping sweat off his brow with a white woman's handkerchief. His brain injuries led to his death. Check out his recordings on disk or online. "That poor boy," said Ardoin's musical partner, the great fiddler Dennis McGee. "Make people cry when he sing."

Joe Falcon and Cleoma Breaux are likewise renowned in Cajun music circles. Their lives and influence are discussed in many books, including *Cajun Breakdown* by Ryan André Brasseaux, *South to Louisiana* by John Broven, and *Swamp Pop* by Shane K. Bernard. Ann Savoy's *Cajun Music: A Reflection of a People* features full discographies of Joe, Cleoma, and just about all the Cajun musical greats. It's loaded with photographs, interviews, and, because Ms. Savoy, her husband Marc, and their family are brilliant musicians themselves, lots of stuff on the instrumentation, lyrics, and melodies that inform the Cajun tradition. My book, albeit in an offbeat if not outright perverse way, was conceived as an ode to a part of the country I loved as a boy. Ann Savoy's book is a native's true love letter.

ACKNOWLEDGMENTS

It's been a kick to write and publish a novel after three nonfiction histories. I'd like to thank some of the folks who helped make it happen. At Thomas Dunne Books, there's Tom Dunne, Laurie Chittenden, Melanie Fried, and Will Anderson. Thanks as well to my copy editor, Christina MacDonald. Harvey Klinger has been my agent for many years, and I hope he'll keep me aboard for a few more. Finally, thanks and love to my family, and especially to my wife, Vicki. To my fretful mutterings about doing this book, she urged me to go for it. Any credit therefore is hers, and any blame is mine.